STUBBORN
as
ELLE

STUBBORN as ELLE

An Elle Riley Mystery

STEPHANIE KINZ

ISBN 979-8-9874789-1-2 (Paperback)
ISBN 979-8-9874789-0-5 (eBook)

In Loving Memory of my Granny Kinzella

1936—2022

If you were blessed to be loved by my Granny,
then you were loved fiercely!

For Shari—and all of the other mothers
fighting the opioid epidemic
on behalf of their children.

Dear reader,

This book is the first in what I hope will become a series. Its characters have many more stories to tell.

Justice is a fictitious town based on my hometown and surrounding areas in Southeastern Kentucky. While there are many instances in which I hope this story evokes laughter, other issues are quite serious—such as the opioid epidemic and economic struggles. I wanted to shed some light on those issues that plague many areas of my home state, while also telling of its wondrous natural beauty and the fortitude of the citizens.

My hope is that this story will evoke more than one emotion to you as a reader. May you enjoy Elle's story.

Happy reading,
Stephanie Kinz

CHAPTER ONE

SATURDAY

The thunder rolls in the distance, announcing the impending storm that is supposed to bring high winds and torrential rainfall. I count off the seconds between the last rumble and the next flash of lightning to figure out how far away the storm is. One, two, three, four... ten. It is eight-o'-six p.m. Storms always make me anxious. Especially the strong gales that are already howling. Hopefully, I will be on my way home before it arrives. This is not how I like to spend my Saturday evenings. This storm, in particular, is making the hair on the nape of my neck and arms stand on end, like something sinister is going to blow in with the tempest.

I take in my surroundings as I sit in my car listening to Country Gold on the radio. Out of my peripheral vision, I can see the blinking "N" in the motel vacancies' sign. I have looked at it for so long that I feel a migraine forming behind my left eye. The earthy scent of the distant rain is mingled with the odor of the dumpster wafting through the air, making me feel nauseous.

An older couple gets out of their white sedan in the row of parking spots in front of me, the gentleman with takeout boxes in his arms, and the lady carrying a Yorkie while trying, unsuccessfully, to keep her skirt from flying up in the breeze. The Yorkie barks at the intrusion as the garment blows up over the lady's head. The gust picks up a plastic grocery bag that was lying in the parking lot and billows it onto the gentleman's trouser leg. He reaches down, fighting against the wind, and trying not to drop the takeout food, to grab the bag. The tall bushes along the iron fence surrounding the pool bend, almost touching the ground, as though they are preparing to do a somersault.

The motel clerk slips out the door to stand under the portico, while trying and failing to light a cigarette. Sticking her head back inside the glass door, she emerges in a cloud of smoke. This is the same motel clerk that I generously tipped, hoping she would call me if either of the current occupants of room one-o-six, whom she said are frequent visitors, were to check in. Three hours ago, the generous tip paid off. I arrived too late to witness the couple enter, so I am waiting for their exit.

I am amazed that either of them chose this location. It is in proximity to their homes. Although the motel is situated away from the highway, with little chance of a passerby seeing who a guest might be, the staff is composed of locals, some of whom most likely have wagging tongues. Arrogance and overconfidence are often factors in people getting caught in situations that they do not wish to be caught in. That same arrogance and overconfidence can make my job much easier.

Finally, after what has felt like an eternity, the couple emerges from the room, neither one seemingly in a hurry to part from the other, despite the weather. My Canon R6 is at the ready. I zoom in. Ironically, the radio is playing Tammy Wynette's "Stand By Your Man," as I snap several pictures. A photo of them emerging from the room, holding hands, laughing as the wind tosses her hair, a heated embrace. Last, an overly passionate kiss before he slaps her on the rear and opens her minivan door. The man is my primary focus. Still, I snap plenty of shots that show both of their faces clearly.

Gotcha!

Having obtained the prized photos, I start the car and pull away just as the first fat drops of rain pelt the windshield.

* * *

My name is Elizabeth Anne Riley. I am named after my Grandmother Elizabeth and my Mother Annie. Everyone calls me Elle. The only time that anyone has ever called me Elizabeth is when I have been in trouble, (which happens frequently), or when someone has had to refer to me by my legal name.

My two namesakes are the strongest women that I know. My Granny Beth became a widow when my grandpa was killed in a mining accident. Her five children were young adults at the time. She then became an independent woman, in a generation that most women were not. She had married at an early age when it was normal for the wife to be a homemaker and raise the children while the husband worked. After my grandpa's death, she enrolled in night classes while working two jobs. She became a registered nurse when she was in her forties.

My mother was also widowed, except she was very young, when my father died in an automobile accident. She was left with me, a toddler, to raise alone. She is a hairdresser who has owned her own salon on Main Street for years.

I have long brown hair and green eyes. I would consider myself pretty but not beautiful—at least, not by today's standards, in which social media promotes looking like a filtered photo. I am five-foot-five and I have to work very hard to stay slim. I often wear my hair in a ponytail or a messy bun rather than styling it, much to the dismay of my mother, the hairdresser. I have always felt that less is more when it comes to such things as make-up. I try to enhance what God gave me rather than trying to fake what he did not. Some days, it works. Some days it doesn't, and I contemplate faking it. I am not a fan of fast fashion. I would rather wear something classic, vintage and comfortable, instead of the current craze. Which, luckily for me, vintage seems to never go out of style.

Two years ago, at the age of thirty, I was living in the Brookline area of Boston. I had the perfect husband and ideal career working as an investigative journalist for a prominent newspaper.

Then, it was as if the universe laughed. I discovered that my loving husband, Liam, was having an affair with his assistant, Astrid—*I know, cliché.* She is five foot nine, has icy blonde hair, blue eyes, and looks like she could be a Nordic princess. Even her name sounds somewhat alluring. It would have made me feel better about myself if she had some quirky physical flaws. Instead, I can only wish she would grow an enormous wart on her nose that cannot be cured, or develop a fungus that causes her toenails to fall off.

Shortly after my split from Liam, I was having a drink after work one evening with my Chief Editor, Stuart. "What's wrong, Elle?" he asked.

"What do you mean," I asked.

"You were a star the moment you came on staff. Seems like lately you keep passing more and more stories to people that are half the journalist that you are. It's like your heart isn't in it anymore. I realize you've had some personal reasons to be distracted lately, but it just isn't like you."

The social, political, and economic climate in America had changed. This new era was a dream for many journalists, who seized the opportunity to sensationalize their headlines. I did not have the desire to interject my own feelings, views, or push an agenda. I have always wanted to uncover the truth—not create it.

"You mean I keep passing on stories to people who are more willing to compromise their journalistic integrity?" He shrugged without commenting. We both knew this was true, even if he did not feel comfortable saying it out loud. "You're right, Stu. My heart isn't in it anymore. I think I quit."

"You what?" he asked, almost choking on his drink. It wasn't the reply he had expected.

"I said I quit. Life's too short to do something your heart isn't in, right?" He did not argue or try to dissuade me from resigning. This told me I had made the right decision.

I was not sure what would come next. Everything that was familiar was now gone. I had left my home, no longer had a husband. My daily routine of getting up and going to work no longer existed. Friends from my college days had all settled into new cities. I had somewhat close acquaintances, but no truly close friends. The few that I had thought were close friends became awkward in my presence. Having been mutual friends of both my husband and I, they thought I was going to ask them to choose sides. They should have known me well enough to know that I do not take part in such childish behavior, as adults picking sides — an activity that resembles picking teams at elementary recess.

Liam had always urged me to invest my earnings. I was happy that I followed his advice. I did not want to dip into my nest egg, but it gave me some security while I contemplated what to do next with my life.

After a week of sitting on the beach and drinking margaritas, I went for a visit to my hometown of Justice. I was long overdue for a visit with my two favorite ladies—Mama and Granny.

Justice is slow paced, rich in natural beauty, and poor in most other things. Located in Southeast Kentucky, it is full of mountains, hills, and hollers (hollows). The area is abundant in waterfalls, creeks, and natural arches. The amazing landscape makes it seem like a heavenly place.

The dialect is Appalachian with a bit of the South tossed in. Everyone knows most everyone else here, or at least some of their family. Most people won't allow you to leave their home hungry, thirsty, or without telling you about Jesus first. The working-class work extremely hard. The criminals work even harder at their felonious activities.

Sometimes I have thought that the name of the town should have been *In*Justice, rather than Justice. Injustices are what the citizens of the town and surrounding areas have often been dealt.

Men dug coal and worked in the coal mines for years. When the mines shut down, the jobs went away. The Federal Government holds the majority of the land, making economic growth impossible. Many people have to travel across county lines and often into other states to find employment. It would be a rarity to find a family in the area unaffected by the opioid epidemic that has swept through the region.

There are many stigmas, stereotypes, and misconceptions, in which the people are perceived as impoverished, lazy, and ignorant. The ignorance belongs to those who believe the stereotypes to be true of all Appalachians. While many of the communities are poor, they are populated with strong, proud, hardworking, intelligent, and talented individuals.

Art Bellamy is the proprietor of the only investigative office in Justice. He and my mother were married for a brief period when I was a teenager. Mama is the last of his three ex-wives. He never remarried after they divorced, and he would often say, in a somewhat joking manner, that if he couldn't have made it work with Annie, then he felt he couldn't make a go of it with anyone.

He never had children, and my being without a father allowed us to fill that void in each other's lives. He is a skilled private investigator, and he cleverly named his office "Art of Investigations." When I returned home, he asked for my help on a case. Of course, I agreed.

As a teenager, I spent weekends and summers working for Art. Sometimes, he would even take me on a stakeout if it didn't involve something too scandalous for a teen to witness.

Looking back, I suppose that is where my passion for uncovering the truth started. Those experiences turned me into something of a cynic and set me on a career path as an investigative journalist. I knew I would never be successful as an on-air reporter because of my accent, something that I was proud of and refused to change. My preference has always been to publish rather than to broadcast, anyway.

It has been almost two years since my return to Justice. That one case I helped Art with turned into another case, then another, and so on. I moved into the apartment above his office. I now work as a freelance journalist and still assist Art.

I have fallen into a comfortable routine. Occasionally, my writing involves travel, which keeps me from becoming restless, and makes me look forward to coming home afterwards. The investigative cases are sometimes entertaining and keep me from growing bored.

Art of Investigations has become a very lucrative business. He now does more traveling out of town, and often out of state, for cases that he undertakes, which leaves no one in the office. He does investigations for a couple of law firms in Lexington and Louisville. The attorneys keep him busy looking into things pertinent to their cases.

I normally work the small in-town investigations. I have suggested that bringing on a partner to share the caseload would be beneficial to him, to which he replies that he does not need to bring anyone in, because he has me. He has agreed to hire a secretary, though. Rather, he has agreed to let *me* hire a new secretary/office manager for him, since I will be the one interviewing candidates.

Reva Lowe, the lady that worked in the office for years, quit about three years ago, when she moved out of state, to be closer to her grandchildren. He wants someone like Reva, who will work for twenty-plus years. No pressure there! I have some applicants scheduled to interview this coming week, and I am not looking forward to the process.

CHAPTER TWO

SUNDAY

The sun comes streaming through the blinds, piercing my eyes and bringing the headache that I have to my immediate attention. The time is seven forty-eight a.m. I intended to sleep in today, after being awake most of the night, because of the storm. The high winds howled, thunder shook the building, and rain slammed against the windows with the sound of someone peppering them with small gravels.

I have never been caught unaware by a tornado, yet that is still my fear. I always make sure my cellphone is fully charged, and I am dressed to run in the event of an emergency, including wearing clean underwear. Nobody wants to be discovered in a field after being carried away by a tornado wearing unclean undies. Okay, I'll concede that chances are they would be dirty when you were found, but still.

The combination of my pounding head and waking up earlier than I wanted is making my disposition sourer by the second. I can tell it is going to be one of those mornings that I don't even like myself. I had to cancel my date with Colton Ryan at the last-minute yesterday evening because of the call from the motel clerk.

I started dating Colt not long after I returned to Justice. He is extremely handsome, with dark hair, which becomes wavy when he needs a haircut, and deep brown eyes. Even if his looks do not make him sexy enough, he has a "devil don't care" attitude. That gives him a bad boy vibe, making him even sexier. His sense of humor matches my own.

He is not the settling down type—which makes him perfect for me! I have no intention of making the same mistake with marriage that I made before. He works out of town during the week for a company that does infrastructure work for highway departments. We usually spend Saturday nights at the Troubadour, a bar at the county line, shooting pool and listening to live music.

Colt and I had a history of dating when we were in high school. When we rekindled our relationship, we agreed that neither one of us wanted anything serious or were looking to settle down. We could even date other people if we wanted. I have dated no one else. I'm not really sure why I haven't. I have never asked Colt if he does. The females fawn over him, so I'm certain he has plenty of opportunities. We aren't star-crossed lovers, which would sound much more romantic, but we share a connection that seems rather kismet at times.

I have fallen into a routine with my love life, the same as with everything else. I am always waiting. Waiting, breath held, for what? Perhaps for divine intervention to flash a blatantly clear sign at me, to show me the way. Preferably before I turn into an old maid and start adopting cats.

* * *

Maybe going for a run this morning will help clear the cobwebs from my head, get my blood pumping, and ease my headache. I groan, untangling myself from the wadded sheets, and rise from the bed, almost tripping over the emergency go shoes that I have sitting next to it.

After dressing in running clothes, splashing water on my face, brushing my teeth, and swallowing two Tylenol, I stumble to the kitchen to get a bottle of water from the fridge. The clock on the stove is blinking as a result of a temporary power outage last night.

A jar of pickles falls out as I open the refrigerator door, landing on my right foot and bringing forth a slew of curse words not suitable for a lady. I hobble around on one foot as tears burn my eyes. I bite my lip, resisting the urge to scream. Looking down, I see the top of my foot is already turning purple. "Screw the workout. I need coffee instead," I mumble. Opening the cabinet, I realize I am out of coffee. I did not make it to the grocery store this past week. My poor attitude intensifies.

I slouch over and rest my forehead on the counter, sighing wearily. As I raise up, I whack the top of my skull on the upper cabinet door that I had forgotten to close. White hot pain sears a line along the top of my head as I see stars. I let loose another stream of expletives. Jerking up the jar of pickles, I think about throwing them, but then I would just have to clean up the mess. I take a deep, calming breath, gingerly placing the pickles back in the fridge while rubbing my throbbing scalp and ensuring that it isn't bleeding.

Heading out the door, I limp across the balcony at the back of the building, and then down the stairs at the side toward Art's office. I know there is always coffee there.

Last night's rain has left everything a soggy mess, other than the places that the April wind has dried off this morning. Several plops of water drip from the eaves of the roof, land on my head, and trickle down the side of my face and neck. Weeds have sprouted up in the cracks of the pavement and sidewalk. A clump of daffodils looks oddly out of place along a portion of chain-link fence across the street. The sight of the flowers is like finding treasure in an unexpected place.

Art opens the door right as I approach, a cup of coffee in his hand. Despite being close to sixty, he still has the same lanky build that he had in his youth, unaffected by the weight gain that often comes during middle age. This is a mystery to me, considering his diet is total trash. His black hair has gone completely gray but is still full and he has a thick gray mustache. His voice is a mellow drawl that sounds easy-going even when he is being stern. He has always reminded me of someone who would make a great cowboy in an old western movie.

"Cup of Ambition," he says, extending the mug in my direction. "A little coffee and a lotta creamer, just the way you like it. I would say good morning but, judging from the sentence enhancers that I heard you yelling upstairs, mustn't be that good. I was on my way to come check on you. You're looking a little like someone pissed in your Cheerios."

"Thank you. Morning could be better. I feel like someone pissed in them twice. Me and a jar of pickles had words. I got into a fight with the cabinet door, and I have a storm hangover. When did you get in?"

He crinkles his nose, giving me a pained look that says he sympathizes with me, then says, "I got back this morning. Came straight here. Would've been back last night, but it rained so hard that I damned near ran off the road. I had to stop and get a room for the night. If April showers bring May flowers, the flowers should be a sight to see this year," he says.

I nod my aching noggin in agreement and then ask, "Productive trip?"

"No Ma'am. Nobody covers their tracks better than a politician with something to hide," he replies, as he props his feet up on his desk.

I chuckle at the truth of this statement. Art is the best there is at what he does. He will outwork the most seasoned detectives and outsmart the sneakiest subjects. If someone covers their tracks well enough for him to have a hard time solving the case, then chances are they have many people aiding them in that task.

"Did you get the photos that I emailed you last night?" I ask, inhaling the aroma of the stout coffee.

"I did. I'm sure you're glad to have finally gotten those so you can quit chasing that pain in the ass around. How many evenings did you end up tailing him?"

"Three this week. That motel clerk proved to be a real gem," I say. "The first two of those evenings were a bust. I followed him to a house and the only thing going on was poker night with a group of men. I was starting to think his wife was just being paranoid."

"At least you didn't have to drive far last night. Either he ain't too bright or he's awfully brave stepping out that close to home," he says, while shaking his head.

"I am guessing it is a little of both!" I say.

"Yep. And it's just as the missus suspected. It's her brother's wife in the photos with him. I'm betting they have some real interesting holiday dinners," he says, laughing. "Oh, speaking of pains in the rear, Gertie left several messages last night. Do you mind swinging by her place today?" he asks, slightly wincing, fearing that I will say no.

"No, I do not mind. I am going to need another cup of coffee first though," I say, as I dig the heels of my hands into my eyes. *Or maybe the entire pot!* Dealing with Gertie Rose can be exhausting.

She is in her eighties and suffers from dementia. A fragile-looking lady who has shrunk in girth and height over the years. The fragility may fool many people that do not realize she is still very sassy. She has long gray hair that her hired home aid usually keeps styled in a long braid, or in a bun for her. Gertie has a large black and white Bernese Mountain dog named Buddy. She adopted Buddy when he was a puppy and didn't realize that he would grow to be as big as he has. Sometimes, she does not remember that she has fed him, so she feeds him a second time. This has contributed to his enormous size.

She often forgets to close the gate to her yard and Buddy escapes. She then calls, saying that someone has dog-napped him. He is always roaming the neighborhood when he escapes, where he finds plenty of table scraps to eat and children to play with. I will drive around until I find him, lure him into my car with treats, and return him home to Gertie. She will then offer me a five-dollar reward for saving him from the dog-nappers. Of course, I refuse the reward. I used to be able to lure him with one treat. Now it takes several. Sometimes, I think Buddy is smarter than both Gertie and I.

Even though Art referred to Gertie as a pain in the rear, both he and I are very fond of her. He would check on her in the past when she would call. She sometimes confuses him for her late husband Joe, who was also tall and lanky. Art never minded, until the day Gertie answered the door wearing nothing but red lipstick and her house shoes, calling him Joe. Art, never easily embarrassed, still turns red-faced when someone mentions it. Ever since that day, I have been the person to respond to Gertie's calls. I never mind going to check on her, although I have thought about refusing, just to see what other humorous situation Art may find himself in.

CHAPTER THREE

I keep an eye out for Buddy as I drive through the neighborhood on the way to Gertie's house. After making three passes down all the surrounding roads, I still have not seen a sign of him. I pull up the hill to her driveway at the back of the house. Gertie, having heard my vehicle pull in, opens the door as I start up the steps. There is a slight incline at the side of the house that slopes toward the back. The steps up to the covered deck are steep. I have often wondered why the rear of the house is still the primary entrance used, when the front of the home, with just a couple of steps leading onto the porch, would be much safer for Gertie. She never seems to have any trouble navigating the steps, though. She is in good physical shape compared to most people her age.

I spot a recent addition to her ever-growing gnome collection, with its hat pointed to the ground, and its bare butt pointed up, mooning everyone. Buddy, seeing me, comes bounding out the door, tongue lolling, expecting me to have treats for him. He plows into me, catching me off guard and almost toppling me over. I grab the rail at the side of the steps to steady myself.

Gertie is dressed in a pastel striped cotton housecoat that zips up the front. She has on a pair of yellow rain boots that go up to her knees and a shade of lipstick that falls more into the orange category than red. Her long gray hair is loose today and disheveled.

Finally, able to pry Buddy's paws off of my chest, I reach down to scratch him behind the ears, offering him a treat. He almost snaps my fingers in his haste to grab it. I try to step around him and he lays down on my feet, blocking my passage, insisting on being petted, nudging my hand back each time that I stop.

Gertie says, "Oh honey, I'm so glad you came!"

"I see Buddy is safe at home. Is that what you had called about?"

"Oh no dear, the most terrible thing happened! I witnessed a murder last night!" she says.

"A murder? Gertie, were you by chance watching the television last night?" I ask, expecting her answer to be yes.

Gertie has her faculties today, and that question offends her. Crossing her arms over her chest, she replies, "No. I was NOT *watching* TV. I saw it with my very own eyes in real life!"

"Did you call the Sheriff?"

"Yes. Fordy showed up. Hmph, that codger is so old he would not be able to find his nose on his face, let alone a murderer."

Bufford "Ford" Smith was the Sheriff of Justice for many years. He is around the same age as Gertie. I almost laugh out loud when she refers to him as old. After he retired, the current Sheriff kept him on as a deputy. The only reason Ford did not contend for office again was because of his age. He is still more than capable of doing the job, and probably would not know what to do with

27

himself if he did not have going to the Sheriff's Office to look forward to.

"Who was the victim? And who is the murderer?" I ask, trying to appease Gertie, but also being curious about her story now. She can spin some pretty wild tales. I try to mentally prepare myself for what she is about to tell me.

"I don't know, but I can tell you what happened." Gertie jumps right in, always eager to tell her story. She becomes very animated, talking quickly. Maybe she thinks she may forget if she does not share what she wants to say immediately.

"Jared had gone out with some of his friends. I don't care much for his friends. They roll their own cigarettes and they stink to high heaven. They are always dirtying up my kitchen making brownies when they come over here. But you know, they probably *are* the best brownies I've ever eaten. They say it's a *special* recipe," she says.

Jared is Gertie's grandson. Gertie's son, Joe Jr., sent Jared to live with her when she refused to go into an assisted living facility. Gertie is still left to her own devices most of the time. Jared spends most of *his* time in his room in the basement, smoking pot and playing video games. His appearance is pretty much in accord with his lifestyle—pale skin, from lack of time outdoors, brown hair that constantly needs a haircut, a stubbly face, and a very chillaxed attitude.

The living arrangement turned out to be ideal for him. He does not have to work and can keep to his own schedule. He rarely emerges from the basement with the purpose of checking on Gertie. Most of the time, if he darkens the door leading upstairs, it is to get something from the kitchen. He depends on Gertie's aid being there during the day, which allows him the freedom to sit up half of the night, and then sleep until well past noon.

Gertie is more than happy to be left alone. She is pert enough that she does not like to be told what to do. She still looks for her car keys every day that Joe Jr. and Jared hid from her, after she accidentally ran over Mona Davies's foot in the senior citizens' center parking lot. I am not entirely convinced it was an accident, considering she had been complaining to me that Mona was cheating at bingo, and knocked Gertie out of winning the super prize. Apparently, bingo can become pretty cutthroat at their age. Fortunately for Mona, she was wearing orthopedic shoes that were a little big on her, so the only injury she sustained was a broken big toe.

"Anyhow," she continues, after getting sidetracked. "I couldn't find Buddy anywhere, so I figured Jared must have left the gate open and Buddy got loose. I think maybe it's Jared that leaves the gate open most of the time and it gets blamed on me!" Her eyes go squinty, as if this is a revelation that just occurred to her.

She pauses for a few seconds, then places a finger on her temple and says, "Where was I? Oh yes, I got the flashlight and went to find Buddy before it started storming. He is terribly afraid of the storms. I usually have to put one of those special vests on him to keep him calm. I went through the woods back there, calling him and calling him, but no Buddy in sight."

"Turns out he was in the house, hiding in the bathroom upstairs. But, when I was looking for him, I got down close to the creek and there were two men down there. There was a lot of yelling and begging. And just like in a movie, the one shot the other. I hightailed it out of there before he saw me. I've seen what happens to witnesses on those crime shows!"

"Can you show me where the crime took place?" I ask, patiently.

"I sure can. But can we drive? That is a long walk, and I already had enough walking last night."

My foot is still throbbing, so that sounds like a fine idea.

Gertie, Buddy, and I load into my vehicle. Her small stature makes her look like a child riding in the passenger seat. If she shrinks anymore, she will probably need to ride in a booster seat. Buddy has his nose stuck to the window before I can hit the button to lower it, leaving smudges and dog slobber all over. Now it matches the other window, courtesy of his last ride with me.

I drive around the street, then take the narrow gravel access road to the creek. Last night's rain has beaten the gravel dust down, and prevents it from looking like a cloud following along behind us, as it normally would. The woods behind Gertie's split-level brick and vinyl siding home back up to the creek. Gertie owns the land on this side. The land on the other side of the creek is part of the national forest. Regardless of the "No Trespassing" signs posted, this is a popular swimming hole in the summer for the locals, and even more popular for the teenagers looking for a place to party. They roll in, light their bonfires, party, and then roll out, often leaving their trash along the creek bank. I cannot imagine, with the terrible weather last night, that anyone would have been here partying, and it is too early in the year for swimming.

I park farther back from the creek today than I usually would have, just short of what seems to be a bottomless mudhole. The water levels, higher than normal due to the rain, have risen to the top of the bank. The gravel ends in front of where I park and the dirt road that leads down to the creek is thick mud and mire, dotted with mud puddles. I put the gearshift in park and Gertie immediately launches back into her story.

"Right there, in front of where you parked, that is where it happened. The truck engine was running, and the headlights were shining on them. Lightning was flashing and made the whole scene seem wicked, like I was looking at a devil. It was starting to rain, and I was about to tell them, youns are going to get struck by lightning and need to get off my property, anyway! But then,"- she pauses for effect- "the tall man with dark hair started shouting at the smaller man something about blackmail. The smaller man sounded like he was making promises and begging. The man with the gun acted like he was going to let him go, but then.... raised the gun and shot him!"- as she goes through the motions of slowly acting it out. "Like he was toying with him like they do in movies!"

"I was awfully glad for the noise of the storm, so they didn't hear me. I am sure that I squealed like a pig when he shot the gun. That's when I took off. I was afraid he would see me. I went a little ways into the woods and hid behind a tree until I got my heart rate under control so I could walk back to the house. I was scared half to death and soaking wet when I got back home. My bun had come loose, and my hair was plastered to my head. I looked like some ugly creature."

I had wondered why Gertie's hair is not styled today. That explains it. I suppose I arrived before her home aid this morning.

"I hate to think what Fordy thought I looked like," she says, as she reaches up, running her hand over her long locks.

Was that a blush creeping into Gertie's cheeks as she said this? Maybe she is fonder of the old codger than she would lead people to believe.

"You didn't recognize either man, or hear anything more specific that was said?"

"No, I didn't know either of them. I probably wouldn't, though. With them being from Florida and all."

"What makes you think they are from Florida?" I ask.

"Well, because the truck had Florida tags on it. Honestly, Elle, keep up!"

"Do you know what kind of truck it was?" I ask, rubbing my eye as my headache returns.

"No, but it was really big, black, shiny, and it had a lizard on the back window."

A lizard? I am starting to think I needed something stronger than coffee this morning.

"Gertie, you did not eat any of Jared's *special* brownies last night, did you?" I ask.

"I wish. He hid them from me," she says, disappointed.

I tell Gertie to stay put because of the mud. I walk around, scanning the ground and the surrounding area. The impressions of my footprints in the soft mud and sand fill with water. No tire tracks were imprinted in the muddy terrain. Tracks made by Ford or anyone else would have been quickly beaten away last night during the hard rain. I navigate to the creek.

The murky, rushing water gurgles as it forcefully cascades over the rocks, creating strong ripples. A deer stands across the creek, looking unalarmed. Not seeing anything to validate her story. I turn to head back to the vehicle. There stands Gertie, knee deep in the mudhole, and Buddy rolling around beside her.

After convincing Buddy to wade into the creek water enough for me to rinse him off, I find a blanket in the back of the vehicle to dry him off. I remove Gertie's boots and get her situated sideways on the passenger seat. I tote her galoshes to the creek and swish them in the water to rid them of the mud.

"I'm sorry, Gertie, but I found nothing helpful here," I say, as I back the vehicle up to turn around. I feel as if I have let her down, but I am happy that there is no evidence of a murder.

"That's what Fordy said too," she says, in a discouraged tone. "I swear I saw the whole thing!"

I drive Gertie back home. As I am seeing her safely back in the house, I ask her, "Have you ever thought of having security cameras installed? They could be helpful when Buddy comes up missing, too."

"I have never felt the need to have them. Besides, I feel safe with Jared living here. And Buddy always ends up back here one way or another."

'Safe' is not the word I would use to describe my feelings if I had to depend on Jared. Maybe….. if a crime occurred late in the afternoon and he was in the kitchen when it happened, he might be of some assistance. He does not seem like he would be very brave to me, though, since I saw him jump two feet into the air and shriek like a girl one day when he saw a spider.

"You know, dear, you should date my grandson, Jared. The two of you would make a cute couple."

"Oh Gertie, you know Jared's standards are probably much too *high* for the likes of me," I say.

"Well, you are probably right, dear. But you are a lot sweeter than the girl he brings over with the snake tattoo up her neck and hot pink hair. She does make a mean pan of brownies, though!"

"You remember I am dating Colton Ryan, don't you?" I ask.

"Yeah, I remember. Sowing your wild oats with that one, no doubt. Since you haven't mentioned settling down with him, I figure you must be looking for another fish in the sea. It never hurts for a girl to keep her options open," she says, winking at me.

I tell Gertie that I will keep my eyes and ears open for this mysterious murderer as I am leaving.

CHAPTER FOUR

I decide to stop at Granny's on my way back to the apartment. Sundays are a great day for a visit. Other relatives usually drop in and out on that day, so I am sure to get to spend time with them while I am there. I park behind a line of other cars crowding the driveway.

She always cooks fried chicken, chicken and dumplings, or some other equally delicious meal on Sunday. Today is no exception. She has pork chops, a kettle of pinto beans, pone of cornbread, and sides, along with a peach cobbler for dessert. Entering the kitchen, I see steam rising from the kettle of beans, smell the grease in the cast-iron skillet the pork chops were fried in, and can practically taste the melted butter on top of the cornbread. I have heard other people say their maternal figures are the best cook in the world. They are wrong. My Granny Beth is. I think I have gained five pounds just from the aroma drifting through the air.

Her house is average sized. The living room and eat-in kitchen are larger compared to the bedrooms and one bathroom. When I was a child, the house seemed huge to me. Now, as an adult, I wonder how she managed to raise five children here. The home seems to be busting at the seams when those five children of hers, their children, and grandchildren, are gathered here for holidays and special occasions. No one seems to mind that it is overly crowded or noisy. Least of all, Gran. The more the merrier. She loves having her family together.

Granny is in her seventies. She wears her hair in a mid-length bob haircut. Her tresses are still more brown than gray. My mother and I both inherited her green eyes, although my grandmother's have faded some with age. She finally retired from working a few years ago. She is still very active, both in her home and in her church. She has spent her entire life caring for others, whether it be her family, her patients, or people in the community. She is the most selfless person that I have ever known. Living a life of helping others seems to be her passion. If you are loved by my Granny, then you are loved fiercely.

My Uncle Mike lives with Gran. He moved in temporarily after his divorce and never moved out. She is still more than capable of looking out for herself and others, but the company, help around the house, yard, and garden, is beneficial to her. He allows her to think that she is tending to him, but he is actually looking after her.

"Hey Gran. It smells delicious in here," I say, while giving her a big hug.

"Do you want me to fix you a plate?" she asks, always being a mother hen, and my stomach growls on cue.

"No, Ma'am. Thank you, but I can help myself. You sit down and rest." I say.

After finishing my plate, she offers to get me seconds. "Gran, I honestly could not eat another bite. I am as full as a tick." If I were wearing jeans, instead of the running tights I donned this morning, I would have to undo the button on them.

"You should try to eat more. You are looking too thin. Has Art been working you too hard? I know it is a lot to work two jobs." It would not matter if I gained fifty pounds overnight, my Granny would still say that I look too thin and need to eat more.

"No, Art goes pretty easy on me. I know you did not mean it as a compliment, but I appreciate you telling me I look thin." I smile and wink.

"She never tells me I look too thin or accuses me of working too hard," says my uncle Mike, while patting his stomach. His stomach does seem to have grown since moving in. That is understandable, since my grandmother's love language seems to be to make sure people are well fed. I would probably have to be rolled out the door if I spent too much time here.

This sets off a lot of laughter around the table, from my cousins and myself, which is usually the case when any of us are in each other's company. It always turns into comedy hour and I end up laughing until my side hurts.

My cousin Renee's daughter, Kenzie, comes tearing into the kitchen along with my cousin Gayla's son, Hunter. They have drawn mustaches and beards on each other using a permanent Sharpie marker. Hunter is thrilled with his artistic facial hair, but Kenzie is wailing in hysterical sobs because her older sister told her that the other children at preschool will make fun of her tomorrow. Uncle Mike tells her it isn't so bad, as he takes the marker, offering to let her draw elaborate designs on his face. This seems to pacify her as her sobs turn into giggles.

I help clean up the kitchen, then announce that I should be on my way. I need to do grocery shopping, laundry, and some household chores. My pantry and fridge are as bare as my canister of coffee.

I will take the long way around town, doing errands on the way home, so that I can be on the lookout for any trucks that may match Gertie's description. Finding a big, black, shiny truck should be easy to do in Justice. Finding one with a lizard on the back window may prove to be more difficult, and it is possible that Gertie may have confused that detail. It is possible that Gertie confused *all* the details, and the event did not actually occur. I am intrigued by solving the mystery of her story, however not as intrigued about a murder occurring.

Murders rarely occur in Justice. When they do, the case is usually open and shut, with no question of who the guilty party or victim is. The possibility that there could be a murderer walking freely in our town is very discomforting. I really hope that Gertie is mistaken about what she says she saw at the creek last night.

* * *

Driving around town, I check out parking lots of every business along the way. I see plenty of black trucks but none matching Gertie's description. I decide to do a drive through of her neighborhood, and maybe speak to some of her neighbors before I go to do my grocery shopping. If I wait until much later, many of them will be gone to church.

The houses along the road to Gertie's are spread out considerably. Nobody was home at the first house. The couple who live in the second home told me they did not see or hear anything out of the ordinary last night. Dottie Hamlin lives in the third house. She is a family friend who attends church with my Granny. I notice she has security cameras as I pull into her driveway, and I become somewhat hopeful that I may discover something helpful here. I ring the doorbell, and it is not long before Dot answers.

"Hello, Elle. How are you doing, Hon?"

"I'm well, Dot. Thank you for asking. I am sorry to disturb you, but I was hoping you may help me out with something? I promise I won't take up much of your time. I know you are probably getting ready to go to church soon."

"Well, I will certainly help you with anything I can! What can I do for you?"

I explain the situation. Dottie did not see or hear anything, but she immediately offers to let me see her security camera footage. After trying to remember her password and several failed attempts to log into her system, she finally succeeds. She allows me to take over and search through the recordings from last night.

I rewind to an hour before the approximate time that the storm would have begun, and become excited when I see a black Chevrolet truck matching Gertie's description drive by. The windows are tinted, and, considering the weather and time of evening, it is impossible to see anything inside of the vehicle. The camera only offers a view of the front of the truck. Nothing significant stands out about the front of the vehicle. I record the images with my phone before I fast forward, hoping to get a view of the back of the truck on its return route. The screen goes black for a moment and then static replaces the abyss of nothingness playing. My heart sinks. I hit the fast-forward button. More snowy, gray and white fills the monitor.

"Do you know why the cameras stopped recording?" I ask.

"That's probably about the time we lost electricity. That storm wreaked havoc last night. Thankfully, it wasn't out too long," Dot says.

Although I am disappointed not to be able to see more details about the truck, at least now I know, that Gertie did most likely see something occur last night. What that something was might be hard to figure out, with no more clues to go on. I cannot fathom that it was really a murder, but my gut instinct is screaming that something isn't right. One of the first things Art taught me, was to never ignore your instincts, even if it seems ridiculous to your mind.

"Thank you for allowing me to do this. It has been very helpful. I will get out of your hair now so you can get ready for church," I say.

"You're most welcome, sweetheart. It sure is a blessing that Gertie and Buddy have you to look out for them. I hope to see you at church again soon," she says, while giving me a hug. She smells like Avon perfume, pot roast, and spearmint gum. The scents are comforting and reminiscent of my grandmother.

"You will," I say, returning the hug.

CHAPTER FIVE

MONDAY

I awoke at five o'clock this morning, eager to get my day started. I got in a longer than normal run, which I needed after the meal I ate yesterday at Gran's. I was not blessed with a fast metabolism and the older I get, the harder I have to work to avoid gaining weight. My love of food does not help the screeching halt that my metabolic rate has crashed into.

After I stopped viewing my workouts as torture and started looking at them as therapeutic, they became somewhat less miserable. It also helps if I conjure a scenario in my head, in which I have a chance meeting with Liam's mistress, and I wow her with my stunning figure, making her feel as insecure as she deserves to feel.

Thinking about Astrid usually makes me angry enough to work out my frustration on the pavement, and leads me to darker thoughts, such as wishing she and Liam would both develop an itchy rash in private places. I realize this probably isn't a healthy thought process, but it seems to make me feel better.

I know Liam well enough to know that he is probably miserable. Astrid looks great on his arm at social functions, and apparently the sexual attraction is there, but I am familiar enough with the real Liam to understand that she is not who he connects with on a deeper level. The fact that he still calls and texts me also tells me he isn't happy. Those calls and texts go unanswered on my part.

After my post-run shower, I settled in at my computer to finish an article that I have been working on. It is now a little past noon, the piece is completed, and my coffee mug is empty. I did not have to do any traveling for this story, and the work did not entail any investigation or commentary from sources. Instead, it mostly consisted of citing statistics. Writing about Consumer Price Index measurements, supply and demand, unemployment rates, and numerical data is not very fulfilling, or investigative, but it pays the bills.

The downside to being a freelance journalist is that I often cannot be as picky about the articles I write, because if I don't work, I don't get paid. The upside is that if I truly don't want to do something, I don't have to. I have been toying with the idea of writing a novel since returning to Justice. One day, I will find the motivation to get started. Until then, I seem to have plenty to keep me busy.

As easy as this job has been, I have had a difficult time concentrating. I sigh as I stand up from my desk chair, stretch, and walk to the kitchen to refill my coffee mug. My mind keeps wandering to Gertie and her story.

It is quite easy to assume that Gertie is confused or imagined the whole thing. It is surprising to me that she had the same story yesterday as the night before. Her memory is not usually that consistent with such detail when she is confused. She was spot on about the truck. Then there was the appearance of her hair, which suggested that she had in fact been caught out in the bad weather, as she had said. Is it possible that she was mixed up about what transpired during the storm? Perhaps she just saw the truck drive by, and she had been watching television, blurring two things into the same story.

What if the lady that everyone assumes doesn't know what she is talking about did, in fact, witness a crime? Even if the supposed crime did not really happen, it seemed very real to Gertie. I dislike the thought of her being scared and upset because nobody believes her. I think she saw *something*. My gut instinct punches me again, telling me that there is something there that needs investigating. Or perhaps, it's hunger, as I remember I haven't eaten today.

I pull a container of steel cut oatmeal from the refrigerator that I prepped last night for the week. As I place the plastic bowl back in the fridge, I notice a piece of peach cobbler that I brought home yesterday evening. I dump the oatmeal back into the storage bowl and heat the cobbler up. This is probably the easiest choice I will make all day. Besides, I do my best thinking when I am on a sugar high.

* * *

Sheriff Jack Lennox is a couple of years older than me. His family moved here when he was in high school. His father was a career Marine. The family moved around a lot before settling in his mother's hometown of Justice. Jack has always been strikingly handsome, tall with sandy blonde hair that gets blonder in the summer, ocean blue eyes, and long dark lashes that set those blue eyes off. He was the second born of four children. All of his siblings are girls. And they were all blessed with the same beautiful blue eyes.

Jack followed in his father's footsteps and joined the Marines fresh out of high school. He did several tours overseas. He came home with muscles, tattoos, and a couple of scars that he did not have when he departed. He does not talk about those years of his life. I am sure that he returned with more scars than just physical ones. This lends a mystery to him. That, combined with his all-American good looks and muscles, makes him a favorite with most of the ladies. His being a Marine, and now a no-nonsense Sheriff, makes him a favorite amongst many of the men.

After his baby sister passed away from an overdose, Jack ran for Sheriff. Winning, he waged war on illegal drugs. It's a war in which he seems to win few battles, but he still gives the drug industry hell every day. For that, he is a favorite of everyone — except those involved in the drug trade.

Almost two years ago, I drove into Justice, in my Audi, windows down, hair blowing in the wind, breathing in the mountain air, Eric Church's "Springsteen" blasting through the speakers. Sheriff Lennox pulled me over for speeding, just inside the county limits.

I pointed out that the speed limit sign had a branch in front of it, obscuring my view. He found this ridiculous, so together we went back and looked at the sign.

"This?" he asked, pointing to the small branch that barely covered a portion of the sign.

"Yes," I said, arms crossed and chin jutting out indignantly.

"You and I both know that limb isn't big enough to have kept you from seeing the speed limit," he said, while rolling his eyes.

"A clever attorney could argue otherwise. The wrong time of day and lighting.... In fact, a *really* clever lawyer could argue that it is by design, so that you can pull people over, and write tickets. Maybe that you even target people such as me, with out-of-state tags."

"That is complete BS, and you know it!" flinging his arms out to the side. "You may have out-of-state tags, but you are from here. I would think you would know me better than to think that!"

"Yeah, but how did you know it was me when you hit your lights to pull me over? I am just saying that it could look bad," as I shrugged.

After much back and forth, he eventually became so exasperated that he let me off with a warning. Every encounter that we have had since then has been equally vexing for him. Knowing that I can ruffle his feathers, I take great humor in it.

According to my friend Daphne, who works at the S.O. (Sheriff's Office), the day after my initial encounter of being pulled over by the Sheriff, he took a chainsaw out to the speed limit sign and cut the whole bush down. She and I shared a great laugh about it.

I no longer have the Audi. I now drive a blue Ford Bronco, and I often drive the Investigations office's black Toyota Camry, when I am working on a case. He still pulls me over every opportunity that he gets. What can I say? I like to drive fast. It is the only law that I ever break. I happen to be the safest speeder that I know, though.

Smiling as I think back to it, I pick up my phone, dialing the non-emergency number to the Sheriff's Office. Jack himself answers. "Sheriff's Office."

"Hey, Sheriff. You don't sound nearly as pleasant as Daphne does when she answers the phone."

45

"Well, if it ain't the most impossible thorn in my side herself."

"Does that mean I am your favorite?" I ask.

"I don't play favorites, but you are prettier than the others."

"Oh, so you think I'm pretty?" I ask, as my heart unexpectedly does a little flip-flop. The only explanation I can think of for the jerky pitter patter is that I do not know many women, that would not like being complimented by Jack. He is the type of handsome that can make a lady turn into a blithering idiot just by looking at them.

"Yeah, yeah, don't let it go to your head. Most of my thorns are hardened criminals that look a little rough around the edges."

I can visualize him blushing on the other end of the phone, having been caught giving me what could be considered a compliment. I don't think he knows how to interpret my banter with him most of the time. Like I said, many ladies fumble in his presence, so he has no idea what to do with one that doesn't. He seems to be rather oblivious to the effect he has on the female population. I think he assumes they are nervous because he is the sheriff.

"Sorry. All I heard was that you think I'm pretty," I say, trying to further antagonize him.

Once again, he is stumped at how to respond. After a few seconds, he says, "Daphne is off today. What can I do for you, Miss Riley?"

"I received a call yesterday and just wanted to follow up on any information that you may have regarding it," I say. Apparently, the interaction that was bordering on flirtatious has turned to seriousness.

"Oh yeah? Who's cheating who this week?" he asks, chuckling at his own quip.

"That joke never gets old," I say sarcastically. I admit to myself that was an unexpected, funny comeback from him. "I happen to be all caught up on catching two-timers red-handed. I actually wanted to check on a call you may have received from Gertie Rose. She said Ford came out to respond last night," I say, becoming serious.

"If she called after the storm started, then I'm sure it was Ford that took the call. He was the only one left here. The rest of us were out having to reroute traffic due to flash flooding on a couple of roads, and some trees down across others. There was also an accident where a SUV hydroplaned and wrecked. Thank God, no serious injuries."

I have no doubt that the weather created a whole slew of problems that had to be handled by emergency crews. One good thing about living in a community like this one is that volunteers and neighbors usually pitch in, to cut fallen trees from the roadways, or do whatever else that needs done. People do not have the "that's not my job, not my problem" outlook on things. Regardless of if they like, or dislike, their neighbor, they will lend a helping hand when the situation warrants it. If they dislike one another, they may quarrel the day after, but they are sure to help when aid is needed.

"I'm glad to hear that nobody was hurt," then, I ask, "Did Ford mention Gertie's call, or can I speak to him if he is in today?"

"He isn't here today. I told him to take the day off, since he had to man the station all night. He didn't mention it, but you know with Gertie, we're at her house pretty regular, and unless it was an emergency, he wouldn't have called me about it. I can check the log and also call him to see what happened, if that will help you."

"I would appreciate it. Thanks for your help, Jack, er, I mean Sheriff." I can practically hear him smiling on the other end of the phone, as he usually does when I am trying to decide whether to call him Jack or Sheriff. He never objects to either name that I choose to use.

"Anytime, Elle. I'll call you back in a few."

I pace back and forth, worrying a thumbnail, as I wait for his return call. I replay everything that Gertie told me. Nothing sticks out in my mind that could be a clue regarding a murder. The only hint to go off of is the truck, which I know exists because of Dot's camera footage.

Gertie said that the truck had Florida license tags. Why would someone from Florida be at the creek committing such a heinous crime? A Florida swamp would seem like a more logical choice for a murderer to get rid of a body. But, then again, there is no body. My pacing slows as I reach up, trying to massage away the tension that has settled into my shoulders. Maybe, the perpetrator took the body with him. Maybe the victim was only wounded and ran off into the woods to escape. It had to be someone familiar with the area to even know where the creek is located. Just because the truck had Florida tags, it does not mean that the people were from there. At least one of the men must be local or have knowledge about the area. But who is he?

About fifteen minutes after hanging up with Jack, my phone vibrates, and the Sheriff relays the same information from Ford that Gertie had given me. I had expected as much, or else Jack would have already been made aware of the situation by Ford.

"What do you think?" I ask.

"I'm not sure what to make of it. You never know with Gertie. If there was a crime, it is not a good thing that she was the only witness. Obviously, Ford thought nothing had happened. And *if* — that's a big if — it happened, there is absolutely no evidence of it. No missing persons, no crime scene, and no body. Not to mention, how would I even know where to begin looking for this mysterious man, with the only lead being a lizard on the back window of a black truck?"

"I cannot argue any of that logic with you. As outlandish as her story sounds, I still cannot help but think she saw something, though. Maybe not a murder, but something she was not supposed to see. You should speak to her neighbor Dottie. She has security cam footage of a truck matching the description driving past last night. Unfortunately, the electricity went out and there is no video of the truck exiting, so no view of a license plate or decal on the back window."

"How about I swing by there today, speak to Gertie myself, and then I'll stop by Dottie's?"

"I would appreciate that," I say.

"No problem. I know you like to look after Gertie. I've grown quite fond of the ole gal myself."

I call Gertie, after hanging up the call with Jack, to let her know the Sheriff will be out to talk to her about the murder that she says she witnessed. To which she replies, "Are you talking about a television show, deary?"

Well, at least I do not have to worry about her being upset today, seeing as how she is confused and does not remember her story. If only I could put it out of *my* mind.

CHAPTER SIX

Not long after Jack called, my phone rings again. Glancing at the caller ID, I see it is Colt. I answer and he says, "Hey Sweetness, you busy?" If anyone can distract my thoughts away from Gertie's recounting or recollection, it is Colt. I smile at the familiar endearment that he used as a greeting.

"Not at all. Are you working hard? How's Alabama treating you?" I ask, falling back on the couch.

"Nah. Not working at all. Actually, that's why I'm calling. To make a long story short, someone forgot to cross their T's, and dot their I's, so there is an issue with the job. I came back home until tomorrow night. I wondered if maybe you would be up to go out tonight? I sure missed you this past weekend."

"That sounds great. I missed seeing you, too." I say.

"Okay. I will pick you up at five. Oh, and dress nice," he adds, as an afterthought.

"Am I not normally dressed nice?" I ask, raising my eyebrows, as if he can see me.

"You always look great! But I mean, wear a little black dress or something."

"For?"

"It's a surprise," he says, drawing out the word surprise.

"Oh crap, we aren't going to the funeral home, are we?" My heart sinks at the thought.

This causes him to laugh. He says, "No, I'm not taking you to a viewing at the funeral home. I think you'll like what I have planned."

"Okay. I will take your word for it. I'll be ready at five," I say, cautiously. Colt is an adventurous type, and I never know what kind of plans he has in mind. Depending on his mood, we could end up hiking to the top of Mt. Kilimanjaro or going boot shopping. I'm guessing since he told me to wear a little black dress, it couldn't be anything too extreme.

* * *

It is ten minutes until two o'clock, and I have settled into Art's office, psyching myself up for the interviews that I will conduct this afternoon. The first candidate is scheduled for two o'clock. I spot a moped coming up the street. The rider hits a pothole so hard that it bounces him into the air like a trampoline. I see it pull onto the sidewalk in front of the office and park. A man who seems more round than tall hops off, removes his helmet, and does some stretching and squats. He does one last lunge before opening the door.

"Hello. May I help you?" I ask.

"Yes. I am here for an interview," he says, in something of a baby voice I can barely hear.

"My name is Elle. You must be John," I say.

"Johnny," he squeaks. His brow is covered in sweat.

"Nice to meet you, Johnny. I see you arrived early. Punctuality is always a plus. Can you tell me a bit about yourself?"

"I live with my mom and I have four cats," he says, almost inaudibly, looking like a deer caught in headlights.

I open the top desk drawer, grab a bottle of acetaminophens, and shake two out into the palm of my hand. Something tells me that the blurry headache that I have may worsen in the next hour or so. I spot Art's bottle of whiskey and contemplate swallowing the tablets with a drink of it. Nah, best not to give a prospective employee the wrong idea about this office being unprofessional. I pick up my bottle of water and gulp down the tablets, as I say, "Well, that sounds nice. Would you like something to drink? Water? Soda? Coffee?"

"No, thank you," he chokes out.

"Can you tell me about your last job?"

"I've never had a job," he squeaks. Now, he looks like he may pass out. I'm no expert, but I think Johnny may have a serious social interaction disorder. I tend to be socially awkward, but his behavior is on another level. I cannot help but to feel bad for him.

"Can you tell me what interests you about working here?" I ask.

"My mom says I need to get a job to help her pay for hearing aids because she can't hear a damn thing I say," he says, slightly louder than a whisper.

The investigative skills that Johnny has listed on his resume consist of searching for his cats when they do not come home. He has also mentioned some rescue work, which is getting one of the aforementioned cats out of a tree if it becomes stuck.

This is going to be a long afternoon.......

The next interviewee walks through the door at ten minutes past the scheduled appointment time. I look up to see the young lady, with vibrant pink colored hair, wearing a studded leather jacket, with a snake tattoo wrapping around her neck. Her name is Stevie.

She slouches into the chair opposite of my desk and asks, "Can you tell me what the hours are before we get started?"

"The office hours are eight a.m. through five p.m., Monday through Friday, and an occasional Saturday," I tell her.

"That's not going to work for me. Could I maybe come in around eleven?" she asks, while squinting through what looks like yesterday's mascara, with a hopeful look on her face.

"I'm sorry Stevie, but we really need someone who can work *all* the hours that the office is open."

"Well darn! Thanks anyway," Stevie says, as her face falls.

I cannot let her leave the office without appeasing my curiosity. "Do you happen to know Jared Rose?" I ask.

"Dude. Jared is my ride or die. I party with him a lot. His grandma loves my brownies!"

A long afternoon, indeed. I retrieve Art's bottle from the drawer and take a big swig. Darn.... Stevie seemed like she would be a lot of fun to have around the office.

The mention of Gertie draws my mind back to her story and the possibility that there is a cold-blooded murderer roaming Justice. I do not have long to ponder, because the next candidate arrives five minutes early. A professional-looking lady named Sandy. She is wearing a smart navy-blue skirt suit. Her jewelry and make-up are understated. Her hairstyle is as neat as the rest of her appearance. I have seen Sandy around town. She always seems equally as pleasant as she does today.

After introductions, I ask the standard interview questions. Her responses are ideal, until I say, "We handle a lot of sensitive information here and confidentiality is of the utmost importance. We need to know that anyone that works here will take that seriously and use discretion."

"Oh yes! I never tell anything that I am not supposed to! Except to my best friend. But you wouldn't have to worry because she never tells anyone!"

I grimace, disappointed at her response. *Three strikeouts for today.* After she exits the building, I open the desk drawer, reaching for Art's bottle again, while sighing. If it keeps going at this rate, I may develop a drinking problem.

The last of the scheduled interviews is a no-show. Hiring a secretary is proving to be even more difficult than I had initially thought. People can find plenty of tips and clues of how to enhance their resumes by utilizing the internet. Points given for being computer savvy and being able to type, but the interview portion seems to be where the process will end, for most of the candidates.

After the way these first meetings have gone, I am relieved that the last applicant was a no show. This will allow me extra time to get ready for my date with Colton. I lock up the office and head upstairs.

* * *

While going through the motions of showering and getting 'all dolled up,' my mind wanders again to Gertie's story. Where would I even start looking for this mysterious devil, as Gertie referred to him? I suppose I could go back to speak with any neighbors that I have not already spoken to along the route, to see if they saw the black truck, or anything out of the ordinary. Chances are that Jack has already done so.

Colt knocks on the door at a few minutes past five. I opted for a little red dress that bares much of my back. I took some extra time with my hair, pinning the loose waves at the nape of my neck, to show off my exposed back and shoulders. My make-up is on point — working with what God gave me, working out today. I chose strappy black heels. The bruise on the top of my foot is not noticeable unless someone were to closely examine it.

When I open the door, he says, "Oooh la la! Maybe we should just cancel and stay in!" He raises my arm above our heads, spinning me about getting a good look at me, before pulling me into an embrace and kissing me on the neck.

I am thinking the same thing as I take in his appearance, of a coat and tie, that looks like they were made just to be worn by him. Instead of agreeing with him, I splay my hands on his chest, pushing him away slightly and say, "Oh no, I do not think so, Champ. I invested a lot of time to look like this. Besides, it is not often that someone offers to surprise me in a good way."

He chuckles and says, "Well, alright then, we'd best be on our way."

Grabbing the shawl that I have hanging on the back of my barstool; we make our way out to his truck. He opens the passenger door for me and takes another opportunity to embrace me. "Are you sure you don't want to just stay in? I have really missed you."

I have a hard time making myself say, "Yep, I'm sure," and it sounds more like I am trying to convince myself than offer a reply. Staying in is sounding more attractive, but I am like a kid on their birthday, curiously looking forward to whatever he has planned.

CHAPTER SEVEN

olt makes the two-and-a-half-hour drive in just under two hours. We pull into a lavish new restaurant that everyone has been raving about. He chooses to park his Dodge truck himself, rather than have it valet parked. The restaurant is on the first floor of a posh new hotel, boasting a menu of exotic foods, along with an expensive wine list. He, no doubt, had to make a reservation. The hotel is said to be just as exotic as the restaurant's menu.

"What made you decide to bring me here?" I ask, as I move my arm in a semi-circle, indicating the fancy restaurant along with its ambiance. We normally only eat at places that have a drive-thru or offer curbside pickup as a convenience. Sometimes, he drops subtle hints that make me think he wants our relationship to be more serious.

"I have been wanting to try it out, and I knew if I brought anyone else here, they would think I was trying to be romantic."

Okay, maybe I am mistaken about those subtle hints.

"Besides, it never hurts to be seen with the prettiest girl I know on my arm."

Giggling, I say, "Nice save, but I am still ordering the most expensive item on the menu." It is just as pleasing, to be called pretty by Colt, as it is by Jack. Colt has never made me wonder if he thinks I'm beautiful. He not only tells me often, but makes me feel beautiful too.

"Sweetheart, looking like that, you can order it twice if you want."

"You are cutting a fine image tonight, also, Mr. Ryan," I say, and he beams a broad smile at the compliment.

We enjoy an expensive wine that lingers in your mouth. An hour after being seated, our food arrives. I was not adventurous enough to try the gator tail, fried rattlesnake, elk, or any other similar items on the menu. I played it safe by ordering lobster and Colt chose the venison. Probably the same cut of meat that can be found in his freezer at home. We enjoy the food, which is good, but we both agree is overrated. It is now almost ten o'clock, both of us are giddy from the wine, and neither one of us is ready to call it a night.

"What do you say we get a room here instead of making the drive back tonight? Check out a club while we're here?" Colt asks.

"That sounds like a good plan. I think the wine was stronger than we expected, and you probably should not drive, anyway. But…. no karaoke," I say.

"Now *that* sounds like a great plan. Besides, I am not nearly drunk enough to listen to you sing," he says. We both laugh because it's true.

We leave the room hoping to find a club to listen to live music. To our disappointment, two in the area, within walking distance, are closed on Mondays. The only place open is a seedy looking dive bar, with several motorcycles parked out front. A neon sign advertises live music nightly.

"Do you think this is a motorcycle bar?" I ask, nervously.

"Doesn't look like one. Only one way to find out," Colt says, holding the door open for me.

The bar looks a little less seedy on the inside. It reminds me of one of those hole in the wall restaurants that doesn't look very attractive, but offers the best food you've ever eaten. The patrons are a mix of business suits, college kids, and bikers. The live music is actually karaoke. Colton and I both laugh at the irony, as he says, "Remember, you promised no karaoke."

We take seats at the only empty table in the room, which happens to be next to the group of bikers. I am sitting in close proximity to the largest man I have ever seen. He is closer to seven- feet tall than six, broad shouldered, and big-boned. He looks like a linebacker and a pro basketball player gave birth to Bigfoot. The other men keep referring to him as Teeny. He has a gray beard that looks like a steel wool pad that has come unraveled, hanging down to his chest, and a ponytail that goes all the way to his lower back. The men are all dressed similarly in jeans, leather vests covered in patches, and black boots. That is where the similarities end. Their physical appearances are unique to each man, but they all share that tough as nails look.

Two middle-aged ladies are on stage crooning and doing a fabulous job. They look like a modern-day Thelma and Louise. Everyone cheers and claps when they finish. The drunken college kids whistle, hoot, and holler things such as "Cougar" and "MILF" at the ladies. There is much murmuring from the bikers about how they would like to teach those assholes some respect.

Next, a stuffy-looking man in a business suit takes the stage. He loosens his tie and starts timidly singing. He lost a bet with his buddies that landed him onstage. His singing is even worse than mine and the crowd boos. Teeny yells "Get off the stage! My dog's howling sounds better than you! An animal caught in a trap, yelping, sounds better! Hell, even I sound better than you!" he laughs.

It seems that most of the tables in the establishment are occupied by assholes. I turn to Teeny and say, "Prove it."

"Huh? What'd you say?" Teeny asks, like he cannot believe his ears.

"Elle, I really don't think—" Colt says.

"I. Said. Prove. It. You go next." I nod toward the stage that the businessman has just vacated.

His fellow bikers laugh, and he says with a wave of his hand, "Whatever. I don't crack skulls all day to get bullied into singing by a five-foot three brunette."

"I'm five-foot five! Guess you don't have the guts to embarrass yourself," I shrug. I may be five-foot five, but the wine that I drank earlier is making me feel ten feet tall and bulletproof.

"Excuse her, sir, she didn't mean it. She drank some wine earlier that went to her head," Colt says, panicked. His normal adventurous spirit seemingly disappeared.

The other bikers are getting a kick out of the conversation and start cajoling Teeny into performing. "You gonna let a little girl show you up, Teeny?" hahaha. "Too sensitive to get booed off the stage?" hehehe.

"Fine!" Teeny says, as he stands up, revealing the leather chaps that are covering his tree trunk legs. "But you're going with me." He points at me demandingly.

"Oh, I can't," I stammer. "I promised I would not perform karaoke. Unlike you, I know that I'm a terrible singer."

Teeny cracks his knuckles, looking at Colt sharply, and asks, "You always tell her what to do?"

"Who me? No way! Never! She never listens to anyone else, anyway. Go sing your heart out, Elle. Have fun," Colt says, practically shoving me from my chair. My dress gets snagged on his watch. I roll my eyes, untangle my dress from his wrist, get up, and accompany Teeny to the stage.

It isn't that I cannot sing. I just cannot sing alone. I have no problem following along with someone on stage with me. The issue is when I have too much to drink; I think I can sing alone, since Colt does not like to perform karaoke. Drunken karaoke can be very entertaining for the audience, but nobody wants to end up as a viral video or meme as the butt of a joke.

We choose "Islands in the Stream" and the crowd goes wild at our performance. Teeny has the most melodious voice that I have ever heard, and some very agile dance moves. I look at him and say breathlessly, "They love us!"

"Yeah, they do! Wanna do another one?"

"Okay, sure," I say, feeling like a superstar.

During our next duet, a couple of drunk men start yelling lewd remarks at me. "Whoo! Take it off! Show us some more skin in the front! Nice breasts! Let us see both of them!" I glance down and see that the strap of my dress came unraveled from getting snagged on Colt's watch, exposing my black lace strapless bra. I stop singing, frantically trying to cover my breast, as I rush off the stage.

Colt stands up to make his way over to the drunken sots. Before he gets halfway there, Teeny has jumped down off the stage. Teeny stalks over to the table, where he lifts one of the men out of his chair by his shirt collar. He delivers an open-handed slap to the man's pallid face. Smaaaaccckkk, the microphone in his hand echoes the sound. "Apologize to the lady!"

"So-so-sorry," the man says, as his feet dangle in the air, and a wet spot trails down his trouser leg. One of his buddies is holding up his hands defensively, afraid that he will be the next recipient of Teeny's thrashing. The third lush fell out of his chair in his haste to try to get away before Teeny could reach him.

The biker's chairs make a loud scraping sound, as they all stand up. One of them breaks a beer bottle against the table, brandishing the top half as a weapon. The bartender yells, "You're all outta here!" He has a baseball bat in one hand and a cordless phone in the other. He is red-faced, has broken out in a nervous sweat, and is trying to show bravado that he clearly doesn't feel.

"Says who?" asks Teeny, dropping the man, and crossing his arms over his chest.

"Says the cops, who'll be on their way before you get too out of hand!" says the bartender, holding up the phone. We can hear "911, what's your emergency?" on the answering end of the line.

"Come on Teeny, you can't afford to break parole, let's go," one of his buddies says.

"Damn it, me neither. I ain't even been out two weeks yet," another member of the gang says.

Teeny drops the microphone on the floor. It echoes making a deafening thud sound. He says, "Elvis has left the building," as we parade like a band of miscreants out the door.

"Thanks for defending me in there," I say to Teeny, as Colt wraps his jacket around my shoulders to hide my wardrobe malfunction.

"Don't mention it. I like you. People never challenge me. Guess they're afraid of my size. It was refreshing when you back talked me in there. Put my number in your phone. If you ever need a karaoke partner, or need me to crack some skulls, call me," he says, giving Colt the evil eye.

Colt takes a step backwards, eager to leave.

"Aw, thanks Teeny. My name's Elle Riley, by the way."

"I think I'll just call you five-foot five," he says, laughing. "Where are you from, anyway?"

"Kentucky."

"Oh really? What part?" he asks.

"A place you have probably never heard of. Justice."

"Heard of it? Hell, I've been there. Did a scenic route over to the Cumberland Gap through there. Small world," he says.

"Sure is!" I say.

Colt nudges me on the back and says, "Um, we should probably be going. *If* it's all right with you, five-foot five."

"See you around five-foot-five Justice," Teeny says, making a saluting motion with two fingers, as he straddles his bike and slips on his brain bucket.

"See you around, Teeny dancer," I say.

"Are you crazy? Telling him where you live?" Colt asks, after we get out of Teeny's earshot.

"And here I thought you were the adventurous one," I say. "Besides, with my line of work, it never hurts to have unexpected friends."

"That is true, I suppose. Could you maybe not make any new friends that want to crack my skull open, though?" he laughs, glancing nervously back over his shoulder, as we make our way down the block to our hotel room.

CHAPTER EIGHT

TUESDAY

I am sitting in Colt's truck at a convenience store an hour outside of Justice, thinking about how dreary the sky looks today. He is pumping gas and I watch as a man, shirtless, rides in on a youth's hot pink bicycle. I cannot help but wonder if there will be a little girl crying somewhere today because her bike has gone missing.

The man gets off of the bicycle, tosses a cigarette onto the ground, and struts to the door, while pulling his low hanging pants up over his boxer briefs that are covered in cartoon characters. He opens the door at the same time a lady with her hands full is coming out. She assumes he is going to hold the door. Instead, he side steps around her, leaving it to shut in her face.

She comes out, after picking up the items that she has dropped, and shoots a middle finger toward the man. She climbs into an older model truck. A minute later, the man exits, gets on his bike, and starts to pedal away. The lady pulls out, her truck backfiring. The man apparently thinks he's been shot and wrecks the bike. The lady shoots him a middle finger again and speeds off.

The sound of the truck backfiring and the sight of the man falling to the ground, draws my mind back to the scene Gertie says she witnessed. I have not heard from Jack, so I assume nothing new has turned up. With no leads to go on, this case could be dead in the water before it begins. I cringe as I think 'dead in the water' is too accurate of a description concerning this case.

Colt gets in the truck laughing. "Couldn't have happened to a better person," he says, referring to the man wrecking his bicycle.

"Karma does have a way sometimes," I say.

I misinterpreted Colt's actions last night when he took me to the restaurant. Which means that I have read the other signs wrong too, and he does not want our relationship to become serious. I tell myself that I am relieved. I have avoided thinking about why my mind says to be glad about it, but my heart feels a tinge of disappointment. It is not that I do not care for Colt; I care a great deal for him. The idea of falling in love again is daunting. Having agreed that we do not want a commitment takes away any pressures, obligations, and possible heartbreak.

Colt and I have always been great friends. Our arrangement makes it possible to maintain our friendship if either of us decides that we no longer want to be involved romantically. So why, then, do I feel that tinge of disappointment? Is it sadness that Colt does not want to become seriously involved, or is it regret with myself for giving up on the idea of love and happiness? I know I want those things again someday. I just do not want to take a chance on getting burned so soon after having last touched the flame. *Someday though....*

I must have dosed off. Which is unexpected, considering Colt drives like he is a contender in a drag race. Coming awake, I see we are almost to the Justice county line. I look at the parking lots of the bars as they speed by. When we pass by the Troubadour, I notice a big black Chevy truck with a lift kit. On the back windshield is a large decal of an alligator. I am still a little groggy, and it takes a minute or two for my synapses to kick in. Then I wonder if that is the same truck from Gertie's story, and the lizard that she saw on the back window could have actually been an alligator. I am intrigued by the possibility of finding the mysterious murderer from her incredulous story—especially this easily. Maybe it's karma sorting this out.

I look over at Colt's striking profile. I had told him about Gertie's story last night at dinner. Now, I do not mention my thoughts about the truck, or that I plan to go to check it out as soon as he drops me off. I know I can tell him anything, but I also know he will insist on accompanying me, and I would feel silly if it's a wild goose chase. Hopefully, the truck will still be there by the time I can make my way back. My excitement about it makes the short drive seem to take forever.

Colt pulls over in front of my building. "I had a really great time last night," he says. "Well, aside from being terrified of your new biker friend," he laughs.

"I enjoyed it too. It *was* a delightful surprise. Thanks for it," I say.

"I dread having to make the drive to Alabama." He sighs. "You know, you can do your writing from anywhere. You should come with me."

I consider the possibility for a split second, but then remember the truck parked at the Troubadour. "I wish I could. Unfortunately, I have an investigative case to work on this week." I do not volunteer to tell him it may, or more than likely, may not be a murder investigation, and the client is Gertie, whom I am working for free of charge. "Raincheck?" I ask.

"Sure, raincheck. But you and I both know that you always have something going on. Just like last Saturday, when you canceled on me," he says, while looking out the windshield, refusing to meet my glance. The flex of his jawline tells me he is irritated.

"That isn't fair. You said you didn't mind that I canceled! You've done it plenty of times!"

"And I didn't mind. I was just using that as an example," he says. He looks over at me, the hard set of his jaw relaxing, and being replaced by a softer expression. "Look, Elle, I'm just saying that it seems your personal life always seems to take a backseat to whatever else is going on. You spend the majority of your time solving problems for others and ignoring your own."

"That isn't fair either," I say quietly. "I don't ignore my problems. I just don't bitch and moan about them like other people do." I feel the sting of his comment knowing that it was loaded with much more than what he voiced aloud. Apparently, he had really minded that I canceled. I try to put myself in his shoes. When he has called off plans with me in the past, I have felt let down, but chalked it up to; that's what I should expect with a no strings attached relationship, and that's what I should expect from Colt. If that relationship is taking a turn for one in which we point out each other's flaws and bicker, I'm not so sure I want that.

"You're right. I'm sorry," he says. My anger fades at the contrite expression on his face. I can read so much in the look he is giving me. Regret that he said those things out

loud. Regret that he had put his hurt feelings on display.
Regret that he has hurt my feelings. A dark curl hangs
down on his forehead, his eyes search mine. I can never
stay upset with him for long.

I slide over in my seat, grabbing his hand, pulling it
to my chest. "Colt, I am sorry. I can be a real jerk and
a pain in the ass. It was very inconsiderate of me to cancel
our date last minute."

"Forget about it," he says, in his fake Italian accent,
his demeanor changing back to his easy come, easy go
attitude. "Besides, it's not like I haven't canceled on you
before. And I'm sorry too." He looks down at his hand
that I had placed on my chest, wiggles his eyebrows, and
seizes the opportunity to cop a feel. I roll my eyes. He
laughs and pulls me in for a heated kiss.

I tear myself away from the embrace and say, "I will try
to make plans to come to Alabama to hang out with you
soon. Deal?"

He looks at me with a sheepish smile and says, "Deal."
I smile back and give him one last kiss before climbing
down out of his truck. He toots his horn twice as he
pulls out onto the street, the diesel engine drumming.
Everything seems to be back to normal between us, still
I cannot help but feel that maybe it isn't. Colt and I may
debate about common issues occasionally, but we never
argue over personal matters. I worry that this argument
may indicate that we both have some unresolved feelings.

I rush around to the side of the building, holding my
tied shawl over my torn dress, almost colliding with Art,
who is carrying a fast-food bag.

"Whoa sweetheart. Where's the fire?"

"Sorry Art. No time to talk. I may have an iron in that
fire," I say, as I dash up the steps.

"Take care to watch your back and if you need me, holler."

"Will do," I say as I round the corner.

I burst through the door, flinging my purse onto the couch. The apartment is three rooms that consists of an open living room with a kitchenette, a bedroom, and a bathroom/laundry room. I love the openness of the space, with exposed brick walls and wooden beams that are original to the building. My decorating style is minimalist. Everything in my home serves a purpose. I prefer things uncluttered. This same space in Boston would cost a small fortune. In Justice, it is considered too small for most people to want to live in. Of course, most people can buy a house in Justice with a mortgage payment that is cheaper than monthly rent on an apartment like this would be in the city.

Having already showered before leaving the hotel this morning, it does not take me long to get ready. I quickly style my wavy hair and put on a bit of make-up. I slide on my favorite jeans and a black sweater that droops down off of one shoulder. I pull on a pair of low-heeled boots and pop some hoop earrings in my lobes. I am out the door in less than fifteen minutes and on my way to the county line.

* * *

I always seem to fall behind the slowest drivers when I am in a rush. I have had to follow a car for several miles, driving ten miles per hour below the speed limit. Finally, coming to a passing lane, I push the gas pedal down on my Bronco, passing the car like it is standing still.

I see Jack's Ford F-150 with Sheriff emblazoned on the side, coming down a side road. *Crap!* I know he is going to pull me over for speeding again. I watch for the blue lights in my rear-view mirror, amazed when I do not see them. He must have not seen me or clocked my speed. Maybe I lucked out for once.

As I pull into the gravel parking lot at the Troubadour, I note that the shiny black Chevy truck does indeed have Florida tags on it, giving credence to Gertie's story. I snap a picture to show her. Then I enter and take a seat on a bar stool.

CHAPTER NINE

The Troubadour used to be a little too worn looking. When it was handed over to a new owner five years ago, the establishment received a makeover. There are now modern industrial style light fixtures hanging from the ceiling. The mirrored wall behind the bar is lined with various bottles of liquor and a unique collection of shot glasses. Full sized drinks are served in Mason jars. The base of the center tables are whiskey barrels. The walls feature framed pictures of the beautiful scenery that is local to the surrounding area, and a couple of photos of local musicians that have graced the stage here, and then gone on to play with well-known artists. There is a dance floor, stage for live music, and pool tables that are located in a back room. The jukebox has been here as long as the bar has.

During Friday and Saturday nights, the place is always filled to capacity. There is never an empty seat on those evenings and the dance floor is always packed with people enjoying the live music. Anytime that the University of Kentucky is playing a ball game, the place is filled past capacity. Men and women of every age group, over 21 years old, cheer or shout obscenities at the large screen television. Even if they do not agree on much else, they all come together to root for their beloved Wildcats.

Sally, the bartender, asks, "Hey Hon, the usual?"

"Yes, please."

"You little rebel. You just might be the only born and bred Kentucky girl I know who drinks Canadian whiskey instead of Kentucky bourbon."

"What can I say?" I shrug. "I like to be different."

"Honey, I'd be disappointed if you weren't."

Sally is small statured, standing just over five-feet tall, with a big personality. She has shoulder-length blonde hair and keeps a great tan all year long (thanks to her tanning bed). She wears cropped tank tops and tight jeans. She doesn't take any bad attitude from anyone. Even men twice her size fear her. She is in her forties and wise beyond her years. She has seen it all, and heard it all, during her many years as a bartender.

I sweep my eyes around the room. The few bar stools that are occupied are taken up by the regular patrons, who occupy them every afternoon on a weekday. There are two men at a table, probably having a drink on their way to or from work, still wearing their yellow protective vests. A couple holds hands across a booth in the corner of the room. Two tables in the center have been pushed together to accommodate a small group of ladies around my age. I recognize most of them. They are probably having a day drinking lunch while the kids are at school and their husbands are at work.

Rachel, one of the ladies that I know, waves at me. A man who is unashamedly flirting with them turns to see who she is waving at. I wave back at her, noticing that his is the only unfamiliar face in the establishment. This must be big, jacked up Chevy's driver. I also notice that Rachel is the only one of the ladies who doesn't look loaded. She must've drawn the short straw to be a designated driver today.

One of the young women has danced her way up to the counter to get another pitcher of margaritas. She asks Sally about adding some new song, which sounds more like pop than country, to the jukebox. "Sorry, Sugar. We only play the good stuff here."

The somewhat tipsy day drinker giggles and I cannot help but laugh out loud. Sally always shoots straight from the hip, saying exactly what she wants to say. Yet, nobody is ever offended and they all still love to talk to her. I suppose having the power to withhold pouring libations for people could have something to do with this.

Sally is also an AA sponsor. This does not seem to cause a conflict of interest for her. And it certainly does not deter anyone from coming to the bar—unless she is their sponsor — which may have the intended effect.

"Hey Sal, what do you know about that guy over there?" I ask, after the lady dances away, sipping straight from the margarita pitcher on her way back to the table.

She follows my line of sight and says, "Ya mean, besides him making my skin crawl? Not much. Been coming in for the last month or so. Sometimes during the day like today. Sometimes at night. Sometimes both. Hits on every girl around and still ends up leaving alone. Please tell me you haven't set your sights on that," she says, almost shivering.

"No worries there. I just didn't recognize him is all."

"I think his name is Clay. He said he moved here for work, but I have no idea what that work is. The only person who I've seen him talking to that acts like they might've known him already was Kurt Abbott. Now, Kurt's N.A. sponsor told me he has been missing his meetings lately, which makes me wonder if it has anything to do with him," she says, tilting her head in Clay's direction. "I haven't noticed him doing anything that would make me think he was dealing, and if I ever do suspect it, he's outta here!" She leans in and lowers her voice, saying, "Between you and me, I think little redheaded Lexie, there at the end of the table, meets up with him on the sly. Must not be serious though, considering he hits on every other female in the place and she doesn't seem to mind."

"Hmmm. Interesting. Thanks Sal."

It does not take long until Clay makes his way over and plops down on the stool beside me.

"Are you tired?" he asks me.

"Excuse Me?" As I think that my lack of sleep must be showing.

"From walking through my dreams all night."

"Ha. I think you may need to come up with a more original line," I tell him, as I try to keep from rolling my eyes.

Laughing, he says, "You're probably right. I haven't seen your pretty face here before. Name's Clay. What's yours?"

"Elle. I do not make it in as often as I would like." I take in his appearance more closely now. He is tall and broad shouldered. Dressed in faded jeans, a tee shirt, and cowboy boots. At first, I thought his dark hair was greasy but now it appears that he has used too much hair gel in it. He has a beard that looks as oily as his hair. Even with the grooming product, his facial hair still seems to look scraggly and unkempt. The overpowering woody smell of his cologne almost makes my eyes water.

I suppose he is handsome, yet there is something totally off putting about him. I can definitely understand what

73

Sally said about him making her skin crawl. We continue with small talk, allowing me time to finish my assessment of him. He tries to come across as a smooth talker but instead, sounds like he is trying too hard. I peg him as an ex-con. A talker who thinks highly of himself. Definitely a bragger. Chances are if he has committed a crime, his big mouth will boast about it.

"So, what do you do for a living, Elle?" he asks, while casually leaning back against the bar, sticking a toothpick in his mouth.

"Um, I am a photographer," I say. Out of the corner of my eye, I see Sally smile, as she realizes I must be working some kind of angle.

"That sounds really cool. What type of pictures do you take?"

"Mostly couple photos," I say. Sally's shoulders shake with stifled laughter.

"What line of work are you in?" I ask, genuinely interested to know.

"Contract work. Self-employed," he says.

That is a vague term that could mean a broad range of things. My mind at once conjures up contract killer or drug runner. I shiver internally at the possibilities of what his self-employment is. "What type of contract work?" I ask, as I feel a tap on my shoulder. I turn to see Sheriff Jack Lennox standing there, looking disgruntled.

"Sheriff. Something I can help you with?" I raise my brows questioningly. I know he isn't here to talk to me about Gertie's story, because I can tell by the look on his face that I have done something with which he is displeased. Probably the speeding.

"Why yes, Miss Riley. I was hoping I could have a word with you." He tilts his head, indicating outside.

"Actually, I am kind of busy having a drink with Clay here," referring to Clay with my hand palm up. "Is this something that can wait until a better time?"

"Now, Elle," he says, impatiently.

This brings forth a huff from me and Clay says, "Now what would the Sheriff be wanting with a sweet little thing like you?" directing this at both Jack and me.

Jack says, "Don't let the sweet little thing act fool you. She's been known to have a potty mouth, throw hands, and have anger issues."

"That was just the one time!" I say. He is referring to when I decked a deputy who pulled me over for a non-existent traffic violation, then offered not to write me a citation in exchange for a sexual favor. To Jack's credit, he fired the deputy on the spot and almost decked him himself.

Clay laughs and says, "Damn girl, I knew I liked you!"

"Well, it has been a pleasure making your acquaintance, Clay. Unfortunately, I must be needed elsewhere." I cannot hide the annoyance in my voice and this causes Clay to let out his sleazy sounding laugh again.

I follow Jack out the door, walking very slowly just to irritate him. As soon as we get to the parking lot, he starts. "What do you think you're doing?"

"Well, I was having a drink and making a new friend, until you interrupted." I cross my arms over my chest in a defiant stance.

"Since when do you drink in the afternoon on a Tuesday?" he asks.

I arch a brow. "Since the last time I checked, I am a grown ass woman, and it isn't any concern of yours."

"Having a drink with what appears to be the man who is Gertie's mysterious murderer? Do you think I didn't notice the truck?" He hooks a thumb over his shoulder, indicating said truck. "I went in there looking to get an idea about the guy, after following you here, and find you saddled up to the bar with him."

"Oh, so you were stalking me?" I ask, incredulous.

"Nooo! I clocked you going almost eighty-five in a fifty-five! By the time I got pulled out onto the road, you were long gone! I knew you were coming in this direction."

Hehehe

"You know what? You aren't even Sheriff here! We are technically across the county line," I say in a slightly raised voice. My accent always seems to become more pronounced when I become irritated, and my language can sometimes become colorful if I am angry. To my credit, I have been working extremely hard not to let as many curse words escape lately. Other than when the pickle jar fell on my foot, of course.

He sighs, trailing his hand through his hair, and says, "Look Elle, I'm just worried about your safety. I ran the guy's tags to see who he is and then ran his name. Clayton Butcher. Has a rap sheet thicker than your stack of speeding tickets. Most recently, for kidnapping an ex-girlfriend. And he has a history of domestic violence against that same girlfriend. Theft by deception, battery, unlawful entry, the list goes on and on. If he isn't the person who Gertie saw, then I can almost guarantee that he is engaged in some other type of nefarious activity."

"I appreciate your concern Sheriff," getting my temper under control, "but, I, like you, was just trying to get an idea about him. I was going to call you after."

"Well, it's good to know you were going to call *after*. Did it ever occur to you to call *before*?" he asks in a sarcastic tone.

"You know what? You are impossible," I say, uncrossing my arms and placing them on my hips.

"Oh? I am impossible? Have you looked in a mirror lately?" He gesticulates.

"I am going home now!"

"Good, Elle! Home is where you need to be. At home, leaving any investigating up to the actual police! This isn't like writing one of your stories. This is real life, with a real-life criminal!"

I stop before getting into my vehicle, with all sorts of snarky retorts on the tip of my tongue. I reign them in, realizing that it is better to cut my losses in this instance.

"Goodbye *Sheriff.*"

"Goodbye Elle. And remember to watch your speed on your way home! I would hate to have to write you another ticket!"

HA! You would love to write me another ticket! I give him the evil eye as I climb in behind the steering wheel. Pulling onto the road, I head in the direction of my apartment. I am smart enough to wait until he pulls out, rather than to let him follow behind me. After about four miles, the Sheriff turns off onto another road. I make a U-turn, backtracking toward the bar. I park at a convenience store across the road, planning on following Clay when he leaves, to see where he goes, or even better, where he lives.

CHAPTER TEN

I backed the Bronco into a parking spot at the convenience store across from the Troubadour. It offers the perfect view of Clay's truck, which is still parked in the gravel lot. At least it did offer the perfect view, until a diesel truck towing a horse trailer pulls in, blocking my view and my exit. I look around to see if I can navigate to another spot, but a semi-truck advertising something about death, taxes, and beer has everything else blocked.

I take this opportunity to grab a snack and see if I can keep an eye on Clay's truck from the store window. I enter the busy store, sidestepping other patrons. I get a coffee, hot enough to scorch the fuzz off my tongue, a package of chocolate donuts, and a jumbo package of Twizzlers, all the while glancing out the window. When I get to the checkout line, I have to look around the customers in front of me, while trying to act nonchalant, to see the parking lot at the bar.

The lady at the counter is slowly counting coins to pay for her purchase. "Good grief, lady! I don't have all day!" the store clerk snaps at her. He slaps his hand down over the currency, sliding it in his direction, counting it himself. The lady's face flushes with embarrassment. She comes up twenty-seven cents short, and the clerk tells her she will have to put her purchase back. A man in line right behind her slaps a dollar bill down on the counter to pay the rest of her balance.

The line moves up, as the cashier finds some way to be rude to each customer, almost making me dread my turn at the register. The patron in front of me tosses his items onto the candy rack in front of the counter and walks out, apparently having enough of this jerk.

The clerk has noticed me looking out the window, and he stares at me like I am a weirdo. He does a complete turnabout, looking outside for a few seconds with his beady eyes. His mouse-brown mullet sways as he quickly turns back to face me. He has probably had the hairstyle since the first time it was fashionable, and it has gone from a mullet to a skullet. Finally, he asks, "You got a problem?" as he curls his lips in a snarl.

"Nope. Just worried that the lion cub that I had in my back seat has gotten loose. I can't see it from here." I crane my neck past him, making a big production of looking at my SUV. "If he has, he won't go far. He hasn't eaten today."

He looks out the window and sees the dried dog slobber, nose prints, and mud on my back window, that look like they could have indeed come from a lion cub, instead of Gertie's behemoth dog. Then he sniffs the air, inhaling all the food scents inside the store. He looks around, taking in the hot dogs spinning on the roller, the hot sandwiches behind the glass at the counter, and finally down at his chest, as if he realizes he may make a tastier piece of meat for a lion. His Adam's apple bobs as he gulps, and he quickly gives me my change.

I almost feel bad for fibbing to the clerk. Almost. Maybe thinking he will have an encounter with a lion will make him more humble and less discourteous.

I do not have to wait long when I get back to the vehicle. The horse trailer and semi are gone, and as soon as I climb in behind the steering wheel, I see Clay's truck exiting the gravel parking lot. I guess he struck out with the ladies and decided to call it a day. He slings gravel as he pulls onto the highway. The truck almost turns sideways as he floors it, leaving a billowing trail of dust, and the smell of hot tire treads, in his wake.

Maintaining my distance, I tail him. I allow a couple of vehicles to get between my Bronco and his truck, just as Art taught me to do years ago. After driving about six miles, he turns onto a small side road. I am familiar with the area. The street is a dead end, with some small rental houses and mobile homes. I park at a carwash close to the road entry and wait fifteen minutes. Clay has not returned from wherever he went, and I feel enough time has passed that I will not be noticed if I follow.

I cruise onto the road and see his truck parked under the carport of one of the small rental homes halfway down. His is the only vehicle in the driveway. The house has pale blue siding and a tiny lawn in need of a mow. The little concrete porch is bare of any decoration or plants. A lack of another vehicle or a feminine touch makes me think he lives alone. I turn around at the end of the street, headed home to do a few errands and grab a power nap, with plans to return later to stake out the house.

* * *

After having a rotisserie chicken sandwich on a ciabatta bun slathered in sriracha and a side of broccoli slaw for dinner, I head out. I dressed in dark clothing, as I usually do when on a stakeout. This allows me to blend into the night surroundings if I have to exit the vehicle for any reason. It is now dusk and I decide to drive the black Toyota Camry. It is less conspicuous when doing a stake-out.

I know the owner of a vacant house down and across the street from the one that Clay is renting. I called to ask her if it's okay for me to park there and she told me it was fine. The last thing I need is for someone to call the Sheriff about a strange vehicle being parked on their private property.

I have been here less than twenty minutes. The Camry is backed into the driveway, which gives me a full view of the house that Clay is renting. I am now settled in, eating strawberry Twizzlers, and hoping I can gather some more intel on Clay. I am so focused on watching the house that I do not hear anyone approach the car until the passenger door is opened. I gasp while grabbing the gun that I have laying on the console. The interior light in the vehicle is off, so as not to alert anyone to my presence. It takes a second for me to see that it is Sheriff Jack Lennox that has ducked his head inside the car.

"Please tell me you have a permit for that thing," he says, as he lifts the items lying on the passenger side and slides in.

"Geez, you should start wearing a bell around your neck. You realize that I could have shot you, right?" I ask, palm placed over my heart, trying to slow the beat. "You almost scared me to death."

"I wasn't too worried. I've seen your hand to eye coordination and I'm guessing you don't have real good aim," he replies.

"I will have you to know that Art taught me to shoot, and he says that my marksmanship is expert."

"Shot many people, have you?" he says.

"No, but I still might shoot you, just to prove that I can."

He shakes his head and laughs. Then asks "What are you doing here? I told you to leave the investigating up to me."

"Did not seem like you were doing much investigating since you were not following him," I say, pointing my licorice toward the house across the street.

"I don't need to follow him. I just need to follow you. I knew you were too persistent to leave it alone," he says.

"Where did you come from, anyway? And why haven't you questioned him?" I ask.

"I parked behind the carwash and walked through the woods," he says. "And say what? A lady that has Alzheimer's said that you committed a murder that we cannot prove happened? That we need you to fess up and tell us all about it since we don't have a body or even a missing person? And alert him to the fact that Gertie saw him?" he asks.

"Well, when you put it like that...," I say.

"Besides, you catch more flies with honey." He slides the seat back to accommodate his long legs. "Better to let him think I suspect nothing until we have proof of a crime," he says.

"Oh, I get it," I say. "So, we can be like good cop/bad cop?"

"No! We are cop," pointing to himself, "and pain in cop's butt," pointing to me.

"What happened to the whole catch more flies with honey thing?"

"Doesn't apply to you," he says, as he reaches onto my lap and grabs my bag of Twizzlers and tears into one. I can smell the clean, masculine scent of him in the small space of the car.

"I'm glad to see you are in a better mood. What are you doing, anyway?" I ask.

"On a stakeout, right? I figure you can either go home and leave it to me or I can sit here with you. Since I know you're not going to take the first option, here we sit."

I am seriously considering taking option one. This is going to be the longest stakeout ever.

"I think it is worth mentioning that Sally said she has seen this guy Clay interacting with Kurt Abbot and it seems they know each other," I tell him.

"Could be worth mentioning. I will follow up with Kurt and see what he knows about him. Kurt did a bit in Florida when he got caught trying to run drugs out of there. Judging from this guy's rap sheet, maybe they served time together," he says.

"I have been out to Gertie's three times now," he continues. "She seems to be having a memory lapse. I have searched up and down the creek, the woods, and anything else that I can think to do, and come up empty. No one in the area saw the truck or anyone matching Clay's description. I just have the footage from Dot's security cam. I probably would have just chalked it up to her vivid imagination, had we not seen the truck and put two and two together."

"You're welcome, by the way. Had I not been speeding; you would not have been led to the truck." I say.

"Yeah, yeah. I'll give you a pass this once," he says.

When you sit alone for hours, you become good at entertaining yourself. Eat snacks, reflect on things, scroll through radio stations, or maybe even listen to a podcast to pass the time. When you sit for an extended period of time with someone else, eventually one of you chatters to fill the silence. Tonight, Jack is the one who starts the small talk after we have been sitting quietly for a while.

"Do you miss living in a city?" he asks. "It must have been culture shock coming back to a town that only has four traffic lights."

"Not really. There is something to be said about a simpler life. One that is less rushed. Farmer's market on Saturday morning with my Mama, occasionally Sunday School with Granny, having time to visit with family. The city lights can mesmerize, but they do not compare to the beauty that we have here. The natural arches, waterfalls, lakes, and streams. There is so much here that the city does not offer. The entire atmosphere is unique, you know?"

"You should write tourist brochures," he chuckles. "I know what you mean. I love this town too. So, you came back because you were homesick?"

"Oh, come now. I know you have probably heard the rumors. The ones that say Elle Riley couldn't hold on to a husband or a fancy job, so she ran home with her tail tucked." I park my gaze on my window to hide my shame over what some would consider failures on my part.

"Do I look like the type of person who people gossip to? I have never put any stock in gossip, anyway. Besides, I know if you wanted those things, you would still have them." I turn to glance at him, and he looks me squarely in the eyes. I think this last part may be the sweetest thing that he has ever said about me. Probably the *only* sweet thing he has ever said about me.

"If I am overstepping, just let me know, but why did you get divorced?"

"Irreconcilable differences." I lift my shoulders in a shrug.

"Couldn't agree on kitchen tile or politics?" he asks half-jokingly.

"No. Actually, he thought it was okay to have an extramarital affair, and I did not agree with that."

"Oh shit, Elle. I'm sorry. If I had known that I wouldn't make jokes all the time about 'who's cheating who'."

"It's fine. I still have my sense of humor."

"If it makes you feel any better, your ex must've really had his head up his ass," he says.

I am not quite certain how to interpret that comment. He could mean that Liam had his head up his ass for being a cheater in general. Or he could mean that he lost out by cheating on me. The intense look he is giving me seems to indicate the latter. I decide not to read too much into it. Normally, Jack does not ask personal questions. Normally, he does not eat much sugar either, so maybe the Twizzlers have gone to his head.

Thankfully, before this conversation can get any more awkward, a car swings into Clay's driveway. Jack and I both sit up, alert. A lady with a sleek blonde bob haircut and expensive looking clothes gets out of a black Jaguar. Her high heels click purposefully up the drive.

"Is that," I ask and Jack finishes by saying, "Cammie Parker?"

Cammie is married to Andrew Parker, Jr, whom everyone calls A.J. He is the wealthiest man in Justice. There are very few rich people in Justice. Shortly after his divorce a couple of years ago, he went to Vegas for a trip, and came back with his new bride, Cammie, on his arm. Much to the disappointment of several ladies in town who had their eye on the newly eligible bachelor.

Cammie bangs on the door with her fist and Clay jerks it open. Obviously, neither one of them pleased.

"Do you think they could be having an affair?" I ask. Even though I certainly cannot picture this being a great match, I have seen more unlikely pairs than this one.

"Anything is possible, I guess." He shrugs, but the look on his face is skeptical.

Just a few minutes later, Cammie comes out of the house, seemingly in a worse mood than she entered with. "Boy, if it is an affair, someone sure is disappointed," I say. Jack gives me the side eye. "What? I'm just saying she wasn't in there very long and she does not look happy." This causes him to laugh.

She gets in her car, slams the door, and speeds away. As she peels out, another vehicle pulls in. A young man with a red visor on his head advertising pizza gets out, carrying a delivery. Clay answers the door, pays for the food, and then turns the porch light off. Jack and I decide to call it a night since Clay is probably settled in for the evening.

CHAPTER ELEVEN

WEDNESDAY

I awoke early again this morning without an alarm. I tend to not sleep well when I have something on my mind. I know Jack is right and I should leave any investigating up to the Sheriff's department. Not that I find them incapable of handling it, it is more that I have some type of compulsion driving me to solve the mystery.

Perhaps this type of behavior is subconsciously my way of living in the moment and avoiding questions I should ask myself. Most people find or reinvent themselves when they are young, maybe during college or shortly thereafter. I never did that. The wildest thing I have ever done is get a large tattoo of a phoenix on my side. I had always known what I wanted from life, set my goals, and achieved them.

I am now thirty-two years old, living alone in a small apartment and have grown accustomed to not setting any new goals for myself. The question, *where do you see yourself in five years?* keeps coming to mind, and I keep pushing it away. I fear I am becoming too complacent and, as Colt pointed out yesterday, I seem to ignore my problems.

I moved to Boston to attend college, where I received my bachelor's degree in communications and political science. I then obtained a master's in journalism. I met my ex-husband Liam, short for William Riley III, while there. He was a handsome lawyer who had gone fresh faced into a prominent law firm to work shortly before we met. We married soon after I graduated. He was the perfect package: Handsome, smart, and kind, he seemed to be able to see directly into my soul. Or perhaps it was that he was the only man that I had met who bothered to try to look at me that way.

He came from an old money family. One would think that his wealth would have made life easier, yet at times, it complicated things. I had not come from money and I therefore was not accustomed to the finer things that rich people seem to think are important. I have always felt that people and experiences are more important than material items. That's not to say that I do not enjoy certain things, such as shopping and creature comforts. I just enjoy them on a different level than wealthy people do.

After we were married for a few years, the same things that he had said that he loved about me seemed to vex him. He did not understand why I seemed to be unaffected by the wealth at my disposal. Why I wanted to pursue a career in which I had to deal with deadlines and demanding editors when there was no need for me to work? Why I didn't want to become a socialite like his mother, and spend my days shopping or at a spa, and my evenings on his arm, as a trophy wife to the prestigious corporate lawyer? Smiling, nodding, and agreeing with everything that his associates had to say.

His mother never embraced me into the family with welcoming arms. That never seemed to help matters any. It shocked her when Liam had married a "hillbilly girl from Kentucky," as she had referred to me once, not realizing that I overheard the remark. Her small-minded ignorance was on full display with her biting words. The words themselves weren't offensive, but the manner in which they were spoken was insulting and full of derision.

I should have seen his affair coming. He had started spending more and more time at the office. He wasn't clocking hours working as he led me to believe. Instead, he was romancing Astrid. She was someone who was much more suitable due to his family's wealth and influence. Someone I'm sure his mother was thrilled with.

Yet, until the day I found out about the affair, he still acted as though he thought I hung the moon, so it blindsided me. He begged, pleaded, and made many promises, asking me not to leave him. I agreed to try to save our marriage. After a few months of counseling, and regardless of the effort that Liam was putting in, I realized I would never trust him again. Then, I found out that he did not end his affair. He just thought he had gotten better at hiding it. I packed my things that same day and filed for divorce.

The months of trying to make a failed marriage work is the only period of my life that I consider a waste. Even now, stuck on autopilot, I do not feel as squandered as I do about that time of my life.

I kept Liam's last name after the divorce because I penned every piece of work that I ever published under the name Riley. His last name was the only thing of his that I took when our marriage ended. He offered me a handsome divorce settlement, which I declined. I loved Liam, not his money.

A part of me has never stopped loving him, even after his philandering. It's the type of love that makes you care if a person lives or dies, prospers or fails. I am no longer *in love* with him, but a place in my heart still grieves over our lost marriage. Maybe I just romanticize the relationship that I thought we had prior to his affair. I tell myself that it makes me happy to think he is miserable with Astrid. The truth is that I hope he finds happiness. Just not with her. And definitely not with me.

* * *

Picking up my phone, I dial Gertie's number. If the Sheriff has not already done so, I want to stop by there today to show her the pictures of Clay and his truck. Hopefully she can identify him or it will jog her memory if she is having an off day. I let the phone ring several times and the answering machine picks up. Maybe she is at bingo at the Senior Center today, or gone to an appointment. I will try her again later instead of leaving a message.

I blow dry my hair and put it up in a messy bun. I apply moisturizer with sunscreen, lip gloss, a little bit of blush, and black mascara that compliments my eyes. I choose to wear black leggings and a medium weight sweatshirt. This is the time of year that you never know how to dress when going outside. Kentucky weather is so erratic. It could be sunny and seventy-five one day and there could be a tornado the next, or maybe even a snow shower.

There is no better place to gather information about someone such as Cammie Parker than at the beauty salon. My mama hears all the gossip, regardless of whether she wants to. I call her, putting my phone on speaker, while sliding into a pair of casual sneakers. She answers on the second ring, always happy to hear from me.

"Hey Mama, are you at the shop today?"

"I am. I came in early to work on a client who could only come before she went to work. What are you into today?"

"I am currently at home, but I thought I might stop by, if you are not too busy."

"I'm never too busy for my baby girl."

"Great. I'll see you soon."

Picking up my cross-body bag, I pull the strap over my head and take off out the door. The beauty shop is close to my apartment, and it isn't raining, so I decide to walk. I stop at the coffee shop on main street along the way and pick up two iced coffees. Then I finish the short trek to the salon.

I cannot help but admire the newly painted window advertising "Annie's Salon- A Place of Beauty," the new black, gold, and white striped awning above the entrance, and the enormous containers of pansies sitting next to the door. Main street is slowly being gentrified. The businesses it now houses include the coffee shop, a vegan bakery, yoga studio, an antique shop, and several specialty boutiques. Murals painted by talented local artists can now be seen on some of the buildings. Beautiful lamp posts with big flowerpots around them adorn the sidewalks. This new aesthetic makes Main Street more enticing to both the locals and tourists. Mama is doing her part to help make it more attractive.

I open the door, and a chiming sound announces my arrival. The inside of the salon received a make-over recently, as well. New salon chairs, a large caramel colored leather sofa for clients to sit on while they are waiting, floor length mirrors throughout the shop, beautiful glass chandeliers, and wooden floors. The mirrors reflect the beautiful chandeliers and the light from the large window, making the space look twice as big and giving the clients plenty of opportunities to admire my mother's handiwork on their hair. The décor is very stylish and looks like it would belong to an upscale salon in a city, rather than a small main street beauty shop. My mother is very intentional with her interior design choices and the place turned out beautifully.

I hand her the iced coffee and she asks, "How do you always know just what I need?"

"Daughterly intuition," as I kiss her on the cheek.

The shop is empty other than she and I. Neither one of the other two stylists is in yet. Nearing fifty years old, Mama is a very attractive lady. She wears her mid-length brown hair with highlights, stylishly cut. She has always been a fan of yoga and the years on the mat have paid off. She looks much younger than her age. People that do not know we are mother and daughter often confuse us as sisters.

We have a brief discussion about how she knows that messy top knots are the style, but I should really make the effort to do my hair before leaving home. She then tells me she has some time before her next appointment and offers to style my hair, to which I say no. When Mama styles my hair, it resembles 'the higher the hair, the closer to God' method. It always turns out beautiful, yet I feel it would be a little over the top paired with my leggings and sweatshirt.

After some more small talk, I ask, "What do you know of Cammie Parker?"

"I know she drives two hours away to get her hair done." Then she explains toner and the integrity of hair after it has been bleached. My mind wanders off, listening to the information. But I keep nodding my head, trying to make her think I am intrigued by hair chemistry.

"And she's from Vegas, right?" I ask, slurping my iced coffee.

"No, honey. That's where A.J. met and married her, but I think she is actually from Florida."

"Hmm. I did not know that." I say, trying not to seem overly eager for information.

But Mama is too smart when it comes to reading my behavior. Her hand pauses as she brings her cup to her mouth, ice chunks tinkling, and she asks in a very loud whisper, "Are you investigating her?" even though there are no other people in the shop to hear.

"No. I had seen her out and about and it got me to thinking that I know nothing about her. Just curious, is all," I say and shrug my shoulders, as if I could care less.

She looks at me like a hot butter knife slicing through margarine. It's the same look she gives me when I try to convince her I am not overdue for a pap smear. She then resumes talking about blonde hair. "Daphne's hair is the perfect example of a healthy blonde head. Now, mind you, she has dream hair, but still she doesn't drive two hours away to get her hair done," she says.

There are two things that burn my mother's biscuits more than anything. The first is if she thinks someone has been mean to one of her loved ones. The second is people thinking they are too good to get their hair done here in Justice. She takes it as a personal affront to herself and her fellow beauticians. After living in the city, I can vouch that the hairdressers here are just as good as the overpriced ones in fancy salons.

"Daphne does have hair to make people envious. You do a wonderful job on everyone's hair, Mama. Cammie is crazy not to have sought you out for an appointment."

She blushes at the compliment. We continue with idle chatter, excited that the Farmer's Market will be open on Saturday. We make plans for that morning, and then I head out.

"Tell Arty I said Hello," she says.

"Okay, I sure will. Bye Mama. Love you," I reply as I am shutting the door.

CHAPTER TWELVE

I can smell food from the diner wafting down the sidewalk as I step out. The golden oldies music spills out of the speakers onto the street. A few customers sit outside at picnic tables enjoying their food and ice cream treats. My stomach growls at the scents that smell like a heart attack on a plate, and I am reminded that I have not eaten yet today. I decide to stop in for an early lunch.

Entering, I find a booth next to the window, thankful that I have beaten the lunch crowd here. I order a cheeseburger, side of fries, and a vanilla milkshake. They are short staffed today, making the wait time a little longer than normal. I retrieve my phone from my bag and dial Gertie's number while I am waiting. The answering machine picks up and I leave a message this time.

Looking up, I see A.J. Parker sauntering over to my booth.

"Well, lookie here, it's Elle Riley. I haven't seen you in a month of Sundays. Mind if I sit?" he asks in his exaggerated southern drawl. He is already sliding into the booth before I can reply. His dark, thinning hair splays across his head in wisps from the overhead vent blowing on him. His once lean physique is going a little soft around the middle. Overall, he is still a handsome man in his forties.

A.J. is a pleasant person. A conversationalist. He talks so much that the person he engages with usually finds it a one-sided conversation. If he were not such a nice person, I would find this extremely annoying. This is a great opportunity to work Cammie into a conversation, while I have the chance. *If* he will let me get a word in.

He mentions the weather, then prattles on about the new boat he just bought, and how he cannot wait to get it out on the lake with the warmer weather now that he is not so busy with work. I have never been too sure what exactly A.J.'s work is. I think it mostly consists of managing his inherited wealth and figuring out how to amass more of it.

I find an opening during a brief pause and ask, "So, does your wife enjoy going out on the lake?"

"Cammie?" he asks, as if he has more than one wife. "Yeah, which is a wonder to me since she's more of an indoor type of gal. Doesn't care for the mosquitoes, sweat bees, and her hair getting messed up. Likes to get her tan inside in the sunbed. Course, she's been real busy lately too. I guess you probably heard that we're building a new rehab. She graciously offered to deal with the contractors and such, allowing me time to concentrate on my work."

He then trails off talking about red tape, tax breaks, and a whole slew of other things. My mind wanders, listening to him, much like it did listening to Mama talk about hair. My phone vibrates. I look down to see that it is an unknown number and hit decline.

A.J. asks "You need to take that?"

"No. It is probably a telemarketer. I was hoping it was Gertie Rose returning my call."

"Gertie Rose. Now that's a character if I ever seen one! Me and Cammie was just out to her place yesterday. Joe Jr. knows I have been wanting to buy her property forever. I would just love to build a cabin in the woods out there next to the creek. He has been trying to talk her into selling it to me and going into the nursing home."

"Anyway, Joe called, and I went out there. After talking to her, I decided that even if she agreed to sell it to me, I would feel like I was taking advantage of her. What with her mental state and all. She was telling us some convoluted story about seeing a murder down by the creek the other night. Can you imagine?" he asks, laughing, as the waitress walks over and sits my order on the table.

"Well, I'll let you get to it, Elle. It was nice chatting with you. Bye now." He is gone as quickly as he arrived.

"Bye A.J. Have a good day," I say, as he is walking away.

The waitress asks, "Can I get you anything else?"

"Actually, I would like a to-go box if you don't mind. I think I will just take my food back to the office and eat it."

* * *

When I walk into the office, Art is at his desk gathering some file folders and getting ready to leave. He has an office to itself, but uses one of the three desks out front, unless he is meeting with someone. This allows him to monitor the door when he works alone. The space is much like you would imagine a Private Investigations office would be. File cabinets, bulletin boards, and office equipment neatly arranged around the room. The same exposed brick and woodwork that grace my apartment are also present here.

A small kitchen, and two restrooms, one for office use, and one for public use, are in the back.

"Do you mind if I use the office to do some digging on someone?"

"Do you even have to ask?" he replies. "What are you working on?"

"Probably a dead end. I am working leads regarding Gertie's mystery man from the other night."

I had already told Art about Gertie's story and was feeling certain that I had found out who the mystery man is.

"Do you need my help?" he asks.

"Thanks, but like I said, it's probably a dead end, anyway."

"Well, I'm going to head out then. I'm going to drive to Bowling Green and meet one of the aids from the law firm in Louisville to pass off some information. If you need help, holler. Watch yourself not to get mixed up in anything dangerous. And lock up the office when you're done."

"Noted, noted and noted," I respond, which causes him to grin. "Drive safe."

Then I say, "Oh, I almost forgot, Mama said to tell you hello."

This brings a pleased look to his face. "Sweet Annie. I will have to swing by her place to say hello myself soon." Then he is out the door.

I sit down in the comfortable chair and move the mouse to bring the computer to life. I open a tab and start a file on Clayton Butcher. Then, I build files for each person he may be associated with, for cross reference purposes. Cammie Parker, Kurtis Abbott, and red headed Lexie from the bar all get a file. I learned a long time ago that looking into associates of people can often lead to more information on the primary subject. Something seemingly insignificant can turn into a major clue.

I start my search. As I suspect, I do not garner any information about Clay that I did not already have. In his file, I type his rap sheet info, Florida, contract work, his physical description and description of his vehicle. I debate on typing sleaze bag under his descriptors but decide to be a professional.

I then move on to his possible associates. Jack had said that he would speak to Kurt today, so I do not waste time on his file. I will save Lexie for later and concentrate on Cammie now. I cannot help but think that there is something important about the encounter I witnessed between her and Clay last night.

Rather quickly into my search, I discovered that when Cammie married A.J. her last name was Johnson, and Cammie is actually short for Camilla. I then do a search for Camilla Johnson, Florida. The information says that she is the widow of Henry Johnson from Palm Beach. Henry was forty years Cammie's senior and a wealthy real estate tycoon. There are two surviving children listed in his obituary, a daughter and a son. I dig a little deeper, finding contact information for Henry's children. The phone number for his son, Isaac, comes with a message that it is no longer an active number. I then dial the phone number for the daughter, Isabelle, and someone answers on the third ring.

"Hello, I am trying to reach a Mrs. Isabelle Decatur,"

"This is she."

"Mrs. Decatur, my name is Elle Riley. I am writing an article about Mrs. Camilla Johnson-Parker and the great work she is doing in our community here in Justice,

Kentucky," I say. (I actually am thinking of drafting an article about the new rehab being built.) "I was hoping to get some information on her back story from you."

I never know how phone calls like this will go. Sometimes people are cooperative, other times they are rude, and often they just hang up. Isabelle Decatur falls into the cooperative category. She is more than happy to indulge on Cammie's history. The picture she paints is not a pleasant one.

I finish the conversation with Isabelle and end the phone call. Perfect timing. My watch vibrates, telling me it is now time to move and stretch. It is now a quarter to one o'clock. I shut down the computer, grab my bag, turn off the lights, lock the door, and head down to the Sheriff's office to speak to Jack. Hopefully, he will not be out for lunch.

CHAPTER THIRTEEN

I step into the Sheriff's office and its drab beige walls. The desks in the room are metal, and they, along with the chairs, look like they are from the early nineteen-eighties. The floors are ancient, faded green and white floor tiles that are chipped and cracked in places.

This office has a history of being predominantly occupied by men, and most men rarely care about interior design. The little money that is in the budget has always gone to things that help the officers perform their job safely or more efficiently, rather than updating the furniture and décor. New state-of-the-art computers and printers sit atop the old desks, with the exception of an old typewriter sitting on Ford's desk, which he prefers. The vests, tactical gear, and body cams are always top of the line, and two new four-wheel-drive SUVs were just recently added to the fleet.

The only area in the office that has had a feminine touch is Daphne's desk. It is decorated with rose gold office accessories and a framed photo of her husband and children. Peanuts character bobble heads perch on the shelves of a small bookcase next to her desk, displaying her fun personality. Her desk is always neat and organized, in great contrast to the other work areas. Sticky notes with her meticulous penmanship dot the calendar. She keeps the office purring like a well-oiled machine.

She looks up as soon as I enter, assuming that I have come to see her. Daphne has long, thick, strawberry blonde hair and blue eyes. She always has a smile on her beautiful face. She is a cousin to Jack, and those vibrant blue eyes are a family trait.

"I wasn't expecting to see you today," she says, happy with my spur-of-the-moment visit.

"I know. It's good to see you. Unfortunately, I am here for business. Would Jack happen to be in right now?"

"He is," she replies.

We spend a few moments catching up, and discussing our favorite tv show, then I get back on task asking, "Do you need to let him know I am here or can I go on back?"

She waves her perfectly manicured hand and says, "You can go on back. His door is always open, and there isn't anyone in there."

"Thanks, Daph."

"Anytime. Catch me before you leave so we can make plans for lunch."

"That sounds great. I sure will."

I walk past the water fountain that is making a humming sound and then start down the hall with pictures of past officers lining the walls. I do not have to go far. Jack's office is the first one on the right. I knock on the door frame. He has his back to the door, retrieving something from a file cabinet and says, "come in," without even turning to see who it is.

I step into his office and take a seat. He grabs some papers off the printer, then turns and looks a little bewildered to see me. He no doubt thought I was someone that works in the office.

"Elle, what brings you here? Do you not have a stakeout planned for us tonight?"

"My stakeouts work better as a one man show. I get all the Twizzlers to myself that way." He chuckles and I then say, "Actually, I just found out some information about Cammie Parker that you may find interesting."

"Do tell," he says, propping his elbows on the desk, and rubbing his hands together in anticipation.

"Cammie Parker was originally Camilla Butcher," I say.

"Clay Butcher's sister instead of his lover," he guesses.

"Winner, winner, chicken dinner. But that is just the beginning. Camilla was married to a very wealthy, much older, real estate tycoon, named Henry Johnson from Palm Beach, Florida. Mr. Johnson succumbed to a head injury sustained during a yachting accident. The couple had not been married long. His adult children thought Cammie to be a gold digger when they married, and suspected foul play was involved in his death, because he was a master yachtsman. They insist that Cammie and her creepy brother had something to do with their father's death but could never prove it."

"Cammie was very disappointed after Henry's death to learn that he had transferred most of his wealth to his children before he married her, his children having convinced him to do so. The only real money she walked away with was half of his life insurance. The other half being split between his children. Cammie's half was still a substantial amount — half a million. Henry's son and daughter had nothing to incriminate Cammie, but they managed to pull some strings and get Clay's parole revoked, sending him back to serve the remainder of his sentence."

"Where he met Kurtis Abbott as his cellmate." Jack replied, holding up the papers he had been retrieving.

"I made a trip out to Kurt's place this morning. I spoke with his wife, Fiona. She said they have been separated for a while. Regardless of him being on the straight and narrow, he has had a hard time finding steady employment since getting released. Financial problems took a toll on their marriage. She said he is really good about coming to spend time with the kids, but not so good about monetary support for them. That is, until a couple of weeks ago, he shows up with a wad of cash. It wasn't a lot of money, but it was a lot of money for him to have. He wouldn't tell her how he got the money, and she was afraid he might be mixed up in something that would get him sent back to lock up."

"She told me he has been staying with his mom since they split," he continues. "When I checked there, his mother said she hadn't seen him in almost a week. She feared he had fallen into his old habits. I talked her into filing a missing person report on him. I have people out looking for him. Neither Fiona nor Kurt's mom know Clay."

"I paid a visit to Clay's house this morning to bring him in and question him about Kurt being missing. We have the video of Clay's truck driving toward the creek and Sally's account that the two men seemed to know each other. Clay has ditched his truck and is nowhere to be found. Him being in the wind tells me he is guilty of something and knows he's about to be caught. I have a car sitting on his house. Sally is supposed to call me if he shows up at the bar. I can only hope he hasn't returned to Florida," he says.

"You're thinking that Kurt is the other man that Gertie saw at the creek that night?" I ask.

"It tracks. I was just getting ready to head over to Gertie's again and show her Kurt and Clay's mugshots

STEPHANIE KINZ

and a picture of the truck, to see if she can make a positive ID."

"Do you want me to speak to Cammie and see if she knows Clay's whereabouts?" I ask.

"I'm guessing it won't do any good to tell you no. But whatever you do, avoid Clay, we both know he is most likely dangerous."

He opens a drawer, takes out a badge, and slides it across the desk toward me.

"Have I driven you to turn in your badge?" I ask, jokingly.

"Hardly. At least, not yet!" He says, his smile showing off the dimple in his cheek. "That is for you. I figure if you're going to keep snooping, I may as well deputize you. We are short-staffed due to budget issues. There's really no point in me having a deputy do the same legwork that you are going to do anyway. And this way, maybe any information you get, you will obtain by the book. If you're agreeable, I'll call the judge. You can take the oath, and we'll get you sworn in."

Why not? Being a deputy sounds pretty cool.

After meeting with the Judge, we return to Jack's office so I can fill out some paperwork.

"Now, can we be good cop/bad cop?" I ask.

"No."

"Does this mean I get a patrol car?"

"No," he answers.

"Can I get one of those sirens to go on top of mine?"

"Nope."

"Stun gun?"

"Definitely not," he laughs.

"Does this at least mean that you can't pull me over for speeding anymore?"

"No, but nice try," he says.

"Fine. But I sure hope you are not one of those bosses that I have to sue for sexual harassment."

"Get out," he says, pointing to the door, trying not to laugh.

I pick up my new badge and walk out. I can hear him laughing as soon as I clear the doorway.

CHAPTER FOURTEEN

I pull up the long driveway that leads to the Parker residence. Bradford pear trees line either side. The trees are budding with what will be an explosion of white flowers. Hopefully, dogwood winter does not kill off all the promising spring blooms. I park in the circle drive, in front of the massive brick home with immaculate landscaping. Fresh mulch lines the flower beds and hardy spring annuals have been planted. A man on a zero-turn riding lawnmower is manicuring the several acre lawn. The truck with the trailer to haul the mower sits in front of a large barn. The porch and its furniture remind me of an old southern mansion, although I doubt this furniture has ever been sat upon.

I park behind Cammie's black Jaguar. Most vehicles have a yellow-green coating on them this time of year, the pollen making it impossible to keep them clean. Her dark colored car is spotless, looking freshly detailed. Of course, any vehicle that doesn't have doggy nose prints, smudges on the windows, or mud on the tires looks clean to me today. Hers is the only vehicle in the drive other than mine. Meaning that she is the only one home, or the other vehicles are in the garage. I wonder if Clay has a vehicle tucked away in that garage, or maybe the barn.

I ring the doorbell after climbing the wide steps. After a few moments, Cammie opens the one side of the double wooden front door. Dressed in workout clothes, her skin is flushed, and she has a sweat sheen around her hairline.

"Hello, Mrs. Parker. I was wondering if you might have a moment for me to ask you some questions regarding your brother?"

"My brother?" She asks, her face becoming very guarded.

"Yes. Clayton Butcher."

She looks around nervously past me then hesitantly steps back, allowing me to enter.

The home has several pieces of gaudily framed art hanging about. The furniture is all oversized and ornate. The décor is all gold, brass, or some other equally shiny material. It is richly furnished and decorated, but not tasteful. The furniture, art, rugs, and décor all seem to compete with each other. The effect is quite overwhelming. The house seems cold and unwelcoming, much like its mistress.

"Ellen, is it? The private investigator?" She asks, trying to sound like a lofty, rich housewife, while peering through her fake eyelashes to look down her nose at me. I am instantly reminded of Liam's mother.

"Actually, it's Elle. And I only help Art out with investigations, occasionally. I am actually a journalist."

"Well, Elle, I would appreciate it if our conversation can be discreet. You aren't writing a story about my brother, are you? Nobody, including my husband, knows that Clay is my brother. I am sure you are aware of his disgraceful past? Terribly embarrassing!"

"I suppose it is like the saying goes, We can't choose our family," I smile awkwardly as she levels a glare at me.

"No, I am not writing a story. I would just like to ask him a few questions about a mutual acquaintance, but I cannot seem to find him anywhere. I know he is your brother, so I thought maybe you might know where he would be." I can tell by the continuing glare and her icy demeanor that this visit will not be productive.

"No, we certainly cannot pick our family. But that doesn't mean that I want to parade him around either!" she says. "I have no idea where Clay is, and I would prefer not to know." She looks at her manicured nails, as if she could be less interested in anything regarding her brother.

"So, you have never mentioned Clay to A.J. at all?" I ask in wonder.

"I really do not see how that is any of your concern, but no, I haven't. Clay was in prison when I met A.J. I thought myself finally free of him, but then to my dismay, he showed up here about a month ago. He found out that A.J. has money and thought that I would be his free ride. I offered him a job at the construction site, but he refused. He became angry with me, and I haven't seen him since."

Liar.

"Do you know of anywhere else he might stay other than his house? Or do you know any of his associates?" I ask.

"No, I don't. What is this really about?" she asks, balling her fists in her lap. An angry shadow crosses her regal features. She is a lady who is used to getting her way, and having someone questioning her without easily being dismissed is making her angry.

"I just need to ask him a few questions. I'm sorry, I can see that I am upsetting you." Jack had said that you catch more flies with honey and the time may come when

I need to speak with Cammie again. She gives me a frigid stare that would wither most people. "I will be on my way," I say. I have given up on any hope that she may divulge anything that would lead to Clay.

"I think that would be best," she says. "I trust you will be discreet like I asked?" her voice turns as sweet as spun sugar when she asks this, donning the personality that she uses for the public eye, her cold countenance falling away as quickly as my hopes of finding her brother.

"Oh absolutely. Please, let me know if you hear from Clay. I will see myself out. Thank you for your time." I can feel her eyes boring into my back as I step out the door. Clay's sister seems to have the effect of making my skin crawl, too.

Cammie has no clue that I know she is lying about seeing Clay. It is a possibility that she is truly ashamed of him. Maybe they were arguing about his being here, or money, when she showed up at his house. It is also possible that she is a con artist and is lying about more than her recent encounter with him.

* * *

Stopping at the end of the Parker's driveway, I get my phone out of my purse, calling the Troubadour. I am hopeful that Sally is working today. She is the person who answers the phone.

"Hey Sally, this is Elle. Do you have a sec?"

"Why sure, Elle," she says, and then I can hear her voice muffled saying loudly, "Hold your horses. I'll be with you in a minute!" Apparently, she is making the time to talk to me. I do not make small talk. I get straight to the point because I can tell she is busy.

"You said you thought Red Headed Lexie may be having an affair with Creepy Clay?" I ask. When talking with Sally, it is best to speak her lingo.

"Honey, I don't *think* it. I *know* it. Rachel told me yesterday that Lexie's husband found out she is stepping out on him with Clay, and left her, and took the kids. Of course, her husband has no clue who Clay is. Just that she was cheating with someone. Now, Lexie is torn up wondering how she is going to make her expensive car payment and get her kids back."

If I had children, I could not imagine losing them for Clay. I do not agree with adultery, but if I were going to step outside of a marriage, it definitely wouldn't be with someone like him. To each their own, I suppose.

"Wow. Do you happen to know Lexie's last name? She may be the only person who can help track Clay down."

"Hmmm. Let me see." After a long pause, she says, "She's a Baker."

"Do you mean she is a baker, as in bakes cakes, or her last name is Baker?" The name Lexie Baker sounds vaguely familiar. But, in a town such as this, most names do.

"Last name's Baker. It's kinda funny that the Butcher is getting it on with the Baker. If they can find a candlestick maker, it'll really be a party!" I can picture Sally's facial expression as she said this, causing me to laugh so hard that I nearly drive myself off the road. Sally starts laughing too. Then I hear her yell, "Don't get your panties in a wad, I'm coming!"

Trying to gain my composure, I ask, "Do you know where Lexie is living?"

"No, I sure don't. But her sister Abby is a teller down at the bank. You could check with her."

"Thanks, Sal. I will let you go. I know you are busy."

"Anytime, Hon," and she hangs up.

As soon as I disconnect the call with Sally, my phone rings. It is Jack.

CHAPTER FIFTEEN

I ask "Hey Sheriff. Miss me already?"

"I was hoping you could help me out," he says, briskly. I can tell he is driving because of the background noise.

"Hmmm. I don't know. You never seem to be able to help me out with those speeding tickets."

"As much as I enjoy our banter, Elle, I have a serious issue. I have just left Gertie's and I am on my way down to the river. A couple of kayakers found a body floating. No positive ID yet, but I suspect it is Kurtis Abbott."

"And you need me to come to where the dead body is?" I ask, panicked, my voice raising several octaves.

I never considered the possibility that allowing him to deputize me would lead to this. I think I should just go ahead and tell him I resign. I am much too squeamish and not nearly brave enough to look at dead bodies. Especially ones that have been in the water for days and could belong to someone that I knew. I can already feel my stomach lurching at the thought.

"Relax. No. I need you to go out to Gertie's, if you can, and try to settle her down. She took a fall down the steps earlier."

"Oh no! Is she okay?"

"Other than a broken arm, she is fine. She says she was pushed down the steps by someone matching Clay's description. I believe her. Joe Jr. doesn't and took her phone away so she wouldn't be calling people telling them what he considers, to be another one of her crazy stories. She has been asking for you all day. As you can imagine, it is a shitshow over there right now. I'm sure they'll fill you in on everything. I left Ford and Eli there, in case Clay decides to come back and finish the job. I have some officers out looking for Clay. I am not sure how long I will be, but I will check in with you later to see how it went with Cammie. It may be late. Is that okay?"

That answers my question of if Clay could have been hiding away at the Parker residence while I was there. He was busy attacking Gertie. But why? Did he see her at the creek that night? The assault on Gertie makes me angry and more determined to find Clay.

"Of course I will go to Gertie's. I am sorry to hear about the body, regardless of who it turns out to be. Whatever time it is when you finish up will be fine. Be careful, Jack."

"Thanks, Elle. And if you decide to go on the hunt for Clay, please do not make contact with him. I would tell you not to even look for him, but I know you are too hardheaded to listen."

"If I find Clay's whereabouts, I will call you," I say.

"Good. Talk to you later, Elle."

* * *

The sky has grown overcast. A heavy, scattered shower rains down. It takes me less than fifteen minutes to drive to

Gertie's house. By the time I get there, the rain has turned into a devil is beating his wife sun shower. It looks as if someone has turned the shower on while standing in the rays of light beaming down from the sky. I can see a rainbow peeking in the distance, promising beauty after the rain.

Ford walks over to my vehicle, holding an umbrella for me. He has always been a gentleman. In his eighties, he can still outwork men half his age. I have heard tale he was a heartthrob in his younger days. It is hard for me to imagine this because even as a child; he seemed ancient to me. Then as a teenager, I had plenty of opportunities to take in his appearance when Colt, a couple of other friends, and I would find ourselves in trouble and confronted by him. Several times, he let us go without contacting our parents. He would give us a stern talking to and make us think we were juvenile delinquents who were on a path to the penitentiary. He knew we were harmless, though.

The one time he did call our parents was the first time that we all experimented with smoking pot. We did not get caught in the act of smoking it, or with it in our possession, but we were high and dared Colt to streak down Main Street naked. Colton Ryan was never one to back down from a dare. Even without the marijuana in our possession, the Sheriff knew we were under the influence, because not one of us could stop laughing, even when faced with the repercussions that we knew would come from our parents being called. All of us turned out to be respectable adults. But who knows, without the Sheriff's stern lectures, things may have gone differently for some of us.

Ford opens my door, holding the umbrella for me.

"Thank you, Sheriff Smith," I say. Retired from being sheriff, he had held the title for so long that people still refer to him as that.

"You're welcome Elizabeth. You're as beautiful as ever. Spitting image of your grandmother."

"Aw. Thank you."

Officer Elijah Keith is leaning against his cruiser, his cap that says "Deputy" turned backwards. He is oblivious to the rain. Tipping his head at me, he says "Ma'am," and then resumes whatever he was doing with his cellphone. He is probably making a video to post to social media. He has garnered quite the following by posting videos showing off his smooth dance moves while wearing his uniform. This has earned him the nickname, "Officer Sexy," from many females. I suppose he is sexy, but he isn't THE Officer Sexy. That would be Jack—the original Officer Sexy. Not that I would ever tell Sheriff Lennox that I think he is sexy. It would definitely go to his head.

Buddy stampedes towards me, almost tackling me to the ground, leaving muddy paw prints all over my clothing. Joe Jr., yells at him to "*Git* down!"

"He is fine, Joe. Buddy does not bother me in the least," I say. I give Buddy a treat and pat him on the head. Joe yells at him again, and he sulks off, his feelings hurt.

Joe takes after Gertie. He is of short stature and has a wiry frame. He reminds me of the landlord from one of those eighties sitcoms that airs reruns late at night.

I make my way onto the back porch. Gertie is sitting in a patio chair, which is covered in cushions with a large pink flamingo print on them. Her feet do not touch the ground. Her casted arm is in a sling.

"Oh, Elle. I am so glad that you are here! You are the only one who ever believes what I tell them!" she says.

"Gertie, you know that Sheriff Lennox believes you. That is why he has these officers here."

"Yeah, but Joey don't believe me," she says, giving him a petulant look.

"I said I believe that you saw something at the creek. I don't believe your story about somebody pushing you down the steps today. I think you fell and made up the story, so I wouldn't tell you *again* that you need to go into the nursing home!" he says.

"You just want me to go so you can sell my house! You are this close to being scrubbed out of my will, Joey!" she says, while holding the thumb and forefinger on her good arm together.

Jack had not exaggerated when he said it was a shitshow here today. "Where was your home aid today?" I ask.

"She called in sick and they didn't have anybody else to send. She has called in every day this week. Can't depend on them. Yet, another reason she needs to go into the nursing home," Joe says.

Gertie has a defiant look on her face. I can tell that she has something to say to him, but her mouth settles into a hard line. We sit in awkward silence for a moment and then she leans in close to me and whispers, "You know Elle, you should date my Joey here." She rolls her eyes toward the back of her head in Joe's direction.

Seriously, Gertie? You could suggest that I date Officer Sexy. He is closer to my age. At least she did not suggest that I date Ford.

She then whispers, "Maybe you could keep him from putting me in the nursing home if you were to marry him. I always wanted a daughter like you." She pats my hand and I cover hers without responding. She leans back in her chair, bumping her cast and exclaims, "Oh Elle, it hurts something fierce!" referring to her arm.

"Did the Doctor give you something for the pain?"

"Yes. But she refuses to take it," Joe says, rolling his eyes so hard that I think they may get stuck.

"I know from when I had my hip operation that those pills make me loopy. Besides, Jared gave me some herbs to relax me before Joey got here. I think they are worn off now, though. If it hadn't been for Buddy, I'd be a goner now. That devil was up here on the porch trying to grab me and Buddy ran up here and tore into him. He took off to get away from Buddy, knocking me down the steps as he went."

Buddy, hearing his name, thinks he has been summoned, and comes over expectantly waiting for a command. I reach out, scratching him behind the ears. "Buddy the Hero! Good Boy Buddy," I say, retrieving another treat from my pocket. He chews up the crunchy morsel and licks me on the face. "I am glad you were not seriously injured, Gertie," I say, wiping the hot dog slobber off of my cheek.

"She will outlive all of us. She's too damned mean to die," Joe says in admiration, with a look of wonderment on his face. I am somewhat inclined to agree with him. Thankfully, Gertie seems to be like a cat with nine lives.

CHAPTER SIXTEEN

The darkness of night arrived hours ago and Jack still has not called. After the day he had, he probably decided to wait until morning to catch up with me. While towel drying my hair, a knock sounds upon my door. It is rather late to have a visitor and they are rare to my apartment. I open the door, saying a silent prayer — Please don't be Clay, please don't be Clay. There stands Jack, haggard looking, after being out in the rain today. His blue eyes are bloodshot and a five o'clock shadow graces his handsome face. His hair is mussed up from combing his fingers through it one too many times. Purple shadows have taken up residence under his eyes.

"I was going to call, but I stopped to get gas, saw these, thought of you, and decided just to stop on my way home," he says, holding up a package of Twizzlers, with a crooked grin.

"How thoughtful. An officer and a gentleman. Come in. Would you like a drink?" I ask.

"I would love a drink if it isn't too much trouble. Did I catch you at a bad time?" He asks while shedding his rain jacket and hanging it on a hook by the door.

"Not at all. I was just getting ready to have one myself. Have you eaten? I can whip you up something," I say.

"Thanks, I grabbed something on the way. Didn't have much of an appetite, though."

He sits down wearily on the couch. I set the drinks along with the bottle on the coffee table, then grab a pad of paper and a couple of ink pens as I make my way over to the couch. I know he will want to get down to the business of the investigation.

"Positive ID for Kurtis Abbott. I won't shock you with the details other than to tell you that he was shot. His body was sent to Frankfort, where an autopsy will be performed tomorrow. Clay is still nowhere to be found. I got a warrant and hauled his truck in. No blood or evidence of murder. Kurt's fingerprints were inside the truck, but that's circumstantial at best. Clay can always claim that he gave Kurt a ride somewhere or some bullshit story like that." He pauses long enough to down the drink.

I pour him another as he continues, "Our only witness is Gertie, and let's face it, Gertie is not reliable as a witness. If I can track Clay down, I am hoping that he will just confess. Maybe you'll get your chance to play good cop/ bad cop, in order to get that confession out of him. I get to be bad cop though. I called Cammie into the station to question her about Clay's whereabouts. She said that she does not know where he is. I asked her about showing up at his place the other night and she said that she went over to tell him to stay away from her. She did not know Kurt or of any association he may have had with her brother. Maybe she is telling the truth. Who knows? She was just happy that A.J. is spending the night on his houseboat and wasn't home to find out about Clay. I have someone keeping an eye on their property, in case brother decides to pay her a visit," he says.

"She feigned innocence about his whereabouts when I spoke to her earlier, too. My gut instinct tells me that something is off with her," I say.

"Unfortunately, there is no law against being off. But, yeah, she's a real piece of work. Let's put together everything we have on Clay and see if we can think of anywhere he may be hiding out," he says.

"Sally said that Lexie Baker's husband left her because she is having an affair with Clay. I found a phone number for her, but I got a message that the wireless caller I was trying to reach was unavailable. Her husband removed her phone from his cellphone plan. I spoke with the husband and he doesn't know where she is staying, and said that he does not care to know," I say.

"Her sister works at the bank," I continue. "I will speak to her in the morning, to see if she can give me any information and tell me where Lexie is living now. I spoke with the pizza delivery guy from the other night. He said that he has made no deliveries to Clay since then. He said that he would remember, because Clay is the only person around here that ever orders anchovies on his pizza, and he is also a very cheap tipper."

"Red headed Lexie Baker? I never would have thought that," Jack says, as if that is the only part of my report that he found interesting.

"Yep. Speaking of red. Gertie's cheeks turned red the other day when she spoke of Ford seeing her with her hair mussed up."

"Oh, yeah? She and Ford had a short fling after her husband passed away," he says.

"No! You're kidding!"

"I joke you not," he says, amused.

We both laugh for a few moments, then I say, "Okay. Back to the subject at hand. Where is Clay getting his money? He has to have money for rent and food. Seems he does not have a job. He told me he does contract work but did not expand on what that entails. Few cons walk out of prison flush with money. Cammie said that she offered him a job, and he refused."

"Good question. That brings us back to possibly drugs. Kurt has a history of using and running drugs. Who knows what Clay could be into that he never got *caught* doing. Kurt's sponsor says he doesn't believe that Kurt fell off the wagon. His wife Fiona says that she thinks Kurt was clean as far as using drugs, but the wad of cash that he had makes me wonder if he wasn't selling. Other than a scenario such as that, what would drive Clay to murder Kurt? Surely, it wasn't because he snored too loud when they shared a cell. And, like you said, where is Clay getting his money?"

"Maybe Cammie has a closer relationship with her brother than she says," I say.

"Could be. I am going to have another go at her tomorrow when I get back from Frankfort. Maybe she will be more forthcoming if I tell her I plan on bringing A.J. in, too," he says.

"Hopefully, she will be. I feel you have a better chance of getting struck by lightning than of her or Clay confessing to anything."

CHAPTER SEVENTEEN

THURSDAY

I am having the most wonderful dream. I am lying in Jack's arms, with my head on his chest, and he is stroking my hair. I can feel his heartbeat. Thump, thump, thump, in rhythm with my own. It feels natural to be wrapped in the comforting heat of his arms, like that is where I have always belonged. I inhale the scent of him. The smell evokes unexplained emotions in me.

A distant alarm beeps, bringing me slowly awake. But I do not want to wake from this dream! I slowly open my eyes and realize that it isn't a dream at all. Jack is lying on the couch, and I am cuddled up next to him, with my head on his chest. He reaches over to get his cellphone off of the coffee table and shuts the alarm off. I jump up, embarrassed, feeling the heat rush to my cheeks. We are both dressed, so apparently, nothing happened.

"Oh hey," he says sleepily, yawning, and stretching. "Sorry, my alarm woke you. You crashed last night, and you looked too comfortable to disturb. To be honest, I was kind of glad I didn't have to drive home. I was ready to crash too," he says, swinging up into a sitting position.

"Oh. I'm sorry I fell asleep on you. Like, literally, on you," I say.

What is wrong with you, Elle? I never say things such as "like literally." This is an innocent situation. Jack apparently does not feel any of the embarrassment that I feel. Stop being a bumbling idiot.

"No problem. I am just sorry to wake you so early. I set my alarm so I would have time to stop at home and shower. I need to get on the road for Frankfort early."

Jack in the shower. Soap lathered up on all those muscles. Water dripping from those glorious eyelashes. The smell of his body wash rising with the steam. Oh, my goodness! Stop it Elle! Seriously, what is wrong with me this morning? It must be the dream having an effect on me. Shake it off! I can feel myself flush with heat as I ask, "What," clearing my throat, "um, what, time is it?"

"Five. Listen, Elle, I'm sorry that I crashed on your couch, too. And I really appreciate your help and insight into this investigation. I will go ahead and get out of your hair. Maybe you can manage to get some more sleep this morning," he says, with a very confused look on his face.

"No problem. I get up early most mornings, anyway. Have a safe trip, Sheriff."

"Okay. I will talk to you later then," he says. He walks to the door and then turns to look at me with a puzzled look on his face before opening it and walking out. No doubt thinking that I am a weirdo for how I have been acting this morning. I cannot say that I blame him.

I see the package of Twizzlers lying on my bar and cannot help but smile. He, showing up with them in hand, was totally out of character for him. There are two versions of him—The Sheriff, and Jack. The Sheriff is no nonsense, straightforward, and fussy. Jack is more relaxed, and much more fun to be around. I have only ever caught brief glimpses of Jack before he turns back into the Sheriff. He seems to be allowing me the opportunity to see more of himself lately. I really like that version of him. It also really confuses me when his behavior is relaxed. I am always on guard, waiting for the Sheriff to reemerge.

Then there is the dream I was having. Is it possible that he was really stroking my hair, and I wasn't just dreaming it? I admit to myself one more time that the dream was nice, but now it is time to put it out of my mind. I am perfectly content in my unconventional relationship with Colt.

Besides, the Sheriff is not interested in me romantically. He has made it clear on many occasions that he thinks I exist just to be a pain in his ass. At least, he realizes I may be an asset professionally. I can only hope that I "wow" him enough that he will cut me some slack on the speeding tickets.

* * *

I enter the bank lobby ten minutes after it opens. It has probably been fifteen years since I have been inside the building. I do my banking online, with an app on my phone, or by ATM. Nothing has really changed in those fifteen years. The flooring still consists of the same marble tiles. The same maroon velvet ropes still map the way to the teller windows. The layout of the lobby is no different at all.

Most of the faces that I see behind the windows of the offices are employees that were here the last time that

I was. The place even sounds the same. The coin counter swirls coins around, and they clang as it drops them into the machine while counting them. Several telephones trill in harmony. Printers whir as they shoot paper out the side. Happy chatter all around. Mellow music flows from the sound system, putting people in relaxation mode as they hand over their money. At once, I am taken back to when I was a child, receiving a lollipop from a teller after Mama would conclude her banking transactions.

A line has formed, waiting to reach the teller windows. I recognize some customers as business owners, who are probably here to do their deposits from last night's till intake. I scan the tellers manning the counter to look for one named Abby, spotting her on the far end. When it comes my turn, I indicate to the available teller that I wish to wait for Abby. The look on her face tells me she is more than happy to have one less person to deal with. The customer at Abby's window leaves and it is now my turn.

"Good morning. I can help you here," she says.

I step up to the window and she says, "Elle Whitley! I haven't seen you since we graduated!"

"Actually, I go by Riley now. How have you been, Abby?" I ask. She must be able to tell that I am having trouble recalling her from the cobwebs of my mind.

"Stearns," she says, referencing her maiden name.

"Oh Abby! Wow! I had no idea that you worked here. It's good to see you."

"Well, you know, losing a hundred and fifty pounds and gaining fourteen years will make you unrecognizable," she says, having noted that I did not recognize her until she revealed her identity to me. "So, you're married then? Someone told me you are a famous writer."

My Mama, with someone seated in her chair at the salon, while she over-exaggerates about me, immediately comes to mind. "Divorced. I am definitely not famous. You look wonderful! Not that you were not beautiful before," I say.

"You always were kind to me, Elle. There were so many bullies that we went to school with. Sadly, some of them are still bullies as adults. You would think they would have outgrown it."

"That is true. They just try to hide it better now," I say.

"So, what brings you in today? Do you need to make a deposit, withdrawal, maybe open an account?" She smiles, all professional now.

Lowering my voice, I say, "Actually, I was hoping I could speak to you about your sister?"

"Let me guess, Lexie." Her mouth turns into a thin, disapproving line. "It isn't your man that she was stepping out with, is it?" she whispers.

"No, definitely not. It is regarding the man that she is seeing, though."

"I get my break at ten-thirty. If you want to come back then, I will meet you out front."

"Sounds good. I will see you then. Thanks, Abby."

As I step out onto the sidewalk, my cellphone rings. Once again, it is an unknown number. The telemarketers must be working overtime. I have gotten numerous calls this week, none of them leaving a message. Thank goodness for caller ID technology.

I have an interview for the position at the Investigation's Office scheduled for nine o'clock. I have plenty of time to swing into the coffee shop on my way. As I step through the door, the aroma of specialty beans hits my nose. The line at the shop is much longer than the line at the bank. The retro furniture is occupied by patrons enjoying their drinks, scones, and muffins. Some tap away at their laptop keyboards, others are engaged in conversation, some murmuring gossip about Kurt's murder. I listen to the talk, while waiting for my order, and hear nothing useful.

The shop has a very cozy feel to it, with its bohemian décor and indie music playing. A walk-up window was installed recently. I prefer to come inside and enjoy the ambiance. I never have to look at the chalkboard menu. I am a creature of habit, always ordering the same flavored iced coffee. I would like to think that I march to the beat of my own drum, but the truth is, I am basic when it comes to such things as iced coffees, wearing leggings, and my hair in messy buns.

Finally, coffee in hand, I make my way to the office, eating a blueberry scone along the way.

"If I had known you would be here, I would have brought you an iced coffee. Or at the very least, a scone." I say to Art when I arrive.

"Now Sunshine, when have you known me to drink those things? You know I prefer bourbon in my coffee instead of those sweet syrups. I like my coffee with a bang."

"If you would ever try one, you would be hooked," I say.

"I'll take your word for it. What have you got going on today?" he asks.

"An interview for a new secretary scheduled at nine. Maybe a visit with Mama if I can squeeze in the time. Then, onto trying to track down Kurt Abbott's murderer."

"Nasty business, that is. Murdering people and pushing old ladies down stairs. What kind of heathen has taken up residence in Justice? You promise me now to keep your distance from him? I know you are helping Jack out with the investigation, but let him handle the dangerous part."

"I am just trying to find out his whereabouts. Trust me, I have no inclination of getting anywhere near him."

"Good. And I'm glad you gave me a heads up about the interview. I think I have somewhere else I need to be," he says.

"Oh, and miss all the fun! You should have to sit through it too. I only wish you had been here during the others." As soon as I tell Art this, the door opens. We both turn to see who is coming in.

"Can I help you, son?" Art asks.

"Yeah, I'm here for an interview," the man says, then he looks over and sees me sitting in the other chair. He immediately turns and walks out the door. It is the clerk jerk from the gas station.

"What the hell was that about?" Art asks.

I simply shrug and say, "It's a long story." I take a sip of the iced coffee and try to look innocent.

Art chuckles and shakes his head.

CHAPTER EIGHTEEN

My mother's Buick is parked in her spot, so I know she is at work already. The ding-dong sound announces my entrance. She peeks out from the doorway in the back, where she is folding towels.

"Good morning. Just in time," she says, tossing a towel at me.

"Hey, Mama." I make way to the back and start folding. She has a particular way that she likes them done. I could do it in my sleep, after so many years of the chore, while I was growing up. She has arrived early again today and is the only person in the salon.

"I know you did not stop by just to help me fold towels. And look at you. You styled that beautiful head of hair this morning and have a flush about your cheeks. Do you have something to tell me? Hopefully some exciting news about Colt?" she asks.

"No, ma'am. Can't a daughter just drop in on her Mama without an ulterior motive?"

"They can. I suppose I was just being hopeful, is all. You're always so secretive about your love life. I still can't believe it took you so long to tell me about Liam's affair."

"You did not give me much of a choice, seeing as how you invited him to our family Fourth of July barbeque!" I say, snapping a towel at her.

"Well, you didn't seem to have anything bad to say about him, and I thought maybe it would be an excellent opportunity for you two to work it out. I can't believe he accepted the invitation! That's what you get for keeping things from me. The highlight of the day was when your Gran threatened to give him a beating," she says.

"That was funny! But, Mama, you know Colt and I will never have a serious relationship, so you may as well give up on that hope."

"That's a shame. You two are good together and would make such beautiful babies!"

I am going to have to change this subject quickly or I will regret my visit with her—even more so than I already do. She changes the topic before I have a chance.

"Terrible news about the Abbott boy! I can't imagine what his family is going through. Fiona was in recently for me to do her hair and she was talking about how Kurt was on the straight and narrow. She was awfully proud of him. According to her, he just wasn't having any luck getting a job. Few people want to hire an ex-con. You know, financial troubles can put a big strain on a marriage, and that's why they separated. She stuck it out with him during all of his other troubles, always believing in him, and according to her, he did change. It's just so sad!" she says.

"It is terrible. I cannot imagine what his family is going through. Jack will see to it that his killer is brought to justice," I say. "We should do something for the family, rather than just sending flowers, don't you think?"

"Absolutely, Elle, that's a great thought. I'm sure he probably did not have life insurance. Maybe we should drop a monetary donation off at the funeral home or with Fiona. Your Gran said earlier that the ladies from her Church are going to drop food off today. I'll pick up a card and we can send it and the money with her."

"That sounds good," I say, going to retrieve my bag.

Having finished with the laundry, we sit down.

"You were telling me about bleaching hair the other day. Tell me about working with red heads. Do you have any clients that are red heads?" I ask.

"I have several. Which one do you want to know about? Come now, Elle, spit it out. I know you well enough to know you could care less about hair terminology."

"Lexie Baker. Do you know her?" I ask.

"I know her. I don't do her hair. But I do cut her husband's hair. Probably soon to be ex-husband. He said she has been cheating on him. Is that helpful?"

"Not particularly. I spoke with her husband yesterday evening, myself. You get an A for effort, though."

She looks at me for a moment, realizing that I must be interested in Lexie for an important reason. "Does this have anything to do with finding Kurt's murderer?"

"Possibly. Lexie was supposed to be having an affair with the suspect. He is in the wind. I am just trying to follow any potential leads to help track him down. There doesn't seem to be much to go on," I say.

"Did her husband tell you how he found out about the affair? Apparently, the guy uses a type of special pomade for men in his hair that is locally made. Do you know that stand at the Farmer's Market that sells homemade soaps, shampoos, and such? He found a container of the pomade in her jeep and knew that it didn't belong to him. Oh, what is the name of that place? They have a store, too," she says, tapping her chin with her forefinger.

"The Bee's Knees Beauty Needs?" I ask.

"Yes! That's it."

"You now have an A plus, Mama. Any clue at all is appreciated, no matter how small it may seem." She beams at me. This tip will probably lead nowhere, but she is happy with the thought of maybe doing anything that could possibly help find Kurt's murderer. I understand that feeling all too well.

* * *

At ten-thirty-two, Abby walks out the door of the bank, lighting a cigarette along her way.

"Thank you for agreeing to talk to me. I know you could spend your break doing something more enjoyable," I say.

"It's nothing. I would be coming out to smoke, anyway. What kind of questions do you have about Lexie?" she asks, taking a deep drag off of her cigarette.

"Where is she staying now? Do you have a phone number for her?" I ask.

"She is staying in one of my parents' rental trailers that was vacant, out on ninety-two. She doesn't have a new phone yet." She leans back against the brick building and inhales another puff from the cigarette. "She has not had the money to get her own plan set up. Her husband pretty much cut her off from everything. Not that he ever gave her much to start with. Simon is a real dick. You know how it is, husband never gave her any attention, never very kind to her, and someone comes along that makes her feel wanted. I'm in no way condoning what she done. I'm just saying…."

"Do you know anything about the other man?"

"Nothing. Of course, she wasn't advertising that she was having an affair. I haven't ever laid eyes on him. Me and Lexie aren't close. The only reason I know anything is because Mom told me. And I reckon Lex is really regretting the affair now."

"I am familiar with the rentals that your parents have. Do you mind telling me which trailer it is? I would really like to talk to her about the man she is seeing. He is possibly dangerous."

"Dangerous how?"

"He's a person of interest in Kurt Abbott's murder," I say.

"Shit! What has Lexie gotten herself involved in?" She shakes her head in disbelief and worry furrows her brow. "It's the last trailer on the left before you get to the pond. Can't miss it. If you come to a cow pasture, or the pond, you'll know you've gone too far. Mom said Lex is supposed to have a job interview today, so if you miss her, maybe try back later."

"Thanks Abby. It has been really great seeing you. I'm sorry it's under these circumstances."

"You're welcome. She is about to worry my mom to death. Now I'm worried too. Give me your number and if I hear anything else, I'll give you a call. It's been great seeing you, too. We will have to catch up over a drink sometime," she says.

"That would be great," I say, while fishing a business card from my purse. I hand it to her and she tosses her cigarette to the ground, stomping the fire out, and heads back into work.

CHAPTER NINETEEN

My bronco has a flat tire. Upon further inspection, Art says that it looks like someone has slashed it. Could it have anything to do with the young man that showed up for the interview? He wonders. I assure him it doesn't. I cannot think of anyone who would want to do such a thing. I have no idea when it would have happened, either. It could have been anytime, from right after I got home from Gertie's yesterday evening, until now. If it happened while Jack was here, then whoever did it was brazen. The perpetrator would have seen the Sheriff's truck parked here. And Jack would have probably noticed the slashed tire when he left. This leads me to believe that it probably happened after five this morning.

I do not mention Jack being here all night to Art. As innocent as the situation was, people may get the wrong impression. I feel it is better to keep quiet about things, rather than to explain them. I am not sure that I can tell of his sleeping over without my face turning red again, either. That would definitely make someone think that it wasn't innocent.

A motorcycle roars down the street, the sun bouncing off its polished chrome. The rider comes to a stop behind our parked vehicles. Art and I both look over, and I see Teeny dismounting his Harley. What is Teeny doing here? Maybe Colt was right and I shouldn't have told him where I live. He struts over to where we are standing.

"Teeny? What in the world are you doing here?" I ask, unable to hide the curiosity in my voice. Art is looking at both of us questioningly.

"I've got a bike rally coming up this weekend. Figured I'd leave a little early and stop by here on my way. You got me to thinking about this place the other night. Thought while I was in the area, I'd look you up. Asked around at the diner about a sassy five-foot five brunette named Elle. The waitress knew exactly who you were and told me where I could find you. P.I. huh?" he asks, looking up at the sign on the brick building.

"Wow. It really is a small world," I say, discomforted that it was so easy for him to find me. If only it were that simple to find Clay. "Part-time P.I. This is the full time P.I., Art, and this is his office," I say, indicating Art. "Art, this is Teeny, my karaoke partner."

Art looks at me as if I have grown a second head. "Uh, nice to meet you, Teeny," he says.

"Pleasure," Teeny replies.

"Did, um, your buddies come with you?" I ask. I chew on my thumbnail as I await his answer, thinking that the Sheriff would not be happy that I unwittingly invited a biker gang to town.

"Nah. I ride solo more and more these days. What cha got going on here?" he asks, pointing to my slashed tire.

"Probably a mischievous kid," I say, with a certainty that I do not feel.

"This your vehicle?" Teeny asks.

"Yeah," I say, sighing as I rake a hand through my hair.

"Huh. That wasn't from some kid up to no good," Teeny says, while twisting the ends of his braided beard. "Look at it. Someone took their time and used a big blade, slicing it. If a kid done it, they would've jabbed it real quick and ran before they could get caught. Probably would've used a little pocket knife. What you got here is someone that is trying to get back at you for something, or is angry with you."

Art and I are both looking up at him now as if he is the one who has grown an extra head on the side of his enormous shoulders.

"What?" he asks. "I read a lot when I was on the inside." He shrugs. "Looks like it was probably a woman that done it."

"What books did you read that helped you learn to discern that?" I ask, somewhat amazed.

"No book. The phallic symbol drawn on the back told me that." He hitched a thumb to indicate the back of the vehicle. "Probably a jealous woman. Did you take someone's man from them? Maybe that pretty boy you was with the other night?"

Art and I both skirt around to the back. I am panicked, Art is curious. There on the back hatch, off to the side of the spare tire of my Bronco, someone had fashioned the long gate handle to look like a penis. I felt my face go pale and wondered if I would hit the ground. "Oh, dear!" is all I could manage to squeak out, as I thought of all the passerby's who had probably seen it. It had been drawn using a dark shade of red lipstick. The sun had been beaming down on it all morning, giving it a dried, aged appearance. I wondered how we had missed it, then I remembered we had walked around the front to check the rest of the tires.

I hear a rumbling sound coming from Art. It starts out quiet, and then builds to a deep belly laugh, as he points at the image, until tears stream down his cheeks. I give him a sharp look and he sobers. I can tell that Teeny has been struggling to hide his laughter.

"Could be a lot worse," Teeny says. "At least it wasn't carved on there with the knife. It should be easy to get it off. All you got to do is rub it really hard. It looks like it's really baked on. You may have to put your back into it." He winces, as he must've realized those weren't good descriptions to use. Art laughs again and I give him another glare.

"Guess I need to get some cameras put up along the outside of the building and at the door to your apartment. Security system on the inside of the office may not be enough anymore," Art says, wiping his eyes, as I frantically try to scrub at the image with spit and elbow grease.

"Maybe I'll stick around a few more days and keep an eye on you Five foot, to make sure you're safe," Teeny says with concern in his voice.

"Thanks, Teeny, but that isn't necessary." I say.

"Ah, I like it here and planned on taking my time going south, anyway."

"You take the Camry, and I'll call the garage and get someone to replace your tire, while you're gone," Art says.

"Okay," I say, feeling very dismayed. "But I'm not going anywhere until that is seen to." I scramble toward the stairs to my apartment in search of cleaning supplies.

I stop on the second step when Teeny says, "I'll check back in tomorrow. Give me a call if you need me before then."

"Thanks Teeny. I will talk to you later, then," I say. He gives me a salute, hops on his motorcycle, and speeds away.

"You're going to have to tell me how that friendship came about, sometime," Art says, chuckling and shaking his head. "Right now, I have to go meet a new client, though. You be careful, you hear? Make sure you keep your gun handy. Oh, and shoot me a text with Teeny's phone number. He looks like someone whose expertise might come in handy sometime."

"Okay," I say. "You be careful too."

Who could have done this and why? I am seething as I walk into my apartment. Colt is the only person I am seeing. Maybe he has a jealous side chick that he hasn't bothered to tell me about. I pick up my phone, stabbing the call button under his contact picture. The call goes straight to voicemail. "It's Colt. I'm busy either working hard or hardly working. Do your thing after the beep."

"Oh, I'll do my thing alright," I mutter as I prepare to leave him a message. I spy the bag of Twizzlers lying on the bar and hang up the phone instead of leaving a voicemail. *Jack.* Jack had spent the night here last night. I wonder if he has a jealous lover who thinks that our all-nighter had nothing to do with work. I recall the vivid dream from last night, and wonder who Jack's lover could be, as I feel an intense dislike for a woman that I am not even certain exists.

CHAPTER TWENTY

I turn onto a side road off of Highway 92. Not much has changed in this area since I was last here. A few new houses have sprung up in an up-and-coming subdivision off of a side road. The land here is relatively flat and beautiful, which makes it the ideal location to build a new home. The property upon which the subdivision is being built used to be a family farm. I suppose the farm was struggling, or was inherited, and the heir decided to sell it, as often happens. I am saddened to see that the old two-story farmhouse with the big porch has been torn down. I had always hoped that someone would restore the home to its former glory. I would much rather own the old farmhouse than any of the new homes being built.

I pass an abandoned house that has been destroyed by a fire and has never been cleaned up and cleared away. The black marks on the white clapboard siding and the blackened broken windows make it resemble some sort of sorrowful creature, crying out for help. The yard is overgrown, making it hard to distinguish where the perimeters were once located. Scraggly bushes grow around abandoned vehicles parked on the property. The trees are overgrown and in need of pruning. Trash from the burned-out house has been strewn throughout what once was the lawn. Someone will probably soon be eager to snatch up this piece of property also, and bring in a bulldozer, to raze the entire area.

The best I can recall, the properties that Abby's parents own are located several miles out, down a side road. I roll the windows down, taking in the breeze, enjoying the ride and the scenic beauty. Mountains spring up in the distance, with a haze of cloudiness above them, much like the popular Smoky Mountains. Cows, horses, and farm equipment dot the fields of the remaining farms. A young man in a neon green and black side-by-side zooms up a long driveway with a dog riding shotgun. I drive over a narrow bridge that crosses a creek that is prone to flood in heavy rains. I remember this as the landmark before arriving at Abby's parent's road.

Seeing the creek also saddens me, making me think of Kurt's tragic death. Kurtis Abbott was not a bad person. He had fallen victim to some vices that he never should have, but by all accounts, he was trying to turn his life around. Society often makes it hard for a person like Kurt to have a second chance. He was a son, a father, and even though separated from Fiona, she still loved him. Kurt deserves justice for what was done to him. And so does his family.

What could have possibly driven him to be involved with Clay? If he was trying to keep on the straight and narrow, then he should have known that Clay is not a person he should be associated with. Could he have grown weary of not being able to provide for his family by respectable means, and turned to something illegal? Clay could have offered to bring him in on whatever his "contract work" is. Perhaps they disagreed over money or drugs and it turned deadly. And what brought Clay to the town of Justice? Was it his sister Cammie, or Kurtis? Did the two men become such close friends in prison that they would have stayed in contact after getting released? If so, what would lead one friend to kill another? And why was their association such a secret from everyone that they know? I hope Clay can be located soon and all of those questions will be answered. The one thing that I do know is that most everything always comes down to money.

Taking a road to the left, I follow it to the pond, then backtrack and pull into the first trailer that I come to. It is situated down a short drive, sitting in a cleared-out spot, surrounded by thickets of pine trees. The property looks quite peaceful and would be the perfect place for someone such as Clay to hide out. He could easily go out the back door and flee into the woods as soon as he saw police cars pull in. The driveway is empty. Lexie's purple Jeep Rubicon is not here. She must be out on her job search. Clay could still be inside the trailer, though.

I know I cannot just walk up and knock on the door. What would I do if he actually is inside? I do not want to come face to face with him. Under normal circumstances, I would agree with Art and Jack about something that I should not do, and then I would do as I wish. It falls closely into the area of being easier to ask for forgiveness than permission. I do agree with both of them in this instance about Clay being dangerous. Even if he weren't a murderer, he gives me the creeps, and I would not want to be alone with him.

Those same woods that would serve as a great cover to sneak away from the trailer would also serve as a great cover to sneak upon the trailer. I think I should try to take a closer look. I do not have cell service here, but

I have my gun and I am quite stealthy when it comes to situations such as this. Besides, I hate to come all this way for nothing. And who knows? Lexie may lie about Clay being here when I speak to her. It is best if I just try to take a look myself.

I back the Camry into the makeshift turn-about and pull out of the driveway. I travel the short distance, park next to the pond, and take off, walking toward Lexie's trailer. A ferocious-looking Pitbull storms out from the lane across the road. He is white with gray spots, very large, and if a dog can be called muscular looking, this one is. He seems to want to eat me, as he snarls, and frothy slobber drips from his mouth. I consider myself an animal lover, but this dog seems like he would be hard to love. I decide it is best to keep my distance and cut across the cow pasture, rather than walking along the road.

Coming to the edge of the pines behind the trailer, I stop, allowing my eyes to scan the area for a few moments. Seeing and hearing no activity, I sneak to a back window. There are some milk crates stacked next to the window air conditioning unit and I turn one upside down to stand upon. I am able to peek through what appears to be a kitchen/dining-room window. Boxes are lined up atop the counters and in front of the cabinets. I can see into the living room area, which is sparsely furnished. The space seems to be dominated by an old, floor model television. The TV is off and there is no other noticeable noise. I jump down, grab the milk crate, and move along to what I think is the bedroom area. I can barely glimpse the bedroom through the closed curtains. I watch and listen. The trailer appears to be empty. That doesn't mean there may not be clues inside the trailer, though.

Trying the knob on the back door, I'm perplexed when I find it unlocked. I debate with myself. Technically, this could be considered breaking and entering. However... I am a deputy now and if I think there is a possibility a fugitive is inside, that may give me carte blanche on the matter. On the other hand, there is no way I would enter if I thought Clay was really inside. Hmm. What to do? The door is unlocked, so I suppose I'm not really breaking anything.

I cast a glimpse over both shoulders and all around me to make certain no one is around. I whisper Sheriff's Department as I peck faintly on the door. Then I take in a deep breath and enter, willing to take any punishment for the deed later. It will be worth it if it leads to Kurt's murderer. Besides, I don't plan on touching or searching through anything. I just want to check things out to make sure there aren't any blatantly clear signs that Clay has been hiding out here.

Nothing seems out of the ordinary. The inside is as sparse looking as it had been looking in from the outside. No men's clothing strewn about. No men's toiletries in the bathroom. Nothing to indicate Clay's presence. I notice a shotgun propped next to the washing machine as I creep to the back door.

The beast of a dog is barking in the distance and I decide it is best to return through the pasture. Cows moo and munch on hay as I walk by. I am about halfway through the pasture, making sure to stay far away from them, when the boot on my right foot gets stuck. Great, I stepped in mud. Looking down, I see that it isn't mud, but a pile of cow manure that is so fresh it almost sucks my boot off of my foot.

Ick!! I suppose it could be worse. At least I did not get murdered by Clay.

I make my way back to the car, gagging all the way. The Pitbull even keeps his distance from me and returns down the lane that he emerged from. I probably smell too bad for him to want to eat me now. I get in the car; my gagging turns to dry heaving. I pull my boots off and throw them into the trunk. I walk on my tippy toes back to the driver's side and slide in behind the steering wheel.

The windows down, the smell of cow manure abates some. I grab some fast-food napkins and blow my nose. Then I rub hand sanitizer on my hands, swiping some beneath my nostrils, which was a burning mistake. I stop at a Dollar General Store and swing in to buy a pair of shoes. I plan on making a trip to "The Bee's Knees Beauty Needs," and cannot exactly walk around barefoot.

The only pair of shoes in the entire store, in my size, are a pair of bright, red, white, and blue, tie dye, clog style, slip-ons. The closest place to buy a pair, other than here, is at least thirty minutes away. Desperate times call for desperate measures. The slip-ons do not exactly compliment my outfit of black jeans, a leather belt, cheetah print tee tucked in, and a lightweight black leather jacket. But they will suffice until I return home. I have another interview for the secretary position scheduled at two o'clock and I need to rush if I am going to have time to stop at the Beauty Needs store.

My phone rings as I am getting into the vehicle. Unknown number again. This has been happening all day. I answer the phone and say, "Listen, whatever you're selling, I am not buying, so stop calling my number!" I hear heavy breathing for a few seconds and a train horn in the background before the phone clicks. That's odd. The sight of the slashed tire and graffiti on my vehicle flash through my mind as I merge onto the highway.

* * *

I park in front of the quaint store that is located off the beaten path. The building is gray, weathered wood, with a porch all the way across the front. Hanging flower pots line the porch, exploding in an array of colors. Metal bee decorations sit on either side of the door.

A cow pasture is located off to the side. The sight of it reminds me of the horrible smell on my boot, and I gag again. Despite the inconvenient location, the business seems to do well. They have many customers that love their signature scents of organic laundry detergent, candles, bath, and beauty products.

An older gentleman and lady are behind the counter when I enter. The lady is compounding concoctions they sell in the store. The gentleman is standing on top of the counter, dusting high shelves.

"Welcome to Bee's Knees. Let us know if we can help you with anything," the kind lady says.

I get sidetracked for a few moments, looking at the attractive array of products, and sniffing candles. Then I remember I am not here to shop.

"Actually, I was thinking of picking up a gift for my gentleman friend. I think he usually buys hair pomade from here. I cannot for the life of me remember what scent he likes," I say.

"We only have the one scent in men's pomade, and that's sandalwood," the lady says.

"Oh," I say. "Well, I suppose that makes it easy enough." I beam a broad smile at her. "I may as well fess up. I met this gentleman, and we really had a connection. I lost his phone number." I turn my lips down in a sad pout. "I know he buys his great smelling pomade here and thought maybe you might be familiar with him or where to find him."

"What's your friend's name?" she asks.

"I'm terribly embarrassed to admit it but I forgot what name he goes by too," I say, shaking my head and rolling my eyes as if I cannot believe how ditzy I am. "I have a picture of him, though." I pull up Clay's mugshot, quickly cropping it down to show his face only and place my phone in her line of vision.

She places the reading glasses that have been hanging around her neck on a beaded chain upon the bridge of her nose, studying the photo. "Oh, that's Clay. He hasn't been here in a while. He really stocked up last time. I remember when he was here because he is so flirtatious," she says.

"Mildred! I told you, he only flirts with you because you give him a discount," the man says, pointing the feather duster toward her.

"Well, he earns the discount. Making an old lady such as myself feel good."

The man rolls his eyes and says, "He stocked up alright. He wears enough of it he could lather a horse with what he uses. I've told him if you use too much, it makes your hair look greasy, and it makes the scent overpowering. He uses the body wash too," he says.

"Don't pay no mind to Jim." She waves her hand toward him as if she is shooing a fly away. "He's in a bad mood because he's having to dust the top shelves for me." She winks conspiratorially.

I smile in return. "Thank you so much for your help. If I leave my number with you and he were to stop in, can you call me? Oh, and don't mention it to Clay," I say, giving her a wink much like the one she had given me. "I would really love to plan something special for him. You know? Maybe be standing in the parking lot as he steps out of the store, like a scene in a movie." She assumes a romantic movie. I'm thinking more of a suspense thriller. Jim shakes his head with a disgusted look on his face.

"I sure can! I love your shoes, by the way," Mildred says.

"Thank you."

"Can I interest you in some other products? We have a beauty cream that our customers swear is like the fountain of youth. And our bath bombs magically erase every bit of stress you may have."

"Yes, please," I say.

Fifteen minutes later, I get into the Camry with two fountain of youth beauty creams, a facial serum, five purifying face masks, body butter, bath bombs, soaps, three candles, and some laundry detergent. It would be easier to list what I didn't buy. I am seeing why Clay stocked up on the pomade. The sales lady seems to put some type of spell over you to make you buy things. This stop turned out to be another dead end, but at least my apartment, my laundry, and myself, will smell sensational.

CHAPTER TWENTY-ONE

I park at the office with ten minutes to spare until the interview is scheduled. My Bronco is not here, so I assume Art must have put the spare tire on it and taken it to the garage. By the time I use the restroom and grab a bottle of water out of the fridge, the front door is opening. I have not even had time to look at the resume of the person scheduled.

I step around the corner and there stands Lexie Baker. This is not great timing, but the interviewee will have to wait until after I speak with Lexie. I feel a tinge of guilt at the thought of invading her trailer earlier, hoping that she doesn't have psychic abilities. Or security cameras, I think as I groan internally.

"Lexie. Hi, I'm Elle. I suppose Abby told you I was trying to reach you?" I ask.

"Please tell me we aren't rescheduling the interview. Or does this mean that I already have the job?" she asks. A look of hope crosses her beautiful, heart-shaped face.

"The job? Oh, you're here for the secretary position!" Now, I realize why her name sounded familiar when I spoke with Sally. "Actually, there is another reason that I was trying to get in touch with you. We will do the interview first and then I will get to the other thing," I say, waving my hand. No need to make it awkward before interviewing her.

I notice she has a black eye that she has tried to conceal with make-up. I wonder who gave it to her—her husband, or Clay? I am stupefied that she chose Clay to have an affair with. Men probably make advances at her often. If it was the attention from Clay that led her to stray, as Abby assumed, then she has more than likely had less sleazy options to choose from in the past.

"Okay," she says, hesitantly.

Ten minutes later, I tell her, "The interview went great, but of course we still have several candidates to meet with." She is by far the best possibility for the position, to date, but I think I should find out if she is aiding and abetting a murderer before giving her a job. She lets out a pent-up sigh of relief.

"I need to ask you about Clayton Butcher? I know that you have been seeing him. I'm helping with an investigation that he seems to be at the center of." I could've knocked her over with a feather. She inhales a shaking breath and seems like she is frozen in place. I open a desk drawer, producing a voice recorder. "You mind?" I ask.

She silently nods, giving me her agreement. I turn on the handheld device, noting the date, time, our names, and getting her verbal consent to record.

"Clay needs to be questioned concerning a murder investigation. He is most likely a dangerous man," I say.

"A murder investigation! I would not know anything about that. I have not seen Clay since the day after my husband, Simon, threw me out. The only reason I saw him then was to tell him it was over. I have no husband, no money, and Simon has taken my kids. I was just having a fling with Clay. He definitely was not worth losing all of that! I wish I could go back in time and tell Clay to piss off. You don't have to tell me he's dangerous. Who do you think gave me this?" she asks, while pointing to her black eye. Her words came out in a rush, the expressions on her face changing with each sentence, but the fear in her eyes remaining through all of them.

"Wow Lexie. That is horrible. You may want to think about filing charges against him," I say.

"No way. He's crazy!" She shivers. "I just want to be done with him. He won't stop calling me. It's bordering on harassment. I have my dad's shotgun at the trailer and I carry it from room to room with me in case he shows up. Please, tell me he isn't the person who murdered Kurt Abbott?"

"It is Kurt's case that Clay is being sought to bring in for questioning." That information would be easy for anyone to guess, since it is the only murder that has occurred recently. Only *known* murder that has happened, anyway. I wonder how many more clandestine meetings take place in secreted places that people do not witness. "Do you know of any relationship that he had with Kurt? Can you think of anything that might be helpful in locating Clay or anything that might pertain to the investigation?" I ask.

She pauses for a moment. I assume she is trying to get her wits about her after being shocked by the information. "One night I was with Clay, we left the bar at the same time, so he could follow me to the trailer that I am staying at now. There wasn't anyone living there. I had a key because I take care of the rentals for my mom and dad, so that's where our meet ups took place. Simon was working out of town and my Mom had the kids over for the night to give me a break."

"As we were walking through the parking lot at the bar, Kurt appeared out of nowhere wanting to talk to Clay. I got in my jeep and waited for him to get in his truck to follow. It looked like their talk got pretty heated. When I asked Clay about it later, he said that it was just some bum hitting him up for money. That is the only time that I ever saw the two of them together," she says.

"You're certain it was Kurt?"

"Yeah, I'm certain. I've known Kurtis my whole life." Her voice grows bitter and tears spring to her eyes. "I knew he wasn't some bum asking for a handout, but I could tell from the way Clay acted that I needed to let it go."

"Do you remember when this was?" I ask gently.

"It was about three weeks ago."

I see the lilt of Sally's head and hear the saucy tone in her voice, as I recall her telling me it seemed as if the two men knew each other. Did she witness their interaction before or after Lexie saw their heated discussion?

"Did Clay mention that he had served time in Florida? Or any friends he may have made while he was in prison?"

"I did not even know that Clay has been in prison. I should've guessed that."

"Did Clay ever mention his sister?"

"Yeah, once. He said she is a real selfish bitch. I thought it was kind of harsh. Abby and I don't always see eye to eye, but I would never talk about *my* sister that way," she says. She drops her eyes and starts picking imaginary lint balls from her pants, perhaps as a nervous tick, or a sign of insecurity.

"Did he tell you who his sister is?"

"No. I just assumed she lives in Florida." Cammie must not be the only one keeping their kinship under wraps. But why? Is he as ashamed of her as she is of him?

"Do you know what type of work Clay does or where he could be employed at? Is it possible he could be involved in the drug business or something else illegal?"

"He says he's a contractor, but I don't know if it's construction or what he does. Our meetings were always a little rushed if you know what I mean. Not much time to really get to know each other. I never knew of him actually going to work anywhere." Clayton Butcher is the type of person who she could have spent all the time in the world with, and still not really known him. I am torn between feeling sorry for her and wondering if perhaps she isn't as smart as she seems, to have made the mistake of being involved with Clay.

"I haven't seen anything that would make me think he deals in drugs," she continues. "He has not called me lately, so I think maybe he has left town and gone back to Florida or somewhere else. I figure he may have crawled back into the hole that he came from — like I told him to do."

"Can I get Clay's phone number from you?"

"I don't have it memorized, and I deleted it from my phone. I hope to work things out with Simon and I don't want him to look through my call log and see any calls from Clay, so I've been deleting them every time that he has called. He has been calling from different numbers, so I figured he must be buying new prepaids or something. If he calls again, I will write the number down before I delete it." She looks at the door anxiously in a hurry to be free of this conversation, like a kid waiting to be dismissed from the principal's office.

"Thanks Lexie. I know you said you do not wish to file any type of charges against Clay, but I am going to recommend that an officer be placed at your place for your safety. Just in case he is still in town."

"Like I said, I think he is probably gone from Justice," she says.

"Still, I will call Jack and see if he can send someone out to your place, just in case."

I dial Jack's number. He tells me that he is on his way back and says he should be in town within the next hour. He will call the S.O. (Sheriff's Office) and have a deputy sent over to follow Lexie home to sit on her place.

"Did you have a chance to grab lunch today?" he asks.

"No. I actually have not even had time to think about eating," I say.

"How about I pick up some food, meet you at Art's, and listen to Lexie's recording while we eat? I can bring you up to speed while I'm there, too," he says.

"That sounds good. I will see you when you get here."

CHAPTER TWENTY-TWO

Jack comes walking through the door of the office with a bag of deli sandwiches and chips. Lexie is safely at home with a deputy parked at her place.

"I didn't know what you liked, so I got ham, turkey, roast beef, and tuna. You can have your pick," he says.

"Twizzlers last night. Sandwiches today. Is this how you plan on paying me for being a deputy?"

"Maybe. I might even throw in some of those iced coffees you seem to like."

"Just to warn you, I can probably drink my weight in iced coffees." I stand up to go to the kitchen in the back to get us drinks and he says, "Um, nice shoes." He has a bemused look on his face and a raised eyebrow. I don't think he meant it as a compliment.

I had forgotten about the clogs until he mentions them. I say, "Thanks. They're DG's," (Dollar General's).

"Never heard of them. Must be expensive," he says.

"I got a very good deal on them."

I eat the turkey sandwich and he tears into the roast beef while he listens to the recording between Lexie and me.

"Good idea to record her," he says. "Thoughts?"

"I believe her. You?"

"She sounds believable. She seemed a little insistent that Clay has left town, though. Do you buy the part about her not knowing Clay's phone number? I could judge better if it were a video and I could see her actions, too."

"Oh well, next time I will have to remember to video record instead," I say, as I roll my eyes. "I assumed it was probably wishful thinking, on her part, that he has left town. Or maybe she is itching for an opportunity to use Daddy's shotgun on Clay and doesn't want a deputy around to stop her. I would not be too happy either if someone had used me for a punching bag. Deleting the calls sounds logical to me if she wants to work things out with the husband. It would be plausible to think that he would no longer trust her and check her phone," I say.

"Maybe. One murder is one too many. I definitely do not want another, whether or not Clay deserves it," he says.

We both turn as Art knocks on the door, his arms full of his briefcase and a McDonald's bag. I had locked it so Jack and I would not be disturbed while listening to the recording and discussing the case. When I open the door, he says, "You wouldn't happen to know why the windows are down on the Camry and it smelled like a perfumed cow patty slapped me on the nose when I walked by, would you?" His nose wiggles as he tries to get the memory of the smell out of it.

I look down at my brightly colored shoes. Jack sees and looks down at them as well. Then Art follows suit and says, "Let me guess. It's a long story?"

"Yep," I say.

"The garage should have your Bronco ready by the end of the day," Art says.

"What's wrong with it?" Jack asks.

"She didn't tell you? Someone slashed her tire last night," Art says. He sets his briefcase and food down on his desk and flops down in the chair. I had been so focused on Lexie and the case that I forgot the tire and the genitals. Which means I forgot to question Jack to see if he knew who might have done such a thing.

"Last night? I didn't notice it when I left this morning," Jack says, turning his head to look at me.

Here we go . . .

"This morning!" Art says, around a mouthful of French fries. He gets choked and starts coughing.

"Relax, Art. We fell asleep while working on the case," Jack says.

"Hmm. I hear that story from subjects of my investigations all the time," Art says, unconvinced, between gulps of his Dr. Pepper.

"Have you ever known me to lie, Art? She and I are both adults. If it was something more, I would've said so," Jack says.

"Hmmm. You don't happen to have a jealous girlfriend that would've been upset you slept over, do you?" Art asks. His eyes are narrowed as he studies Jack.

"What? Jealous girlfriend?" His reflective pause goes on long enough to make me realize he isn't exactly Mr. Lonely. I feel the fingers of envy pinching me, as I think of my dream from last night. "No," he finally replies. "Why?"

Does that mean that he doesn't have a girlfriend at all, or he doesn't have a girlfriend who is jealous? Why do I care, as long as he doesn't have a jaded, tire slashing, artist, girlfriend?

"I guess she didn't tell you about the penis either? Or that Teeny said it was a female out for revenge that done it?" Art asks.

"Penis? What the hell are you talking about, Art?" Jack raises his hands palm up, thoroughly confused. He looks at me to fill in the blanks.

"Someone drew a phallic design on the back of my Bronco," I say.

"A Teeny penis?" Jack asks, the corners of his mouth pulling up in a mischievous grin.

"No, a pretty well-endowed one. Teeny is her new jolly green giant, biker friend, who read a lot of books on the inside that led him to think it's a jealous woman because of the nature of the drawing," Art says.

"Good grief! Can we please stop talking about this and get back to discussing the investigation?" I ask.

"In a sec," Jack says, holding up a finger. "I am a little concerned that your tire was slashed. And I have to see this graffiti," he says, springing to his feet and heading for the door.

"It's gone. I scrubbed it off," I say. His face falls in disappointment.

"I have pictures," Art says, tossing Jack his phone. Jack catches the phone with one hand, flipping it over to look at the image displayed on the screen. He immediately starts guffawing. I allow them the privilege of sharing the joke at my expense before finally looking at them through slitted eyes. Both men seem to take the hint and try to put on serious faces.

"This does concern me," Jack says. "Regardless of what your biker friend says, we both heard Lexie say that Clay is displaying stalker type tendencies. He has already made an attempt on Gertie. What if he somehow knows that Gertie told you about what she witnessed? He could be planning on seeking you out next."

I hope Teeny was right in his assessment. Although I hate to be the target of a crazy, jealous woman, I would prefer that over being singled out by Clay. I think of the phone calls but decide that I am being paranoid and it is a coincidence. "As I told Art earlier, it was probably some kids out into mischief. We all know that I am loveable and no one could possibly be targeting me for personal reasons." This draws several snide remarks from them both. I clear my throat, "Um hmm," I say, while looking at Jack and pointing to the voice recorder.

"Okay, back on task," Jack says. "Kurt's tox screen came back clean. He wasn't using drugs. Cause of death was the gunshot wound—forty-four magnum. He was dead before he went into the water. The M.E. put the time of death as last Saturday, which matches with Gertie's account. With the water levels from the rain, Kurt's body was put in the creek near Gertie's and made its way into the river. The body was caught on some rocks and when the water level started going back down, that is when the kayakers found him."

"We know Clay is our man. We just have to find him. We have been over his truck and house with a fine-tooth comb and there's nothing other than Kurt's fingerprints in his truck. We are keeping an ongoing check with motels, convenience stores, and anywhere else that we can possibly think he may visit, as well as patrolling for him. Clay has no credit, debit, or ATM cards. He pays cash for everything, even his rent. We now have Lexie, who can place the two of them together, having a heated discussion. What else have we got?" Jack says.

"I think that pretty much sums it up. Other than Lexie, there really isn't anything helpful that I have found. I have even chased a lead to the place where he purchases his hair pomade, for lack of anything else to go on. Is it possible to put a tap on Lexie's phone, or a trace, in case Clay calls her again?"

"That would be a long process. By the time I could make it happen, I hope to have Clay in custody. And do we believe Lexie, that he hasn't been hiding out there? I know he wouldn't be now, because of the officer there, but that doesn't mean he could not have been there lying low before today," Jack says.

"I don't think he was. I got a look inside the trailer and around the property. I did not see any sign that would lead me to think so," I say.

"You what?" Art and Jack ask in unison.

"What happened to observing from a distance? Someone has already slashed your tire, and we just talked about his stalker tendencies," Jack says. "And please tell me you didn't enter her residence without permission!"

"Okay, first of all, she was sleeping with the guy. I am not. He has no reason to stalk me. Second of all, I had my gun. And I announced myself before I entered," I say nervously. "And the door was unlocked." I wince up at him, hopeful that he doesn't arrest me for my *non*-breaking entry.

"Well, sweetheart, I can guarantee you from the bullet taken from Kurt that Clay's gun is bigger. And just because I gave you a badge, doesn't mean you can pull crap like entering Lexie's trailer. Is that clear?" Jack asks in a scolding tone.

"Perfectly clear," I say. Perfectly clear that I will keep information like that to myself from now on.

"You know what, Jack, I will just sleep on the couch here in the office tonight to keep an eye on things," Art says, drawing the Sheriff's searching gaze away from me.

"I can come back and stay, if you'd rather me to," Jack says.

"Maybe you can sleep on her couch, and I will sleep down here, or vice versa?" Art says.

"Either way is fine with me," Jack shrugs. Just like that, they are on the same team about Jack sleeping over.

"I will go to my Mama's and spend the night! How about that? Is that satisfactory to both of you?"

"Yes," they say in unison again.

"Maybe one of you can sleep on my couch, and the other on the couch in Art's office, even with me at Mama's house. I can round up some nail polish and hair rollers, and you can have a slumber party out of it."

"Throw in a pizza?" Art asks and Jack laughs.

CHAPTER TWENTY-THREE

Dark clouds gather in the distance and it looks like this afternoon may bring more sporadic, isolated April showers. I open the heavy door leading into the storefront of the garage. My Bronco, sporting a brand-new tire, is parked off to the side of the building. Stepping in, I smell motor oil, hear the whirs from tools, clanging and thumping from working on cars, and hissing noises from air hoses. Mechanics are yelling at each other in order to be heard over the den of noise. A ding-dong sound indicates that someone has pulled into the gas pumps. A young man that had been sitting on a bench out front is quick to approach the vehicle and start pumping the gas.

Different brands and sizes of tires are stacked around the storefront, along with visual aids, to show what the tread on tires should look like. An ancient vending machine is stocked with off-brand potato chips and snacks. The "pop" machine is new. Coffee that smells scorched and looks more like sludge than coffee, sits atop a counter. No one is in the storefront, and I wander around smelling car air fresheners. I grow bored with that and start looking at windshield wipers, as if I know something about them.

Finally, Rob, the owner, emerges from the garage, wiping his hands on a grease rag.

"Hello, young lady. We got you all fixed up," he says.

"Thank you. How much do I owe you?" I ask.

"Don't worry about it. Art has already taken care of it. I owed him for an investigation that he had done for me a while back. He wouldn't take payment for it," Rob says.

Art often does jobs for free. Before the high-profile cases he undertakes now and the business that the website brings in, there were several times in years past that he barely made ends meet with his business. He has always been freehearted.

"Thank you. That is very kind of you."

"Don't mention it. Somebody sure must be angry with you. Really took it out on your tire."

"It's all part of the business, I suppose," I say.

"I hear that," he chuckles.

I dial Mama's number when I get in the vehicle. I would like to assume that she has no life other than me, as most children tend to think about their parents, but I know this isn't true.

"Hey Mama."

"Hey Hon," she says.

"Is it okay if I stay over at your place tonight?"

"Are you kidding? I would love that! We can have a girls' night! But why are you needing to stay over?"

"I'll explain later. I just wanted to make sure you did not have any plans that my staying over would disrupt," I say.

"Nope. I have nothing going on tonight. We can get Chinese food, maybe watch a sappy romance movie. I can even put some highlights in your hair if you want, since summer is coming up."

"Yes, to the food and movie. Raincheck on the highlights. I'll pick up Chinese food on my way."

"Okay, I'll see you this evening, then. Love you, bye."

"I will see you later, Mama. I love you too."

I change my shoes, first thing, when I get to my apartment. Then I pack an overnight bag to take to my mother's house. It is still early in the day, but I would like to do some patrolling of my own, to look for Clay. I spy the bags of items from the Beauty Needs store and bring them along. Mama said she wanted to do a girls' night, so maybe we can do facials and such. I note where everything is placed in my apartment before locking the door and leaving. I think back to the phone calls and the slashed tire and I feel somewhat uneasy. I would like to know if anything is out of place when I return to my apartment.

I drive zigzags around town. The windshield wipers slap, clearing the rain that is constantly changing from steady to a light drizzle. Thunder rolls and sounds much like the train rumbling down the railroad tracks next to the highway. I am looking for anything that may point to Clay. I then drive Highway 27, which is the main road, from one end of the county to the other. My gas light blinks on just before I get to the county line. I have been so distracted by this case. I never let my fuel gauge fall below a half a tank. I seem to be out of sorts today. I still blame it on my dream from last night.

I pull into the convenience store at the county line. It seems to take an eternity before the gas pump kicks off. Gas is three dollars and eighty-nine cents a gallon, making the numbers on the cost gauge roll by much faster than the numbers of gallons pumped. A notice flashes on the screen that the receipt printer is out of paper- see cashier. *Wonderful. I hope the rude cashier is not working today.*

But of course, he is the person behind the register when I enter the store. I get an extra-large cup of coffee and put about fifteen squirts of mix and match creamers in it. He is looking extra surly today and does not take his eyes off me.

"I can pay extra for the creamer," I say.

He does not give me a response, and he never breaks eye contact the entire time — staring at me, deadpan.

Gee, what is it with this guy?

"Seventy-seven-fifty-two," he says.

"Oh, I paid for my gas at the pump, Thomas," I say, looking at his name tag.

"Do you have a receipt?" he asks.

"It said the receipt printer was out of paper."

"All I know is it says you didn't pay."

"I am going to need to speak to your manager!" I say—a statement that I loathe having to make.

This emits a huff and an exaggerated eye roll from him. "Lester!" he yells.

A very pleasant-looking man emerges from the back room. I explain the situation to Lester, who is the store manager.

"Tom, you've worked here for seven years! You can see right here that she paid for the gas. What's the problem?"

"Oops. My mistake," he says, still deadpan.

"The coffee's on the house and here, ma'am, have a free lighter for your trouble," Lester says.

"Oh, I do not smo...., you know what, never mind. Thank you. And I would love a lighter for my trouble."

"And you have yourself a fantabulous evening, Thomas," I say on my way out the door.

Clerk Jerk. Okay, maybe Art was right to wonder if Mr. Personality could be my tire slasher.

After that ordeal, and the thought of listening to Mama pitch marriage and babies to me all evening, I decide I need to trade my coffee in for something stronger. I pull across the road to the Troubadour.

* * *

Entering the bar, I take in my surroundings out of habit. It is not very busy yet. It is still too early for the after-work crowd. Three regulars occupy bar stools. Two couples sit across from each other at a table, laughing and having a great time. An older lady, walking with a cane, is sliding into a booth with a much younger man. Then, there is a man sitting in the back booth, all alone. He seems familiar, but I cannot place where I know him from. The booth that he occupies is darker than the others, due to poor lighting in the corner. It is the last booth along the wall before coming to a short hallway that leads to the restrooms. No one ever chooses to sit in this booth unless it is their only option. On busy nights, if you are seated here and a line forms to the restroom, then you have people standing beside your table waiting. It is slow enough right now that this hasn't become an issue for the man.

"Hey, Hon. Usual?" Sally asks.

"You know it. Do you ever get a day off, Sal?"

"Oh well you know, it's hard to take a day off when you're the proprietor of the establishment!" she says proudly.

"Proprietor? Sally, did you buy this place?"

"Yep. Signed the paperwork yesterday."

"That's awesome! I am so happy for you!" I say.

"I figured I might as well. Been working here my whole life, it seems. I've already got big plans for this place. Going to build on to make a bigger dance floor, expand the parking lot, and a new menu. Lots of good things coming," she says.

"I know it will be great," I say and she blushes.

I turn slightly and study the loner sitting in the back booth. He has unusual blonde hair, large, black-framed glasses, dark denim blue jeans, and a too loose long-sleeved gray tee shirt. He is clean-shaven and is wearing a do-rag with American Flags printed on it.

"Who's that?" I ask Sally, indicating the loner.

"Dunno. I think he may be mute or something. Just walked up to the bar, when he came in, and pointed to what he wanted, took it, and sat down," she says.

"How long ago was that?" I ask.

"Not long before you got here," she says.

"Have you ever seen him before?"

"I don't recall ever seeing him. He seems familiar for some reason, though," she says, as she dries a shot glass.

"That's what I was thinking, too."

I hold my cell phone up high and take a selfie, capturing the man in the photo's background. After a few more minutes of small talk with Sally, in which she detailed more of her plans for the bar, something is still nagging me about the loner. I decide to take a closer look. If I go to the restroom, I will have to walk past his booth, giving me an opportunity to study him.

I step down off of my barstool, taking the long way around to the restroom, feigning confusion about where it is located, allowing me extra time to look at the man along my way. He has his head down, looking at me out of the corner of his eye as I approach. Passing his booth, I get a strong whiff of Sandalwood, and it clicks—this is Clay! He has changed his appearance! I reach back to pull my gun from my back waistband and start to turn. He has been watching me this whole time. He stands, grabs me, and wrenches my arm painfully behind my back. In an instant, he has pulled a forty-four Desert Eagle from beneath his loose-fitting shirt and sticks it to the side of my head. I can see the light gleaming off of the gold on the gun. The other patrons quickly realize what has happened and every male in the room pulls a gun. Every one of us breaking laws by having entered the establishment with weapons. The only problem—I am standing between their bullets and Clay.

Sally jumps up on the bar, brandishing a sawed-off shotgun. She racks it and yells, "Hey, Shithead! Let her go unless you want your brains splattered all over the walls! Won't trouble me none. I'm getting ready to repaint the place anyhow!"

Everyone hits the floor when they hear the cha-cha sound of the shotgun rack, except for Clay, me, and the lady on the cane, who was making her way to the restroom, when he grabbed me.

Clay laughs and says, "You can't shoot me without shooting her."

Exactly!!

"How about you let her go, drop your gun, and maybe we can talk. You shoot her, I'm still going to shoot you, so there's no way you're walking out of here unless you drop it and let her go!"

We hear a "Oooooaaah" coming from the lady on the cane and then a thud as she faints onto the floor. This distracts Clay. I headbutt him and hear a loud pop. I hope I broke his nose. He instantly reaches up, letting go of my wrenched arm. I do a half turn toward his gun hand, pulling his wrist down. I can feel that his wrist is bandaged under the cuff of his shirt sleeve. Probably courtesy of Buddy the dog. I gouge into the wound with all the force I can muster, while hoping he does not pull the trigger on the gun. He lets out a yelp that sounds gurgled from the blood pouring out of his nose, and the weapon clatters to the floor.

Dropping onto my knees, I scramble for the Desert Eagle to keep Clay from retrieving it. I successfully take hold of the gun as Sally fires off a shot, missing him. Shards of glass from a picture frame and splintered paneling careen through the air. The shotgun kicked when Sally shot, knocking her backwards off the bar. Clay springs toward the door. Sally recovers quickly and lets off another shot, missing the moving target.

I take off after him with my ears ringing from the noise of the shotgun blast. The acrid odor of the gun smoke hangs thick in the air. The lady with the cane is starting to come around and raises up off the floor as I am passing by her. I try to side-step around her. She moves to pick up her cane and unknowingly trips me. This causes me to take a nosedive into a corner of a table. Blood gushes from a cut on my forehead, but I ignore it and take off out the door after Clay. Sally is not far behind me with the shotgun. The men, guns drawn, emerge into the parking lot next. We search the surroundings, but Clay is already gone.

Officer Eli Keith is the first to arrive at the scene. After doing a quick sweep of the area, he takes statements. The other responding officers begin canvassing. Eli is now taking a statement from the lady on the cane. She recognizes him as Officer Sexy from his videos and asks him to show her some of his dance moves. After much sweet talk from her, he wiggles his hips and steps from side to side while moving his hands, then does a big twirl and finishes by crossing his arms over his chest, just as Jack walks through the door. Jack stops and has a word with him as Eli takes off out the exit.

The Sheriff saunters over to me. "Did Clay do that?" he asks, referring to the big gash on my head. The amount of blood from the wound makes it appear far worse than it actually is.

"No. She did," I say, pointing to the lady on the cane. "Not intentionally," I add.

I start from the beginning and tell Jack of the entire event. When I am finished, he has the same look on his face that I have after listening to one of Gertie's stories. I suppose the adrenaline is making it difficult for me to make sense. Or it could be the probable concussion that I have.

Officer Keith walks back in, notepad flipped open and says, "EMTs just arrived. Nobody saw anything except a clerk at the convenience store. His name's Tom Thomas. First name, Tom, last name, Thomas. Says he was walking to his car when he got off work, and heard the shotgun blast. He was looking in this direction because he could tell that's where it came from. He saw a guy run out, wiping blood off his nose with a do-rag. The guy jumped on a motorcycle and took off. A couple of minutes later, he saw a lady that he recognized, but does not know her name so he just calls her and I quote, "Josie Exotic," come out, and jog around the parking lot, waving a big-ass gun. Then another lady, that he knows is Sally, came out with a shotgun. Then, a bunch of men ran out with their guns, reminding him of a posse. He then ran back into the store and hid behind the counter."

"Josie Exotic?" Jack asks.

"Probably because of the lion cub," I say.

"Lion cub? You know what? Never mind, you can tell me about that some other time," Jack says.

"Huh, I would've thought maybe it is because of your cheetah print shirt," Eli says.

"Yeah, maybe," I say.

"I met your new friend Teeny earlier," Jack says. "He stopped in at the station to report his motorcycle stolen. He had parked at the grocery store to help a lady load her bags, and someone matching Clay's new appearance jumped on the bike and rode away. I'm guessing it was Teeny's cycle that Clay just fled on."

"Ballsy move," I say.

"*Stupid*, ballsy move," Jack says. "Clay had best hope that Teeny doesn't catch up to him before I do. At least now, we have an up-to-date description of Clay and, more than likely, the murder weapon. You sit tight and get checked out by the EMTs. I will come back in a while and make sure you get to your Mama's safe. I tried calling Art, but his phone immediately went to voicemail. He must be out of range of a signal or his phone is turned off."

"I'm fine to drive myself," I say.

"Um, I don't think you are. You probably have a concussion. At least, I hope that explains it," Jack says.

"Fine. But just so you know, I have to stop and pick up Chinese food on the way."

"I could go for some General Tsao's," Jack says.

"Okay. But I can promise that you'll regret it," I say.

CHAPTER TWENTY-FOUR

I walk through the door at Mama's with my overnight bag. Jack trails along behind me, carrying half of the buffet from the Chinese restaurant and my bags of beauty products from the Bee's Knees Beauty Needs.

My Mother's home is always organized and immaculate. Nothing is ever out of place. If she weren't such a great hairdresser, I would think that her calling would be to become an interior designer. She likes for everything in her life to look classy, much like her appearance always does. She is very meticulous about everything that she does. The house is beautifully decorated and always smells like a hot toddy. I have often thought that my mother possesses some kind of superpower that allows her to accomplish every task that she takes on, alone. As pristine as she keeps her house, it is still comfortable and beckoning. It is home. There have been many times throughout my adult life (especially when I lived in Boston) that I have craved being in this house, with the comfort and safety that it, and her have always provided.

"Hey, Mama. Sorry that I am so late."

"Elizabeth Anne Whitley Riley! I have been trying to call you! I have been worried to death! Why did you not answer your phone? Oh, my goodness! Let me look at your head!"

News spreads quickly in a small town. She has already heard about the fiasco at the bar. She puts her hands on either side of my face, examining it. Apparently, she has some type of motherly X-ray vision and can see through the bandage covering the cut on my forehead.

"My head is fine. It is just a small cut and a minor concussion. I'm sorry that I did not answer my phone. It has been a little hectic, and I knew I would be here soon enough. We have a plus one for dinner," I say.

She looks up and sees Jack standing in the doorway. "Oh, hello Sheriff," she says, immediately putting on her company smile.

"Ma'am," Jack says as a way of greeting.

"Call me Annie. Come in, come in. Make yourself comfortable. I'll get the food set up."

"Please, call me Jack. No need to call me Sheriff."

After getting everything spread out on the table, we sit down and Mama immediately starts interrogating me.

"There really isn't much to tell. I had a chance meeting with Kurt's murderer. Realized it was him and he pulled a gun. Sally brandished a shotgun. He got away, and I fell and hit my head on a table," I say, cramming a crab rangoon in my mouth.

"Not much to tell? You're seriously going to shorten the version down to that? Honestly, Elle, I don't know what makes you not be more forthcoming." She takes her stare off of me and turns to Jack. "She takes that after her dad's relatives. Odd bunch. The whole lot of them. I think she got a double dose," she says, and he nearly chokes on a noodle. "She doesn't like to explain things, except on paper."

I do not take offense to the things that she is saying. I inherited my physical traits from my mother. I am happy to know that I inherited something from my father, whom I never had a chance to know. And I know she is happy about it, too. When she is irritated with me, she blames my quirks on his side of the family. When she is not irritated with me, she finds the behavior that reminds her of my father, endearing. She is also correct that I am much more comfortable putting words on paper than sharing them out loud.

"You never did tell me why you needed to leave your apartment tonight. Is Art doing some work on it or something?" she asks.

Jack is about to open his mouth. I shake my head at him, making a slicing motion across my neck with my fork. He drops his head, avoiding looking at my mother, and stabs a piece of broccoli. "I knew you would be excited to have a girl's night. We haven't had one in a while. What movie did you pick out?" I ask, changing the subject.

"Well, I picked out a real tearjerker, sure to give us the vapors. Jack, do you want to stick around and watch the movie with us?" she asks.

"Mama, Jack has to get back to work. He has a killer to catch. Right, Jack?"

"Yeah, as much as I like tear jerker movies, I should probably get back out there. Elle, I can swing by in the morning and pick you up," he says.

"I'm sure she can give me a ride. Mama?"

"Um, no. Actually, I've got a thing in the morning," she says, refusing to look at me.

"What thing? Can you not give me a ride on the way to your *thing?*"

"Hmm. No, I'm afraid not. It's a personal thing and I will be in a rush in the morning," she says, being extremely vague. It is quite obvious to me that her "personal thing" is for me to get picked up by Jack, as some type of matchmaking ploy. Her dreams of Colt and I sailing off into the sunset on a honeymoon are not working out for her.

"Alright, then. I will swing by around eight in the morning and pick you up," Jack says. He stands and says, "Thank you ladies for a lovely dinner."

"You're welcome anytime, Sheriff," Mama says.

I start to see him out and my phone rings as we get to the door. He waves goodbye and walks on to his truck, as I answer the call. It is Colt. I walk to my old bedroom and shut the door in order to have some privacy from my Mother's prying ears.

Colt has heard about the ordeal. He is concerned and confused as to why I did not call him. I tell him I am sorry, it has been hectic, and the Sheriff dropped me off at Mama's a bit ago. I know when he hears that I am at my mother's house, it will be explanation enough as to why I have not called him.

"The sheriff dropped you off? Is something going on between you two? I heard a rumor that he spent the night at your place last night," he says.

"Is something going on between Sheriff Lennox and me? The same sheriff that makes my life torture half the time when I am out driving? Absolutely not! He was at my apartment because we were working on the murder case. That is the *only* thing that I have in common with him!"

"Alright. Just asking. You know you could tell me if there was something going on?"

"Yeah, I know. A deal is a deal and we are not exclusive, blah, blah, blah," I say.

"A deal?" Colt asks.

"The deal we made when we started seeing each other."

"Oh, you mean the deal that we made almost a year and a half ago? Just to clarify," he says.

"Yes. And while we're on the subject, have you been seeing anyone that would have a reason to slash my tire and draw genitals on my back hatch?"

"Um no. Someone did that to you?" he asks, angry at the thought of it happening.

"Yeah. I've been racking my brain and can't think of anyone that I would have made angry enough to do such a thing. Hopefully, it was just kids messing around."

"Yeah, hopefully," he says. "Listen, I am supposed to work this weekend, to make up for the lost days earlier in the week. Do you need me to come on home? Should I be worried about your safety? Maybe you should go ahead and come down here to hang out with me."

"No worries. I am fine. You get caught up on your work and we will try to catch up next weekend. Maybe things will be settled down for both of us by then."

"Alright. If you need me, call. I'll talk to you later, then," he says.

"Thanks. I will look forward to seeing you next weekend," I say.

After hanging up the phone, I look around my childhood room. It has remained the same, other than the random array of exercise equipment that Mama has added. Old photos still hang on a corkboard, held in place with neon push pins. The throw that my Granny Beth crocheted for me still lies neatly across the foot of the bed. A picture of my father, holding me as a newborn, sits atop the nightstand. He was very young.

He and my mother were high school sweethearts who married during their senior year, after my mother became pregnant with me. My conception caused quite the scandal for them. My father's family were particularly distraught, thinking that any bright future he had was immediately taken from him. Little did they know that three years later, they would bury him. A drunk driver hit his car when he was on his way home from work.

I have never had a close relationship with my father's family. One would think that they would have wanted to spend more time with me, considering that they had lost their son, and I was his only child. Unfortunately, it was the opposite. They still harbored animosity toward my mother, for getting pregnant with me. They chose to punish her by having as little as possible to do with me. Mama struggled with this for years. She would do everything that she possibly could to accommodate their schedules, so they would not have excuses for refusing to see me. A new excuse would replace the old. She finally grew weary of trying, and my visits with them became more sporadic, until eventually they stopped altogether.

My Granny Beth was not happy that my mother became pregnant when she did, either. But she chose to see me as a blessing and always made sure to make me feel as such. She would say that my father's family were the ones that were actually missing out by not having a relationship with me.

I touch the simple gold chain hanging around my neck that I never take off. It has a dainty E hanging from it. It had been gifted to my granny from my grandfather. She passed it on to me, on my sixteenth birthday, saying that she wanted her namesake to have it.

Still, to this day, my mother extends grace to my father's family, out of respect for him. Other than to refer to them as an odd bunch, she has nothing bad to say about them.

My Granny Beth in no manner feels obligated to extend as much grace concerning them.

My disappointments from my father's family taught me at an early age not to expect much from people, and you would be less likely to get hurt.

* * *

"Is it supposed to burn?" I ask Mama of the face masks that we have applied.

"Let's see here. The jar says that tingling is normal. I guess that means it's working. It says to leave on for fifteen minutes, which should time out perfect to when your highlights are done processing," she says.

I gave in to her suggestion of highlights. Summer *is* right around the corner. And with the week I have had, maybe they will make me feel better. After taking forever to get my long hair foiled, we did a brief foot soak, painted our toenails, and then applied the face masks.

"You know, Elle, you should think about signing up for this new kickboxing class that I am taking. It's great. You could use the extra skills that you would learn in your line of work. Not to mention, the instructor is really hot!"

"Maybe. It does sound like fun. But you do realize that I do not go around kung-fu fighting with people all day, right? I mostly sit behind a computer."

"Look at what happened today! And what about your tire getting slashed? Did you really think that Art would not tell me about that?" she asks.

I should've known that Art would have already told her. The two of them communicate about me, like they are attempting to co-parent a troubled teen. She probably already knew about it when she asked why I was spending the night at her house.

"I really wish you had never started helping him out with investigations. It's not like you do not make a comfortable living with your writing," she says as she checks the foils in my hair.

The truth is that I do not make nearly as much money as she thinks. I seem to accept fewer and fewer writing jobs, and an increasing number of cases for Art, rarely accepting payment for them. I do not feel right taking money from him when he is kind enough to let me live in the apartment rent-free. He insists that I get paid for my work. I finally gave up arguing with him, so I started accepting the checks and then depositing them right back into his account. I handle his bookkeeping, so he has no clue.

"This mask is *really* burning. I think I should rinse it off," I say.

"It'll have to wait a few minutes. You're processed. Let's get you rinsed out," she says. She hands me a wet washcloth to wipe my face as she is rinsing the bleach out of my hair. *Hmm. That is odd. It looks like there are faint traces of blood on the washcloth. Must be from the cut on my head.*

She rushes through getting all the bleach out of my hair. She does not take her time, as she usually does, to give me a nice, lengthy scalp massage. "Go wash your face *NOW*," she says, grabbing my arm and pulling me up.

I rinse the mask completely off. It has left my face red, raw, and angry looking. "I think I may be allergic to it," I say.

"Hopefully, it's just made you all red because it works so well. It will probably calm down in a bit," she says.

I can tell by the look on her face that she is doubtful, though. "Let's get some toner on your hair now. I would get you some Benadryl, but with your concussion, I don't want to chance it making you drowsy. I am going to set my alarm for every hour, maybe hour and a half, tonight, so I can wake you, and make sure that you are okay," she says.

"I really do not think that is necessary. I feel fine. I am fairly certain that anytime someone bumps their head, they say concussion, just to cover all of their bases," I say.

"Yeah, but still yet…." she says.

CHAPTER TWENTY-FIVE

FRIDAY

My alarm blares, and I awake from a dream in which I am swimming with jellyfish. I raise up from having fallen asleep, face down on ice packs. The packs are now melted. The jelly-like substance inside of them has turned squishy. At least, that explains the dream. I can't believe that I slept long enough to dream any dreams, being woken up so frequently throughout the night.

I make my way to the kitchen, where Mama is taking homemade cinnamon rolls out of the oven. I put the ice packs back into the freezer and say, "I thought you had a *thing* this morning."

"Oh, it got canceled," she says, waving her oven mitt.

"Wonderful! I can text Jack and tell him you will give me a ride."

"I'm sure he has already left to come pick you up. You might want to go look in the mirror."

I rush to the bathroom, nervous to look at my reflection. The bandage covering the stitches had come off during the night. A goose egg sized bump protrudes from the middle of my forehead. It is the only area on my face that splotchy looking blisters does not affect. I look hideous. My mother is standing in the bathroom wincing at the sight, as if I can't see her in the mirror.

"Can you do something with concealer to hide it?" I ask.

"I don't think that even *I* can hide that, sweetheart. Here, let's go have a cinnamon roll." She takes me by the shoulders, pulling me away from the mirror and directing me toward the kitchen. "Maybe it will make you feel better."

After eating, we do our best to make my face look presentable. When Jack pulls in, I rush out the door before he has an opportunity to come inside. "Here. Mama sent you some cinnamon rolls," I say, passing them off to him.

He looks at my face in horror, and says, "What happened to your face?" Apparently, the attempt to make myself look presentable failed.

"Girls' night facials gone wrong," I say.

He cannot seem to take his eyes off the disaster that is my face. It is a moment before he starts the truck and pulls away. Finally, he says, "Your hair looks nice."

I do love the highlights. However, I cannot help but wonder if they might be accentuating the redness of my face. "Thanks," I say.

"Daphne canceled our lunch date today. She said the phones are ringing off the hook, with people claiming to have seen Clay," I say, after a few moments. It is typical for Jack and me to have long pauses in our conversations. Sometimes, those pauses are awkward. Often, they are comfortable, with neither one of us feeling obligated to take part in small talk.

"Yep. You know how it is when something like this happens. People have good intentions and want to help, but they just end up tying up time and resources. Everyone with a police scanner calls in," he says, after swallowing the cinnamon roll he has in his mouth. "These are really good. Your mom sure is a great cook, in addition to being a real firecracker," he laughs.

"I told you that you would regret coming in to eat with us," I say.

"I did not say that her being a firecracker was a bad thing. I actually agree with her on some things."

"Let me guess. You agree with the part about me being odd?"

"I was thinking, the part where you should've answered your phone when she called, but she's right about you being a little odd, too," he says.

"Gee, thanks."

"Don't mention it," he says, shrugging, and cramming more cinnamon roll into his mouth.

After another moment of silence, I say, "I am not supposed to drive until it has been twenty-four hours after bumping my head. Do you have time to let me drop in and check on Gertie? I promise to be quick about it."

"Sure. I have been going by there every day and checking the woods and surrounding area, anyway. By the way, I checked into your friend Teeny yesterday. I wanted to find out if he was as dangerous as he looks. Surprisingly, Lawrence 'Teeny' Tulane has only served time once. That was recently for tax evasion. The DA said that she was fairly certain that he had been set up, but he refused to roll over on whoever had done it, and served his bit instead of ratting out whoever was funneling money through his name."

"I assumed he had been to prison for cracking skulls. Lawrence, huh? Just doesn't seem to roll off the tongue like Teeny Tulane does."

* * *

Jack drops me off in Gertie's driveway. He pulls out to go check around the creek for any sign that Clay has returned to the property. Buddy must be roaming the neighborhood this morning because he does not greet me. I am rather glad since I do not have any treats for him today. Gertie is sitting on the covered back porch, as she frequently does when the weather is fair.

"Good Morning, Gertie. How are you doing?"

"I am doing fine this morning. How come the Sheriff dropped you off?" she asks.

"I had an accident and I am not supposed to drive today," I say.

"Does it have anything to do with your face?" she asks, squinting up at me. I should have realized that I was setting myself up for that question. She picks up a Tupperware container and says, "Brownie, dear?"

Under normal circumstances, I would refuse. Today, I accept. I sit in the chair next to her, savoring the brownie, and start to feel better.

"Another Brownie, Hon?" she asks.

"Don't mind if I do," I say, giggling.

Gertie and I are laughing hysterically at her gnome collection when Jack returns. "What's so funny?" he asks. I point down at the gnome, with his bare behind stuck up in the air, mooning everyone.

Gertie picks up the plastic container and says, "Brownie, Sheriff?"

Jack rolls his eyes, lets out an exaggerated sigh, and shakes his head. "I should arrest you both." Gertie and I almost fall out of our chairs laughing.

* * *

I am feeling unusually chatty on the drive to my apartment. "Gosh, this weather is going to be gorgeous today. What do you do in fair weather? Fish? Golf? Do you like to deer hunt?" I ask.

"I'm not much of a golfer. I hunt later in the year. I do enjoy fishing, but the job doesn't allow for many off days," he says.

"You seem to be one of those married to your job type of people. Is that why you've never actually gotten married? No dreams of the white picket fence with kids frolicking barefoot through the yard?" I ask.

"Actually, I was married for a short time. Turns out military life wasn't suitable for her," he says.

"Huh. I never knew that about you. Sorry to hear that it didn't work out."

"I used to be sorry. Turns out, it was for the best. I am not so sure I would've enjoyed spending the rest of my life with her. She ended up being a different person after I married her."

"Does she live in Justice?" I ask.

"Nope. She remarried not long after we divorced, and lives in North Carolina, where she is from. She has quintuplets and a set of twins. I'm kinda glad I didn't have to buy all of those diapers," he laughs.

"I bet you would've made a wonderful dad," I say.

"I still hope to be one day," he says.

I suppose I had never thought about Jack outside of his role as Sheriff. The revelation that he has personal dreams makes him seem more human to me, rather than him just being the walking embodiment of law enforcement. I ponder this during the rest of the drive. I wonder if he is dating someone that he hopes will lead to that future. I do not know of any serious relationship that he may be involved in, but then again, Jack is private about his personal life. If he has a girlfriend, apparently he doesn't think she would be a person to vandalize vehicles.

When he parks in front of Art's building, I hop out of the truck and make my way around to the side to go to my apartment. Two men have a ladder precariously sitting on the steps, installing security cameras and blocking my way. I turn around and head into the office. Jack is inside talking to Art. I make my way past them to the kitchen and proceed to look for snacks. I hear Jack tell Art that I have been at Gertie's eating brownies that Jared made, and Art replies, "Heaven help us all!"

"Yep. She's higher than the grocery bill," and I can hear both of them laughing.

"I can swing by this afternoon and take you to pick up your Bronco at The Troubadour, Elle," Jack yells toward the kitchen.

"Okie dokie, artichoky," I yell back.

After eating all the food in the small kitchen, I curl up on the leather couch in Art's office, and take a nap that is akin to being in a coma.

CHAPTER TWENTY-SIX

I wake up a couple of hours later, feeling surprisingly well, other than a dry mouth. Art is gone, and so are the men who were installing the security cameras.

I walk into my apartment, taking note that everything is still exactly how I left it. The tire slasher must not be interested in breaking and entering. I also have not had any strange phone calls today, which is even more convincing, that it was just a coincidence. I was being paranoid, after all. I take a deep breath to inhale the scents in the apartment. No sandalwood, which means that Clay has not been here.

With the weather being perfection, I decide to go for a run to clear my head. It will give me plenty of time to think. Billie Eilish comes pulsing through my headphones, as I take off down the sidewalk, footfalls landing in sync with the music. My ponytail bounces along with the beat, as I go back in my mind to the encounter with Clay yesterday evening. I try to remember if there was anything that I did not notice at the time.

Clay does not wish to be caught, for obvious reasons. But why is he even still in Justice? He could have easily left and gone to another state. What is holding him here?

He does not seem to have a job, but he is getting money from somewhere. He has no known connections, other than his sister and Lexie. Lexie ended her relationship with him. Cammie says the same. Jack has had officers watching both of their homes, and nothing unusual has happened at either place.

Kurt had money after Clay arrived in town and then Clay murdered Kurt, so it has to have something to do with money. Clay has removed Kurt from the picture. With Lexie and Cammie no longer being involved with him, what is keeping him here? He has gone to great lengths to change his appearance and demeanor in order to not get caught. It was an extremely bold move on his part to show up at the bar yesterday. That boldness is what I would expect from Clay, not the quiet, reserved act that he was putting on when he entered the bar. Why take the chance of even going to The Troubadour? Maybe he did it just to see if he could get away with it. Why was he brave enough to steal Teeny's motorcycle from the grocery parking lot, in plain sight, during broad daylight? Maybe for the same reason, to see if he could get away with it.

Clay seems to be an enigma. He no doubt, has already changed his appearance again. Jack has been working this case nonstop, functioning on very little sleep. He has questioned and re-questioned people. He has followed every clue and lead that he could possibly think of. I know Clay is not smarter than Jack or me, so how is he outsmarting us? Either he is much cleverer than I had given him credit for, or someone has to be helping him. But who?

Jack sends me a text saying that he will be by to pick me up in the next hour or so. I turn retracing the route to my apartment. All of the sudden, the hairs on my nape start to prickle. I feel like I am being watched. I do a three-sixty turn scanning the entire area. I do not see anyone in sight. *Damn paranoia.*

I pick up my speed making it back to my apartment in record time. Still feeling a little unsettled when I get there. I shower, and get ready. Jack knocks on my door as I am slipping my shoes on.

* * *

"Hey. Thanks for taking me to pick up my Bronco. You seem to be having to go through a lot of trouble on my account lately," I say.

"Honestly, it's no trouble. I am out patrolling and going from one end of this county to the other, constantly looking for Clay, anyway," he says.

"About that. I think we are going about it all wrong, searching for him," I say.

"We are going about it all wrong by looking for the murderer?" he asks, confused.

"What I mean to say is that someone must be helping Clay. We need to find out who that someone is and they will lead us to him. He may be smarter than I thought, but I still think someone is helping him."

"Is that not what we're doing? I have been questioning anyone known to be associated with him," he says.

"Yes, questioning them and having an officer sit at their house. But what about investigating *them*? Think of them as a suspect. Clay has to be getting his money from somewhere. Maybe whoever is keeping him flush has left a money trail in their financials. Figuring that out could lead to why he is still here, and why he murdered Kurt. When I interacted with Clay at the bar the first time, I did not peg him as having a brilliant mind. Not one

smart enough to keep evading being captured, anyway.
I think that someone smarter than him may be helping
him. If that someone is Cammie or Lexie, they are being
very careful right now, because they know they are being
watched. Either that or he truly is a psychopath, choosing
to hang around, getting a kick out of watching us chase
our tails looking for him," I say.

"That actually makes sense. I see the brownies have
worn off," he says.

Ignoring the remark about the brownies, I continue,
"Lexie has no money, so she isn't Clay's cash cow. But
Cammie has a rich husband and possibly money of her
own from her late husband's insurance pay out."

"That's true. But a half a mil probably would not have
lasted someone like Cammie long. I think A.J. knows where
every penny of his money goes. If she were to be giving Clay
A.J.'s money, he would most likely know about it," he says.

"Have you asked him? Maybe he does, and Cammie's
story about A.J. not knowing about Clay was just to throw
us off."

"He has been out in the middle of the lake on his
houseboat, with no cell service the last couple of days.
Which happens to be very convenient for Cammie. I plan
on questioning him as soon as he returns."

"And you have ruled out a possible drug connection?"
I ask.

"My sources tell me that there have been no new people
on the scene. If it is drug related, it's on a much larger
scale than locally," he says.

"Why don't I help you today? After all, I *am* a deputy,"
I say with a mischievous grin. "I cannot do much
investigating and tracking the 'perp' unless I actually get
out into 'the field.' I'll have your back, Jack."

"Don't try to use cop lingo. It doesn't sound natural coming from you. Your *field* isn't going to lead through a cow pasture again, is it?" he says.

"I certainly hope not. I don't know if you've noticed, but I seem to be having a run of bad luck this week."

"Huh, you don't say," he says, staring at the disaster that is my face. "By the way, I can't take you to get your vehicle."

"Oh?"

"We forgot you aren't supposed to drive yet. So, it's a good thing I'm here and you can ride along with me."

* * *

We spend the next two hours going from place to place, questioning people that we have already questioned, in case there is something new which they forgot to mention. We talk to clerks and cashiers of any business that cell phones can be purchased from. We get the same response that he and his deputies have gotten every time. Some do not recognize either Clay's old or new photo. Some recognize him as a customer from his old photo, but have not seen him lately, and have seen no one resembling the new photo. We question staff at motels, liquor stores, and convenience stores, but none of them have seen Clay.

We stop in at The Bee's Knees. The kind lady and gentleman have not seen him lately. However, the lady did gift me with some ointment that she says is sure to clear up the rash on my face. She assured me that after the rash goes away, my skin will be as soft as a baby's butt.

Jack turns onto the road leading to the house that Clay was renting. We go through everything in the house again, searching for clues of a hobby, interest, or anything that may lead to Clay. Finding nothing, we decide to divide and conquer, speaking to his neighbors. No one that lives on the road has seen anyone at the house, other than the Sheriff's Department. The last time that Clay was seen in the area was Tuesday evening.

I make my way back to Clay's house and see Jack standing in the yard, speaking with Clay's landlady. I open the mailbox on my way by and retrieve an envelope inside. The piece of mail is from a life insurance company and is addressed to Clay. Walking over to Jack and the landlady, I say, "You've got mail," while waving the envelope.

Jack says to the landlady, "I thought you said you would call if anything showed up in his mailbox?"

The landlady, named Doris, says, "I hadn't checked it yet this morning. I would've called you when I did."

When we get back inside the truck, I slide my finger into the corner of the envelope, tearing it open. It is a monthly bill for a million-dollar life insurance policy on Cammie Parker.

"I'm betting Clay is listed as the beneficiary on that policy," Jack says.

"That would probably be a winning bet. Do you think little sister knows about the policy?"

"Only one way to find out," Jack says, as he backs out of the driveway and heads toward the Parker residence.

CHAPTER TWENTY-SEVEN

Jack pulls into the circle drive in front of the Parker residence, where no other vehicles are parked today. We make our way to the door, wondering if anyone will be home.

Cammie answers the door. She has a very annoyed look on her face when she sees who has rung the bell. "Sheriff. Elle. We seem to be making this a habit," she says, stepping back, allowing us to enter.

"Sorry to inconvenience you again, Mrs. Parker. Unfortunately, with a murderer on the loose, some doors need to be rung more than a couple of times," Jack says. I try to figure out if he is being good cop or bad cop, but he has a way of making himself sound like he is both.

"No, before you ask, I have not seen my brother. And no, I have not told A.J. about Clay, before *you* ask," she says, looking at me, then does a double take, having just noticed my appearance. *I really hope that I get to be bad cop!*

"Can we make this quick? I was just getting ready to meet my personal trainer." I take in her workout clothes. Yoga leggings so tight they look like they are melted onto her, a sports bra that looks more like it was meant to wear for a boudoir photo shoot rather than a workout, a meticulously made-up face, and her sleek bob doesn't have a hair out of place. I don't know what kind of workout she does, but I'm guessing it's nothing like the ones I do.

"Oh well, now, I assumed you would call if you had seen him, just like you said you would. Right?" Jack says.

"That's exactly what I said," she replies, again with attitude, jutting her angled chin out.

"Is A.J. still out on the lake?" Jack asks.

"Yes. He will probably be home early next week."

"You didn't want to go with him and stay on the brand-new houseboat?" Jack asks. She just gives him an emotionless look, without commenting. She is especially difficult today. I have already grown weary of her behavior. I decide to forget the whole catch more flies with honey advice.

"I suppose since you are alive, that means that your brother hasn't cashed in on your life insurance and fled town," I say. "*Still* alive, I should add."

"What are you talking about?" she asks.

"Oh, you didn't know? I suspected maybe you didn't. Big brother took out a million-dollar life insurance policy on you," I say, assuming the role of bad cop.

She genuinely looks stunned. She takes a step back and sits down hard on the couch before she loses her balance. Tears spring to her eyes. After a moment, an angry shadow crosses her face, and she says, "I don't know why I should feel shocked that he would do something like that. I am just as expendable to him as anyone else."

"So, it concerns you he may have been planning an untimely death for you so he could cash in on the policy?" Jack asks.

"Oh, I can guarantee it!" she says, laughing bitterly. "I really do not know where Clay is. I didn't lie when

I said that I hadn't seen him. I was honest about wanting him out of my life." Then she continues, becoming surprisingly forthcoming.

"Clay and I had a shit childhood. Our mom ran off when we were little. Our dad was a mean bastard who used us as whipping posts until social services stepped in. We ended up being bounced around from foster home to foster home. Clay is my big brother. He was supposed to be the one to take care of me, but all my life, it has been me bailing him out of one situation after another. I used to think his behavior resulted from the abuse we endured from our father. Now, I think maybe Clay just inherited the same evil gene that our father possessed."

Maybe being bad cop isn't as much fun as I had initially thought it would be. I am feeling genuinely empathetic toward her now.

"Clay has followed me everywhere that I have gone, finding opportunities to scam and con anyone that I have ever been involved with. I am fairly certain that he killed my last husband, thinking I would inherit, and that he would benefit as well. I know Henry's children think I am a gold digger and had something to do with his death. I suppose I was a gold digger, to some extent. I would not have married him had he not been rich. I did not have anything to do with his death, though. I really cared for him, despite his age. After the way I grew up, he offered me safety, stability, and comfort. That was something I craved."

"I was happy when Clay got sent back to prison. I hoped it was my chance to finally be done with him. But he tracked me down when he got out. I can only imagine the schemes that he was probably concocting when he found out that I am married to A.J. I tried paying him off. I gave him half of the money that I had left from my late husband's life insurance. He was supposed to leave town."

"Then, A.J. and I were at Gertie Rose's house, and she told a story about seeing a murder at the creek. I knew when she described the truck that it belonged to Clay. I went to confront him. That's the night you saw me at his place. He, of course, acted innocent, like he had no clue what I was talking about. I told him to stay away again, and I have not seen him since."

"You said before that you did not know Kurtis Abbott? Think back again, are you sure? Did you know he had been Clay's cellmate in prison, or of any association they had after Clay came to Justice? Did you think after hearing Gertie's story that Clay may have killed Kurt?" Jack asks.

"No, I didn't know. I assumed any associations Clay had were made after his arrival in Justice. That's why I figured he may have actually left. I thought I was the only tie he had here, and I haven't heard from him. As for Mrs. Rose's story, I assumed she was confused. A.J. said you can't put much stock in her stories. I figured she probably just interrupted some type of shady deal that the two men were in the middle of."

* * *

"Well, that was enlightening," I say, after we get back into the truck.

"Yeah, well, nothing like inciting a sibling rivalry, to get someone to spill the family secrets," Jack says as he starts the truck and pulls out.

"Now we know where Clay got his money from. And why he most likely made an attempt on Gertie's life. When

Cammie told him about hearing Gertie's story, he would have realized she was a witness. Do you believe Cammie?" I ask.

"She seemed believable. It concerns me that she makes so many assumptions despite knowing that her brother is dangerous. True, we do know where he got money, but we still don't know what his motive was for murdering Kurt, where he is, or if someone is helping him. Or why he has stayed in Justice," he says.

"How did she not think that Clay could have murdered Kurt? She knows too well what he is capable of. I'm sure she did not want to confess that she knew her brother probably murdered someone, and she knew of his whereabouts," I say.

"Of course not. Then A.J. would have found out about Clay. I really do not understand that. Why marry someone if you are going to hide your family from them? I can understand wanting to be estranged from a sibling like Clay, but you would think she would have at least mentioned to A.J. that she has a brother and he's a sack of crap," he says.

"I agree. It would appear as if she would be happy if Clay went back to prison, so why go through all the pains to hide him from A.J.? Why not report that you think he committed a crime? Maybe A.J. is a less understanding man than I would have thought," I say.

"Maybe he is, but I don't see him as the type of person who would hold it against her for having Clay as a brother. If I were to guess, she just doesn't want to take a chance on losing A.J. and her pot of gold. He probably doesn't know the circumstances of her last husband's death and that is what she is truly concerned about him learning. She could possibly just be scared of Clay. If she reported him and nothing came of it, then she would have reason to think he would seek payback. Especially since he would be willing to kill her just to get the life insurance policy," he says.

"It is looking more and more like Clay is a psychopath," I say.

"Yep. Clay only knows one other person that we know of. Maybe it's time we take a more in-depth look at Lexie. Let's go over everything we know about her," he says.

* * *

The trees and passing scenery blur by as Jack drives the truck towards town. We replay everything that Lexie said through our minds and brainstorm off of one another. Jack's cellphone rings. It is the only female deputy on the force, Brittany, calling. He puts her on speaker. She says, "Hey Sheriff. I've got a situation that I need your help with. I'll explain when you get here, but it could be pertinent to the murder investigation." She gives him the address and assures him she is in no danger. He does a U-turn and we head in the direction opposite of town.

When we get out of the truck at the address, a lady is yelling at Brittany. "I told you to come back with a warrant!"

"And I told you that doesn't even make sense! You called us! It's your vehicle that was stolen," Brittany says.

Brittany is one of those "walk softly and carry a big stick" people. People who mistakenly assume that they can disrespect her often learn that they have grabbed a bull by the horns. She is in her twenties, has short auburn hair, is extremely busty and curvy, and an absolute bombshell. Some men make lewd comments or sexual innuendos toward her because of her attractiveness. This leads to those men getting the bull by the horns.

Seeing the sheriff, the lady says to him, "She's got no business nosing around my property." Her name is Rebecca, and she is a law-abiding citizen that considers this an act of overreach on the part of a government office.

"She said someone ditched a motorcycle at the back of her property and stole a car that she had for sale that was sitting up here by the highway," Brittany says.

"How about you walk me back to the motorcycle?" Jack asks. "That's what we're interested in. It could belong to a murderer. I sure would hate to think he was in your backyard and we didn't even know about it."

Rebecca's face goes ashen. "A murderer? Well, why didn't you say so?" she asks, looking at Brittany. "Is it Kurt's murderer? I hope you find the bastard and fry him for what he done!" She becomes extremely willing to help in any way that she can. "You can call me Becky," she says.

She leads us past an overgrown field with abandoned vehicles and a barn that is ready to collapse to the ground. At the edge of the field next to a mud pitted, one lane road lies the abandoned motorcycle. Jack looks at me and I nod my head. It looks like we have found Teeny's hog.

Becky says that she has not seen or heard anything. She discovered that the car, a red 1992 Honda Civic hatchback, was missing when she left her house earlier to go to the Post Office.

Jack gets someone to come out to take the motorcycle in, where it will be checked for fingerprints. It is a probability that Clay was the rider. He issues a BOLO for the car. I wait in the truck while he is wrapping things up, thinking again about my conversation with Lexie while rubbing the ointment from the Bee's Knees on my face.

Immediately, I feel a cooling sensation. I hope that is a good sign. I pull the sun visor down and look in the mirror. I can practically see the rash clearing up before my very eyes!

When Jack climbs in behind the steering wheel, I mention that Lexie manages her parents' rental properties.

"Why did I not remember that?" he asks.

"I didn't either. It seemed insignificant at the time," I say.

"Let's go check out some rental properties," he sighs. "Your face looks pretty normal now," he says.

"Gee, thanks. I'm starting to understand why you may have gotten divorced," I say, and he chuckles.

CHAPTER TWENTY-EIGHT

Jack calls Daphne and asks her to text him the addresses of all the properties listed to Lexie's parents. He worries that if we go straight to the source, and Lexie is helping Clay, she will be tipped off.

We drive the same route that I took yesterday and check out the properties as we come to them. When we come to the trailer that Lexie is occupying, her Jeep is parked out front, and Officer Keith is parked behind her, keeping an eye on things. He has nothing unusual to report. "I followed her for a visit with her kids this morning and then back here. She has had no visitors. I haven't seen a sign of anyone or the stolen Honda. She came out a bit ago and brought me a glass of sweet tea. Everything seems to be fine," he says.

"Thanks, Eli. Keep up the good work," Jack says.

We make our way toward the next rental. Jack laughs as we drive by the pasture, knowing that it was the scene of my cow manure incident. The dog from yesterday darts out chasing the truck. "Demon dog," I mutter under my breath, and he chuckles again. He seems to take great humor in my misfortunes. I suppose it could be payback for the times that I have found it hilarious to exasperate him.

He turns down the next road to the left. It is a one lane drive that winds through the trees. He stops at the end of a bend before coming upon the trailer, pulling out a pair of binoculars to get a look ahead. He passes the binoculars to me and says, "Do you see what I see?"

I spy a small one-bedroom mobile home that is not much bigger than a camper, with a porch that is half constructed on the front. It appears that some remodeling is taking place while the trailer sits un-rented. There are stacks of lumber and various building materials on the porch and in the yard. A very nice metal shed that looks bigger than the mobile home sits off to the left of the yard. A car with a tarp covering it is backed in beside the trailer. Enough of the vehicle can be seen to discern that it is a small red hatchback.

"Yep," I reply, as he grabs his radio and calls it in.

"I'm going to go have a look," he says.

"Shouldn't you wait for backup?" I place my hand on his arm to stall him.

"No time. I don't want Clay slipping away. You slide over to the driver's seat and stay in the truck. If he comes this way, run him over, or shoot him if you have to."

"I really think you should wait for reinforcements," I say. I have a sinking feeling that this may not go well.

"Look, Elle. I know what I'm doing. Just stay in the truck," he says before getting out. I scoot over behind the steering wheel and watch through the binoculars as Jack makes his way through the woods, then maneuvers to the back of the trailer. His military background proves useful in sneaking up on a target.

After a moment, I catch a glimpse of movement through the window of the shed. I grab my phone to text Jack. *Ugh. Of course, no service here! What should I do? There is no way for me to alert Jack. If I just sit in the truck, then Clay may get away, or worse, sneak up on Jack who thinks he is sneaking up on Clay.* I pull my gun and step down quietly out of the truck. I go through the trees and sneak up on the backside of the shed. There is a snow shovel propped against the building. I stick my gun in my waistband and carefully pick up the shovel. If he comes around the side, I will hit him with it. That will be much better than having to shoot him. If that doesn't work, then I will shoot him.

I hear a faint noise coming from the shed. I peek around the side and see Clay attempting to climb out the small window. He will most likely rush toward the cover of the woods and I can play whack a mole with the shovel when he rounds the corner. If he goes any other direction, I can chase him with my gun and yell for Jack.

He drops onto the ground with a soft plop. I can hear his footsteps lightly coming in my direction. I step toward the side of the building and smack him with the snow shovel just as he is rounding the corner. I guess I had forgotten how much taller than me he is, because I ended up hitting him on the chest instead of in the face. The shovel makes a vibrating noise and bounces out of my hands to the ground. Clay is stunned for a second but appears to be uninjured, which is a real shame. His nose is bandaged, no doubt broken. A hit to it would have really brought him down. He grabs me and slams me into the side of the building, then shoves me down onto a pile of pallets that are stacked up haphazardly. He takes off, racing into the trees. I disentangle myself ungracefully from the messy heap and chase after him, yelling for Jack as I go.

Out of nowhere, the Devil Dog Pitbull emerges, barking and growling at Clay. *Good boy. Maybe you aren't so bad, after all.* Clay halts for a split second, then makes a turnabout, veering toward the road. *Oh shit! The truck is parked in the direction he is headed!*

Clay is scrambling toward the truck, the dog is thundering toward Clay; I am galloping at breakneck speed chasing Clay, and I can hear the thud of Jack's footfalls bringing up the rear. There is no way to get a shot off at him. He is moving too fast. Fear of being caught, shot, or attacked by the dog must really have his adrenaline pumping. I can tell that he debates on whether to keep going or jump in the truck. He chooses the truck. He floors it going backwards, slinging dust and gravels, right as Jack and I close in. Jack shoots several times, hitting something under the hood. The dog scurries off at the sound of the gunfire. The vehicle starts smoking, but Clay is still able to spin the truck around and drive away. We chase after him on foot, unsuccessfully.

Jack and I are both panting. I am bent over at the waist and he has his hands on his head as he turns around in circles, stopping only to grab his radio and call it in.

"He probably won't make it too far. I'm sure you probably shot the radiator," I say.

He looks at me, and he is livid. "I told you to stay in the truck!" Hands on his hips now.

"He was going to get away! I didn't have any service to text you and I didn't know what to do!" I say.

"Newsflash, Elle! He did get away! Because you didn't stay in the truck!" He is looking at the cloud of dust from Clay's departure, that still hasn't settled. "Could you not have at least taken the keys out of the ignition?" He looks at me bug eyed.

"I wasn't thinking. I was in a hurry. He was going to escape through the woods. He just lucked out with the truck," I say. Weak excuse, I know, but it's the truth.

"He would not have gotten away through the woods. I would have caught him," he says.

"You did not even see him! So, how would you have caught him?"

"You never listen. Never! One simple instruction and you're too stubborn to follow it! You make choices that can get yourself or someone else seriously hurt, or even worse, killed. You would never really make it in law enforcement." He keeps pointing his index finger at me, as if he is scolding an errant child.

"You mean like your choice to go in without backup? Is that the type of *safe* decision one makes in law enforcement?"

"I am highly trained. You are not. You know what? You're fired," he says in a threatening voice. He places his hands on his hips again.

"Oh wow. So, I don't get to play Deputy anymore? You're breaking my heart," I say, my voice dripping sarcasm.

"That's right. You're fired. Off this case. If I catch you investigating on your own, I will haul you in for obstruction," he says.

"Fine by me! I'm sick of Clay and I'm tired of you too! My life was going well until I got myself involved in this mess!" I cross my arms over my chest and turn my back to him.

He turns around and storms off in the trailer's direction, leaving me standing in the road. I am glad that he doesn't see the tears that I am fighting. I do not know if they are a result of hurt, anger, embarrassment, stress, or a combination of all four.

I am still standing there a few moments later when the responding units pull in. Except for Officer Keith, who stayed at Lexie's, in case Clay decided to make a pit stop there.

Brittany gives me a ride back to the office and I am thankful that I do not have to rely on Jack to do so.

* * *

Art takes one look at me when I walk in and says, "Ah, Sunshine, I'm so glad you're safe!" He has already heard about what happened.

I can no longer stop the tears from escaping my eyes and trickling down my face. Normally, I would be upset with myself for being unable to control my emotions. But I know Art is a safe space for me, and I let the tears fall where they may. He walks over and embraces me as I sob all over his chest and blabber on about what happened.

"Why don't you go get an overnight bag together and I'll drop you off at your Mama's for the night? You don't need to stay here alone. Clay may decide he has it in for you and come looking to take it out on you. I'll stop and pick up a pizza on the way. Maybe that'll make you feel better?" he says.

"Okay. And an extra-large iced coffee?" I ask through sobs and hiccups. I am starting to feel like a blubbering idiot.

"Yep, and an extra-large iced coffee. I may even try one myself. Would that make you feel better?"

"Uh huh, you're going to love it!" I say, smiling, as I head out the door to go put together an overnight bag.

CHAPTER TWENTY-NINE

SATURDAY

I awake in my old bedroom at my mother's house. I lie in bed giving myself a pep talk about how I am determined to make today a good day. Positives are what I focus on. *The horrible rash on my face has cleared up and the goose egg bump has gone down. By bedtime last night, my skin looked radiant. I have not had any strange phone calls. No more slashed tires. I don't have to worry about getting myself into situations where Clay may murder me. I don't have to put up with Jack's Dr. Jekyll and Mr. Hyde personalities anymore. Today is a new day! Make the most of it!*

The thought crosses my mind that Colt will not be home this weekend. That adds a tinge of disappointment to my newfound positive mindset. But I am still determined to have a good day.

Mama knocks on the door, opens it, and comes in before waiting for a response. "Wakey, wakey, eggs and bakey," she says. "Oh good. You're already awake. Come on then. Get up and get to moving. I only had three clients scheduled for today, and they all said it was fine by them if I rescheduled, so after we hit the Farmer's Market, you and I are going to a kickboxing class."

"You shouldn't have rescheduled your clients. I need to get back to work today myself."

"Oh, it's fine. One of them actually rescheduled themselves, and the other two were Daphne and her mother. You know Daphne didn't mind one bit. And you don't need to work today! You could use a nice relaxing day after the week you've had!" she says.

"So, kickboxing is relaxing?" I am very skeptical about this.

"Well, I don't know about that part being relaxing, but it is very satisfying. Just imagine thinking that you're hitting that murderer's face every time you jab or kick. Plus, the instructor is *very* easy on the eyes," she says.

"Alright, I suppose. It does sound like it has potential. Do you think you can take me to pick up my vehicle first?"

"I don't see why not. I'll take you to get it, and then you can park at your apartment and ride with me. Yay! We are going to have so much fun!" She claps her hands together. "I'll whip us up some breakfast real fast," she says.

"No need. If we are going to the Farmer's Market, I plan on having a funnel cake for breakfast."

"Elle, you can't eat junk food for breakfast."

"Tell me what the difference is in eating a funnel cake for breakfast versus a stack of pancakes?" I blink up at her, waiting for her answer.

"Hmm. You know you're right. I may just have myself a funnel cake for breakfast too," she says.

"That a girl, Mama. You should take a walk on the wild side and have a little fun sometimes."

"Last time someone told me to let loose and have fun, I ended up pregnant with you."

"Eww. No. Just no, please," I say, while grimacing and burying my head in a pillow. She giggles as she walks out of the bedroom.

* * *

By the time Mama makes it back to her car, I have powdered sugar all over me from the funnel cake. Always Miss Organization, she grabs some wet wipes from a basket in her back floorboard. "Here, clean yourself up. You look like you have been snorting cocaine. What all did you buy today?" she asks.

"The usual. The funnel cake, an extra-large bag of kettle corn, and some vegetables to offset the funnel cake and kettle corn," I say.

"I don't think it works that way, but I'm still glad you're eating vegetables," she says. Unbeknownst to her, the vegetables usually die a slow, painful death in my fridge until I toss them out.

"What did you buy?" I ask.

"I stocked up on fruits and veggies, some honey, a summer sausage, and some of those facial masks from The Bee's Knees. I also got some of the ointment like she gave you yesterday. That stuff must truly be a miracle!" I nod my head "yes," in agreement about the ointment being a miracle. I may have to start stockpiling it like Clay does the sandalwood hair pomade.

She pulls out from the market and drives painfully slowly, at least five miles per hour below the speed limit. I have never understood how people can be slow drivers. Even if I have nowhere in particular to be and no set time to be there, I still like to drive fast. I realize this is a problem for me. The patience required to drive the speed limit is not a virtue that I possess. I suppose I will have to adjust and try to master that patience. There is no way that I want the Sheriff to have the pleasure of pulling me over anymore, for my "lead foot," as he likes to refer to my driving style.

Even with her cautious driving, we arrive twenty minutes early for the kickboxing class.

"We have time to grab a coffee if you want," I say.

"No ma'am. Do you want to take a chance on throwing it up during class? You're already living on the edge by eating that funnel cake."

"Exactly how hard is this class? And you said you were having a funnel cake, too."

"I changed my mind," she says, without responding to my question about the class, which makes me a little concerned.

We enter the newly opened fitness studio named "Scotto's Fighting Stance." We are not the only people to have arrived early. Several females are congregated around the instructor. When I catch a glimpse of him, it is easy to understand why. He is incredibly gorgeous, with a shaved head, tasteful tattoos, and bulging muscles everywhere. When he sees Mama and I, he excuses himself and jogs over to us.

"Elle? What a pleasure to see you here. Annie, you didn't tell me Elle is your sister," he says.

"Oh stop it, Scotto," Mama says, blushing. I think she may even be breaking out in a sweat. "You know good and well that she's my daughter."

"Honestly, you should stop telling people that. Y'all could pass for sisters," he says. She has definitely broken out in a sweat now. She even starts fanning herself.

"You don't remember me, do you, Elle?" he asks.

"I apologize. I know I should, but I am terrible with names," I say, studying his vaguely familiar face.

"Scott Jamison. We graduated together," he says.

"Scott? Wow! I am so sorry that I did not recognize you! I haven't seen you since high school. How has life been treating you?" I ask.

"Spectacular! I've just launched my own brand of meal kits and my online classes are becoming more popular by the day," he says, rubbing his hands together.

"Wow. That's awesome!"

"It's really great seeing you. You know, I had the biggest crush on you when we were in school," he says.

"I had no idea," I say. Now, it's my turn to blush.

Scott Jamison was a very skinny, awkward boy growing up. He was bullied terribly in school. Many of the mouth-breathers gave him the nickname Snotty Scottie. Turns out, Snotty Scottie turned into Scottie Too Hottie. He goes by the name Scotto now. He thought that name sounded cooler for his brand.

Cammie Parker enters and Scotto excuses himself to go speak with her. Mama fans herself again as she watches him walking away.

"Hmm. You didn't tell me that Cammie takes the same class as you," I say.

"She doesn't very often. He usually gives her private lessons," Mama says, putting air quotes around the words private lessons.

"That is interesting," I say. Now I understand her appearance yesterday when she was going to meet with her private trainer. Maybe Scotto is the reason Cammie didn't want to spend time on the houseboat with A.J.

Scotto claps his hands a moment later, saying, "Y'all ready to get started? Let me hear a 'Hell Yeah,' if you are!" He paces back and forth like a tiger.

All the ladies yell, "Hell Yeah!" It sounds more like we are at a concert than a kickboxing class. It is easy to see why he is becoming popular. He exudes an amazing energy.

"Okay! We're going to do things a little bit differently today. What do you say we incorporate some self-defense into our routine? Someone can have you choked unconscious in six seconds. I'm going to teach you how to prevent that from happening! Sound good, ladies?"

"Hell yeah!" we all respond.

After almost an hour of kicking, jabbing, punching, and learning techniques to get out of choke holds, I am covered in sweat and my legs feel like Jell-O. I considered myself to be in pretty good shape from running and the occasional light weight work-out. Apparently, I was mistaken. I decide right now to sign up to attend the classes consistently. This will really help with my new positive outlook. After just one session, I already feel like a badass. A few more classes and I will be able to break more than noses.

Speaking of noses that I would like to break, Jack walks through the door, scanning the class, looking for someone. Hopefully, it is not me — unless he has come to apologize. He spots Cammie and motions for her to join him. He speaks to her, and she immediately goes to gather her belongings, rushing out the door. Then he spots me. Great. Now he will probably think that I was here *investigating* because Cammie was here. He just nods his head as a way of greeting. I pretend I do not see him. He turns and leaves.

"Now, *that* was interesting," Mama says. I am not sure if she is referring to Jack speaking with Cammie or the interaction between him and I.

What did just happen with Cammie? Not my circus, not my monkeys, I remind myself. However, I still cannot help but ponder various scenarios in my mind. I am much too stubborn to ever concede to anyone that it is driving me crazy, not being involved in the case anymore.

CHAPTER THIRTY

Mama parks in front of Art's office. It looks as if he is in this morning, so she decides to go in, too. We enter, I in my new "Kick 'Em Where It Hurts" tee shirt from Scotto's, carrying my bag of kettle corn, and she, carrying an armful of produce from the Farmer's Market.

"Good morning. Both of my favorite gals," he says. I know it is my mother that he is really happy to see. He sees me almost every day.

"Hi, Artie. I thought you might like some goodies from the Farmer's Market, and you need to eat healthier. I worry about you, you know?" Mama says.

"No need to worry about me, Annie. I'm healthy as a horse. I will enjoy the produce, though. That's awful sweet of you," he says. I cannot help but to smile because he and I both know that those vegetables are going to turn to stew in his refrigerator, just as mine will.

"Alright then. Enjoy. I will see the both of you later," she says.

"Bye, Doll," Art says.

"I will talk to you soon, Mama. Thanks for this morning. I had a lot of fun," I say. She blows me a kiss as she walks out the door.

Art eyes my tee shirt with a raised brow. "What? I'm learning how to be a badass," I say.

"Elle, you're already badass. Everyone except you knows it. And you missed all the excitement while you were at that class with Annie," he says.

"Excitement?"

"Yep. Someone knocked A.J. Parker over the head and threw him off his houseboat earlier. Only thing that saved him is he can hold his breath for an exceptionally long time," he says, leaning back in his chair, hands locked behind his head.

"Wow. That's terrible."

"Mmm hmm. I don't think I told you cause you was so busy helping Jack trying to catch that Clay fella, but A.J. hired me earlier in the week to tail Cammie. He thinks she's stepping out. She hasn't left the house since he hired me until today, when she went to that class you were at. I know it wasn't her that done it to A.J. since she was there, but I wonder if she don't have a lover and he done it," Art says.

"I don't think her lover done it. According to Mama, the kickboxing instructor gives her *private lessons*, if you know what I mean. So, unless she has more than one lover…. My money is on her creepy murdering brother," I say.

"Wait a minute," he says, sitting forward, putting his hands on his desk. "You mean to tell me that Cammie is Clay's sister?"

"I thought you knew," I say, with a confused look.

"Nope. I heard you talking about the Baker girl but never heard you mention Cammie."

"I'm sorry. I guess I dropped the ball on that one."

"Wasn't relevant to it anyhow," he says. The chair makes a creaking sound as he leans back again. "Unless she's been sneaking out to meet her brother and A.J. thinks she's been meeting a lover instead. I saw the personal trainer at her place yesterday. A.J. told me she has a trainer and isn't concerned that he could be her lover. Guess he's wrong about that!"

"She went to Clay's house Tuesday night. Other than that, I could not say. She says that they are estranged, and she wants nothing to do with him. He is a psychopath that follows her around, creating havoc in her life, and she thinks he murdered her first husband. It makes sense that he may try to murder her second one. I feel pretty certain that if he had succeeded, he would not have profited, though. He took out a substantial life insurance policy on Cammie and she knows about it. She isn't happy," I say.

"Well, I'll be darned. That sounds like something straight out of a made for television movie," he says. "She's at the hospital with A.J. now. I went by there to check on him and he said she's going to stay there with him tonight. He's fine, but they want to keep him for observation. You going to stay at your Mama's again tonight?"

"No, I think I will be fine at my apartment, with the security cameras and all," I say.

"I really wish you'd reconsider. I'm going to be tied up staking out Cammie in case she decides to sneak out of the hospital. I'd hate to have to call the Sheriff to keep an eye on you," he says.

"You wouldn't!"

"Yes, ma'am, I would. You said so yourself. Clay is a psychopath."

"Fine. I will go to Mama's. Just for tonight. And just because you threatened to call the Sheriff. I do not need a babysitter. You said so *yourself*, I'm a badass. Besides, Clay could find me at Mama's too."

"I realize that, but with the two of you together, he wouldn't stand a chance! Plus, I'm going to send Teeny by to stakeout the street there," he says. I look at him askance. "What? He's growing on me. I told him he could drive the Camry until he got his motorcycle back. He seems to be more than happy to be your bodyguard *and* to keep an eye out for Clay. I guess you're feeling better today?" he adds.

I hoped he would not mention the ugly crying melt down I had yesterday. Now, having my emotions under control, I am embarrassed by it. "Yep. I guess it was a combination of stress and hormones," I say. He falls silent. Just as I suspected, at the mention of hormones, I can now practically hear crickets chirping.

I open my e-mail and start the process of elimination. Junk e-mails, trashed. E-bills, paid. Now onto job prospects. The first is a request for an article about a politician. It is the same politician who is the subject of an investigation that Art has been handling for a law firm. I respectfully decline the job. It could compromise Art's investigation. Next, I have a couple of requests for articles that will be a breeze, which I accept.

Art offers to go and get us iced coffees. I knew he would be hooked if he tried one. I take the opportunity to call Colt while he is gone.

He picks up on the third ring. "Hey Colton, how's it going?" I ask. I can hear heavy machinery in the background and I know he is at a job site. I can picture him in a white tee shirt with or without a flannel over it, a hard hat, and a clipboard in his hand. It's a very attractive picture.

"You know, another day, another dollar," he says. The background noise quietens as he takes a seat in his truck, closing the door. "Sad that I won't be seeing you this weekend. How's everything going with you?" I launch into telling him about yesterday's events.

"You should probably go a little easy on the sheriff, Elle. I'm sure he saw some terrible shit when he was overseas. Sounds like he really is worried about your safety."

"Maybe," I say, somewhat disgruntled at being called out for my bad behavior. I can actually see things from Jack's perspective. What makes me angry is that he is never willing to see things from anyone else's perspective.

"I'm kind of glad he threw you off the case. I don't like the thought of you being wrapped up in something dangerous. Plus, the fella lost his truck. That's like a personal injury. We give our trucks names and everything," he says.

"Oh yeah? Does your truck have a name?"

"Yep. Diesel Dolly. She only drinks the high dollar stuff, is beautiful, blonde, has an attractive rear bumper, and big headlights."

"Hmm. Maybe I should think of a name for my Bronco," I say.

"I'll be working on helping you come up with something," he chuckles.

We chat for a few more minutes before hanging up, and Art walks back in with the coffees.

"What have you got going on today? You working on an article?" he asks.

"I have an article to do, but it isn't due until the end of the month. What do you need?" I ask.

"Got a call from Mags a few minutes ago. She's needing us to track down a young lady for her. Thinks she's staying somewhere down next to the county line. The girl's uncle just passed away and his estate's going to her. She can't reach her by phone and thought we'd check it out, rather than her driving all the way down here," he says.

Maggie Turner owns a P.I. firm in Indiana. Art often works out of her office when he is in Louisville. In years past, families often uprooted and moved from Kentucky to Indiana or Ohio for jobs. They would settle into those places while still having ties and family in Kentucky. Chances are that this girl's uncle was a transplant from Kentucky who moved to Indiana for work.

"Sounds simple enough. I'd be glad to help out. I do need to shower first, though. I definitely smell like a badass," I say. I would much rather be tracking down Clayton Butcher, but...

"Alright, then. I appreciate it—You helping Mags out and showering," he pinches his nose, then waves his hands in front of it, pretending to be offended by my odor.

"Funny," I say, rolling my eyes as I head out the door and up to my apartment.

I take my time showering and getting dressed, enjoying being in my own space. My thoughts are all over the map today. I would love to be able to find Clay. I would also like to look at this case with indifference so Jack will not have the satisfaction of knowing how being "fired" had its intended effect on me.

Thankfully, Clay has bungled his last two murder attempts. Gertie and A.J. must have guardian angels that were watching over them this week. I think back to my strange phone calls, vehicle vandalism, and feelings of unease. I remind myself that I am being paranoid and that these occurrences were coincidences. I still cannot help but to hope that my guardian angel is working overtime too.

CHAPTER THIRTY-ONE

I park in front of a small brick building that houses two apartments. Each residence has its own concrete stoop and front entrance. It appears as though the apartments have an upstairs, but neither one could possibly have much square footage. The door to the right belongs to Dana Miller, whom I have come to see. I make my way up the walkway. A man sits in a quad chair on the stoop to the left, whittling. The surrounding ground is scattered with fragrant cedar shavings. "She ain't home," he yells over toward me. "She works two or three jobs and she's at one of them now."

"Thank you. Any idea when she'll be home?" I ask.

"Who's to say. Depends which job she's working today, but she's usually home by a couple of hours from now. She comes in and gets a few hours of sleep before going to her third shift job," he says.

"Mind if I sit in my car and wait for her?"

"Suit yourself, so long as you ain't here to make trouble for her," he says, spitting tobacco juice into a tin can.

"Nope. No trouble. Promise," I say.

"Hmph," he says, not quite convinced.

I return to my vehicle and the man goes inside his apartment, no doubt watching out the window, in case I am here to make "trouble." I probably have time to go home and return later, but I don't want to take a chance on missing her. I do not want to disturb her after she has gone to sleep, so I will wait and try to speak with her as soon as she gets home.

About an hour into my wait, my bladder feels like it is about to explode. I am regretting the iced coffee from earlier. I have three options. Knock on the neighbors' door, I'll pass. Squat behind the SUV and hope nobody sees me, pass again. Drive two minutes to the county line and use the restroom at the Troubadour or the convenience store. I am still a little traumatized after my ordeal at the bar. Besides, if Sally gets me into a conversation, I may be there awhile. Convenience store, it is. Maybe Thomas will not be working today.

I rush into the store and make my way to the restroom. When I emerge, I grab some snacks and make my way to the counter. Just my luck, Thomas is working.

"Hello. How are you today?" he asks cheerfully. I glance over my shoulders to see if he is speaking to someone else. I am the only customer in the store.

"I'm fine," I say, hesitantly. "You?"

"I'm finer than frog hair." He rings up my purchase, hands me my change and says, "Listen, I was hoping I would see you again, so I could apologize for my behavior. I've had a rough month or so and I've been angry at the world. My best friend played a joke on me with a lottery ticket, making me think I had won. I immediately called Lester and quit my job, only to find out it was a joke. I had to beg for my job back and he hasn't let me have a day off since. Then I found out my fiancé was cheating on me with the same best friend. I've been doing some online anger management classes and I think they are really helping." He breathes in deeply and I can hear him counting under his breath.

"I totally get it," I say, thinking back to the horrible week that I've had. "I just signed up for kickboxing classes yesterday. It's very satisfying if you imagine you are punching and kicking the people you are angry with. Is that something you may be interested in?"

"That sounds great! Sign me up! By the way, my friends call me TNT. You know, because my initials are T and T. I think it's also because of my dynamic personality, though."

"Hmm. Clever," I say. *I'm guessing it's because your personality is explosive, rather than dynamic.* I write down the name and address of Scotto's for him. I step away from the counter, hesitate, and turn back to him. On second thought, since we are on friendly terms now, I ask, "You haven't happened to see the man that ran away from the bar the other day come in here, have you?"

"He was in here that same day before you and Sally went all 'Annie Oakley'."

"Do you remember what he bought?"

"Can't remember for certain. I was distracted looking at the small numbers on my paycheck," he says. I reach into my pocket, draw out a twenty, and lay it on the counter. He smiles. "Now that I think of it, I remember him trying to buy a six-pack, but he wouldn't show me any ID. But he did buy a Rand McNally, a do-rag, and a pack of zip ties. Figured he was going on a trip."

"And the zip ties?"

"Did not want to know. Dude's creepy as shit," he shivers.

"Did you tell the deputy when he came over to talk to you?"

"He didn't ask," he shrugs.

"Has he been in the store since that day?"

"Maybe. Can't remember," he says, eyeballing the twenty-dollar bill with his beady, pale brown eyes. I reach into my pocket, pulling out the change he had just given me, including the coins, and lay it on the counter. Smiling, he unfolds the bills. "Nope. Haven't seen him since. Told the deputy I would call if I did." I narrow my eyes at him, and reach to take my money back. He places his hand over the top of the money and taps the handwritten sign on the back of the register that states all sales are final. He sticks the money in his pocket.

I can't decide if it is better to have him as an archnemesis or an extortionist friend. I backstep away from the counter, turning my eyes into slits. "Thanks so much for your help. *Thomas.*" I make it a point not to refer to him as TNT.

"Pleasure," he says, patting his pocket.

I make my way back to Dana's apartment. As I sit in my SUV waiting, I go over everything Thomas just said. I think of the zip ties and the stint that Clay did in prison for kidnapping. What is he up to? Maybe he needed them for a legitimate reason, but I seriously doubt it. He is racking up on attempted murders and the life insurance policy on Cammie may mean that she will be next.

I glance up as an older model silver Nissan Altima pulls in and a young lady gets out of the car with what looks to be a three- or four-year-old little boy. Her thin frame is dressed in maroon scrubs, and her long, dark hair is pulled back at the nape of her neck.

"Dana Miller?" I ask.

She pulls her son to her side and says, "Who's asking?"

"My name is Elle Riley. I have been asked to contact you for a private investigation firm in Indiana. Do you know an Abraham Miller?"

"I think my grandpa had a brother named Abe," she says. The door to the adjacent apartment opens and the little boy's short legs bustle to the lady standing in the doorway. "That's my son Brendan. I'm able to take him with me to my cleaning job in the morning, then he stays with the neighbors while I get some sleep. Sorry about being rude. I came from an abusive relationship and I'm always on guard," she says.

"Everything okay?" the neighbor yells.

"We're fine. Thanks," she yells back.

"It's good you have neighbors to look out for you," I say. "I'm sorry to tell you that your uncle passed away."

"Someone sent you to tell me that? I honestly didn't even know he was still living."

"Yes. You are his only living relative, so you are the sole heir to his estate."

She looks very puzzled. "Is this some kind of scam? Nobody has ever given me anything unless it's a hard time," she says.

"No scam. It's legitimate. Here's the contact information for the lawyer handling his estate and the Private Investigation firm that has been trying to reach you. Good luck to both you and Brendan. If you need any assistance, you can reach me at Art of Investigations." I hand her my card as well. I turn as I am walking away and say, "Dana, I mean it. If you need help with anything at all, please call me."

She is still standing beside her Nissan, looking at the business cards in amazement as I pull away. I hope her uncle left her a fortune, she never has to work three jobs again, and she and her son will always be safe.

* * *

I step through Mama's back door with my overnight bag and a double order of chicken fajitas for our dinner. "Oh, Elle. I didn't realize you would be over again tonight," she says.

"I forgot to text. I brought fajitas for dinner." I set the tin foil containers down on the kitchen table.

"I'm actually getting ready to leave for a date."

"A date? You need me to leave? Who's this date with?"

"Yes, a date. No, you're welcome to stay. You probably don't know him. His name's Melvin and he works at the Federal Prison. This is our first date. We're going to dinner and to see a movie."

"Ick. Melvin. He sounds hideous."

She rolls her eyes and says, "Be on your best behavior and I'll bring you back some popcorn."

Melvin arrives a few moments later. He's very handsome, charming, and seems like he is as straightlaced as my mother. They look like the perfect match. I whisper, "Are you sure you don't want me to leave in case you decide to bring him back home? You know, you may decide you want to play prison guard and bad female inmate who needs punished."

She gives me a harsh look and hisses, "No popcorn for you."

After they leave, I am alone with too much time on my hands to think about the case that I am not supposed to be investigating. *Just let it go, Elle. Curiosity killed the cat.* Instead of letting it go, I pick up my phone and call Daphne. I know she will update me on the details. I have to know if Clay is close to being caught.

"I've started to call you several times today, but I had a bet with Art about how long it would be before you started pumping me for information," she says. "Congratulations. You toughed it out longer than either one of us thought you would."

"I'm glad to know that I am a source of entertainment for you two," I say.

"Lexie feigned innocence about knowing Clay was at one of her parents' rentals. There is no proof otherwise. A.J. did not get a look at his attacker. It is still suspected that it is Clay. He now knows that Clay is Cammie's brother and is being very understanding and supportive to her, in light of her brother being a psychopath and all. No sightings of Clay. Jack has been moping around like he lost his best friend. Everyone has been treading lightly around him because of his foul mood," she says, breaking everything down for me.

"I'm very sorry about Jack's truck. According to Colt, that would be very traumatic for a man," I say.

"It has nothing to do with his truck, Elle. It's you. He's sadder about losing *you* than his *truck*," she says.

I remain unconvinced. Nobody else was there yesterday to witness how angry he was. That ire was not only for Clayton Butcher.

CHAPTER THIRTY-TWO

SUNDAY

I awake so stiff and sore that it is painful just to get out of bed. It is 10:30 A.M. and I cannot believe that I slept so late. Rather, I can't believe my mother allowed me to sleep so late. I amble to the kitchen, trying to walk straight legged. I ask my mother, "Are you out of ibuprofen? There isn't any in your medicine cabinet," as I pour myself a cup of coffee and grab the jug of vanilla creamer from the fridge.

"Check in my purse. What's wrong with you?" she asks, looking up from her Facebook scrolling, eyeballing me over the top of her reading glasses.

"I am convinced that you and Scotto tried to kill me. I am so sore that I can barely move this morning." I groan as I reach down to pick up her purse.

"Don't be dramatic. You just need to do some yoga to stretch those muscles out."

"Mama, I would rather pluck my eyelashes out than attempt to do yoga this morning." I rummage through her purse until I find the medication and down four of the tablets. As I try to sit in a kitchen chair without bending my knees, I groan again. I glance over the top of her phone and see that she is perusing Melvin's page.

"Suit yourself." She is prone to use reverse psychology on me. As usual, it works and I end up finding myself in a painful downward dog position. After the ibuprofen, yoga, and a hot shower, I am feeling much better. We are now ready to go to Gran's for a visit. She has made breakfast foods for lunch. She has biscuits, gravy, fried potatoes, bacon, sausage, and scrambled eggs. It is a dreary, rainy day today. The perfect weather for comfort food.

"See? I told you the yoga would help!" she says, when I am able to bend my knees getting in the car. I scrunch up my face at her. I really hate when she is right.

"How was your date last night?" I ask. I have been waiting on her to tell me about it but she has been tight lipped on the subject, both last night and this morning. "I'm guessing it went good since you were looking at his social media page this morning."

"I had a nice time. I'm still trying to decide if I like him well enough for a second date."

I study her profile. I suppose that's all the information she is willing to dish on the subject. I decide not to pry any further. I do not like it when she is nosy concerning my love life, so I try to respect hers.

I have often wondered what led to her and Art's divorce. It wasn't infidelity and the two of them obviously still love each other. Her only explanation was that they were two very opposite people. They both work long hours and have opposite interests. After I moved away for college, Art started sleeping at his office. Then before long, they were getting divorced. It saddens me that their marriage failed.

I am happy that they remain friends. It perplexes me that they choose to pine for each other from afar. I suppose whatever led to their failed nuptials is what keeps them from renewing their relationship.

As soon as we walk through the door at my Grandma's, she says, "I missed you ladies at Sunday School this morning."

"Sorry, Ma. We overslept," Mama says.

"Yeah, we were up late because Mama had a date. She got home late, and I had to sit up to make sure she made it home safely without turning into a pumpkin," I say.

"A date? Who'd you have a date with? Anyone I know? Is it serious?" Gran asks.

My mother shoots me an "I can't believe you told her" look, then proceeds to vaguely answer the questions. I am not the only person who doesn't like their mama meddling in their business. I suppose my mother gets it from hers. I flash my most innocent looking smile at her as I grab a plate.

I take a seat at the table and my Uncle Mike says, "So Elle, have you had any trucks hijacked today?"

Mama slaps him on the back of the head and says, "I told you not to mention it!"

"What? It's not like everyone doesn't know about it. I heard about it at the diner before you even mentioned it," he says.

"Hilarious. Nope. Not since I got 'fired' from my deputy job and banned from investigating the case," I say, putting air quotes around fired.

"You seriously going to let Jack tell you what to do? He's been telling you to quit driving too fast for years now and it hasn't taken. I know it's gotta be eating you up inside being told you're not allowed to do something."

"Well, he made it pretty clear he would arrest me if he caught me meddling in his case."

"He isn't going to arrest you. The only thing he might do is make a show of throwing you in a cell for a couple of hours." he says.

Now Gran slaps him on the back of the head saying, "Don't encourage her to get caught up in this mess again. She doesn't need to be chasing and getting chased by murderers!"

"What?" he says. "You two should be glad I encourage her to do what she wants. You know, the whole 'I am woman, hear me roar' thing." This gets him slapped on the back of the head by both of them.

I chew on a piece of bacon as I contemplate what Mike just said. Do I want to help put Clayton Butcher behind bars? Definitely, yes. Do I want to give Sheriff Jack Lennox the satisfaction of tossing me in jail, even if it's just for a couple of hours? Definitely, no. Also, Clay makes my skin crawl and I'm not certain I want to encounter him on my own.

We visit with Gran for a couple of hours, and then return to Mama's so I can pick up my Bronco. I plan on stopping in to check on Gertie and then grocery shopping.

"Come on back and stay tonight," Mama says, as I am leaving.

"Thanks, but I can't abandon my apartment forever. The security system is in place and Art has our new friend Teeny babysitting me. I will be fine."

"Okay. But promise me you will be careful. I love you."

"Always. Love you too."

* * *

Gertie isn't sitting on the back porch today. The dreary day has driven her indoors. I knock on the back door, expecting Buddy to bark, but he isn't in sight. I can see Gertie through the glass door and she motions for me to come in. She is sitting in an oversized recliner in the family room. The chair appears to be swallowing her whole. She is wearing a long black skirt with a floral print on it, a pair of sneakers, a black tee shirt that says "In Your Wildest Dreams" in neon colors, and bright pink lipstick. The cast on her arm is covered in various Sharpie colored signatures. Her outdoor gnome collection seems to be expanding indoors to her family room. She has a gnome shooting a middle finger sitting on her coffee table.

"Nice shirt," I say.

"Thanks. I like yours better," she says, referring to my "Knee 'em in the Nads" tee that Scotto gave me.

"How are you doing?" I ask. "Do you have big plans today?"

"I'm doing good. The arm's a lot better. I've got a date today," she says, beaming a smile at me.

"A date? Do tell, Gertie." I rub my hands together in anticipation.

"Well, I guess you could say that I'm robbing the cradle. He's a lot younger than me. He's seventy-two. He lives in a senior living complex and we met when they brought some of the residents to bingo at the senior center. His name's Oscar. He ain't much to look at, but he's got a real good personality. He still gets around good and has hair. He can't hear real well even with hearing aids, though. Jared is going to take me over to visit him today."

"Good for you, Gertie. I'm excited for you."

"Thanks, dear. You know, he has a grandson you should date. He's a paranormal expert. Hunts ghosts," she says.

She looks around the room as if she thinks she has some ghosts in her house.

"No thanks. I'm not brave enough to date someone like that," I say.

"I would offer you a brownie, but I gave them up. I don't know why those things are so addictive. I gained three pounds from eating them! I need to watch my figure now that I have a man," she says, smoothing her bony hand down her shirtfront.

"Gertie, you do know that those are pot brownies, don't you?"

"No, they make them in a baking dish, not a pot."

"No, no, Gertie. Pot, as in mar-i-juan-a," I say, stressing the word.

"Are you kidding me?" She looks at me as if I am playing a joke on her.

"Nope."

"Huh. I went my whole life without trying drugs and turned into a pothead at eighty-three. Who would have thought? Hopefully I don't start knocking over liquor stores when I turn eighty-four," she says, and we both laugh. I do not bother trying to explain to her that apparently she has turned into a cougar, too.

"I should be going. I just wanted to stop and check on you. Where's Buddy? Do I need to keep an eye out for him when I leave?"

"Nah. Joey is keeping him tonight. He's going to take him to the vet for his shots bright and early in the morning."

"Okay. Bye, then. Have fun on your date," I say.

"Bye. I'll try to remember to call you tomorrow to let you know how it goes. Tell you if I get lucky. By lucky, I mean neither one of us breaks a hip!" *I'm glad she clarified the part about getting lucky!* I am also glad that as far as her memory goes, she seems to be having more good days than bad lately.

CHAPTER THIRTY-THREE

I swing in Rodger's Grocery on my way home to pick up groceries for the week. I smile, thinking of Gertie, as I toss a box of brownie mix into my buggy. Someone jostles into me rather roughly. I envision Clay grabbing me. When I turn, I see that it is a lady who pushed her way in behind me, trying to get a box of cake mix off a top shelf. I reach up and get the box for her, despite her rudeness and lack of apologizing or thanking me.

I am really on edge because of Clay. I have been noticing every unfamiliar male face I see, trying to figure out if it could be him. I reason and tell myself that the paranoia that has settled into the back of my mind is not rational. If Clay were out to get me, surely he would have already done so. Both terrible encounters that I have had with him were more his fault than mine. I just happened to be in the wrong place at the wrong time.

The fact that Art and Jack worry Clay may seek me out is what really concerns me. Who knows? Maybe he isn't even in Kentucky anymore. I do not necessarily think it's a good thing if he is not. I really want to see justice done for Kurt's murder. But I worry that if he remains in Justice, there may soon be another body added to his count. He has already attempted to commit two murders, in addition to Kurt's.

I pay for my purchase, assure the bag boy that I can carry the groceries out myself, but he insists on being helpful. We chit-chat as he is loading the bags into the back of my SUV. Then, I slide into the driver's seat and notice something under my windshield wiper. I get out of the car and see it is a matchbook from the Troubadour that someone has scrawled "see you soon" on. Now, I am hyper-alert. I look around. The only person I see is the retreating back of the bag boy. I do not touch the matchbook. I have read too many stories lately about items with fentanyl on them being left placed in public places. I hurriedly get back in my vehicle and lock my doors. I turn on the wipers and the matchbook flies off into the parking lot.

I notice a black sedan with dark tinted windows sitting at the edge of the parking lot with the engine idling. When I pull out onto the road, the car follows. I make an unnecessary turn to see if the driver turns behind me. He or she does. My paranoia is really in full gear now. I reach over onto the passenger seat and get my gun out of my purse. The next turn I make, the car does not follow.

I am still jittery when I pull in at the apartment and park. Someone knocks on my window. I jump, gasp, and instinctively point the gun. It is Lexie, and she scrambles back, alarmed. I put my hand to my chest as if it will slow my heart rate and lower the window apologizing. I get out of the vehicle and I now notice her jeep parked across the street. She must have been waiting for me. I also notice the Camry is parked in front of the office and I can see a light on. Teeny must be on babysitting duty tonight. Art probably knew I would refuse to stay at my mother's again.

"Sorry, Elle. I didn't mean to scare you," she says.

"It's okay. I'm sure I scared you worse. Again, I am sorry. I just seem to be on edge today."

"Trust me, I understand that feeling! I was hoping I could talk to you about something," she says, biting her lip.

"Sure. But if it involves Clay or the investigation, then you should call the Sheriff's Office. I'm no longer on the case," I say.

"The Sheriff probably wouldn't believe anything I have to say to him. He thinks I'm guilty of something. Now, Simon thinks so, too, and won't even let me see my kids," she says, her eyes growing damp.

"I'm sorry to hear that, Lexie. That must be really hard."

"Yeah, it is." She hitches the shoulder strap of her purse higher on her arm and says, "Anyway, there's something really important I need to tell you." We both turn at the sound of a vehicle coming to a stop behind mine. It is the Sheriff. Lexie instantly goes silent and looks scared.

"Ladies. Everything okay?" Jack asks, as he gets out of the squad car he is driving. He leans against the side of it, folding one leg over the other and crossing his arms over his chest.

"We're fine," I say, giving him a shooing motion with my hand. Whatever she has to say, she will not disclose with Jack here. I get the sense that it is something important.

"Yeah, we're fine. I should be on my way, Elle," Lexie says.

"Are you sure? I think the Sheriff just stopped to say hello and is getting ready to leave himself." I give Jack a pointed look.

"I'm sure. I'll talk to you later," she says, and dashes across the street to her Jeep.

"What was that about?" Jack asks.

"Guess we'll never know since you spooked her. And no, I wasn't investigating. She was waiting for me when I pulled in," I say.

"Be careful around Lexie. She knows a whole lot more than she is letting on. Her dad sent in a lawyer when we found Clay squatting at the rental. She claimed she didn't know he was staying there. I have someone sitting at the end of the road, but I can't put anyone on her property now."

"Thanks for the advice," I say, as I swing the back hatch open to get my groceries.

Jack walks over, reaching in to get the bags. "I've got it, thanks," I say, my voice crisp.

"So, I guess you're still mad at me, then?" he asks. "Maybe we should talk about it."

"Doesn't seem like there is anything to discuss." I shrug. "We both said what we wanted to the other day. My only regret is that I didn't stay in the truck and shoot Clay. If presented with the opportunity again, I'll shoot first, and ask questions later," I say.

"I hope you don't have to be faced with the opportunity. Just, please be very careful. We've had a couple of reported sightings of Clay that seem to be legit. He's like a piece of slime that just keeps oozing out of our hands. I have a feeling he's getting ready to make a move on whatever is motivating him to stay here."

"Noted. Thanks. I'll be cautious. Take care of yourself, too," I say, as I start up the steps without looking back.

CHAPTER THIRTY-FOUR

My phone rings, jarring me awake. I had fallen asleep on my couch watching *The Gilmore Girls*. My television is lit up with a message asking if "I'm still there?" It's almost 1 A.M. The caller ID says "unknown." *This had better not be my nuisance caller or they are going to get a mouth full.* I answer the phone groggily. "Hello."

"Elle. Thank Goodness you answered. It's Lexie." The connection is very staticky and I have difficulty hearing what she is saying, but she sounds panicked.

"Lexie? What's wrong? Did you call the Sheriff's Office?"

"If I call the Sheriff's office, I'm a dead woman! I have something to tell you...." She says, and the line goes dead.

"Lexie? Lexie, are you there?"

What should I do? Should I call Jack? She sounded very serious and also very adamant about not calling the Sheriff. If Clay were there, I do not think she would have been able to call me. I do not even know where she was calling from. I would guess the trailer since cell service is so spotty in that area. That would explain the dropped call. She must want to tell me what she came to say earlier before Jack showed up. She said she had something important to share and apparently I am the person she wants to tell.

My gut feeling is telling me that something is wrong. My gut feeling has been misguiding me lately, though, playing tricks on my mind and causing me to be paranoid. I know that if I call Jack, Lexie will not divulge whatever information that she is willing to share with me, and she will no longer trust me. There should be an officer parked on the road to Lexie's. I will just make sure to be seen on my way in. I am sure the officer will call Jack, and by the time he gets there, hopefully, I will have the information from Lexie. Besides, Teeny will probably follow me.

I try to call Art and tell him what I am about to do, rather than letting Teeny call him. It goes straight to voicemail. He must be working. I leave him a message so that someone will know where to start looking for me if something goes wrong.

What are you doing, Elle? This is exactly why Art and Jack think you need a babysitter.

I hesitate, second-guessing my decision, then hurriedly get dressed and check my gun before tucking it into my waistband. The gun is fully loaded and my cell phone is fully charged. I watch the security monitor for a moment, noting the Camry is missing. Things must be secure if Teeny has abandoned his post. I reset the alarm on my way out and rush down the steps to my Bronco before I can change my mind.

I place my wallet and keys in the cupholder. I poise my finger over the push start button. My passenger door is wrenched open and Clay is there with a gun pointed at me. I reach down to get my firearm and he says, "Na-da-da-da," while wagging his finger back and forth at me. He grabs my defense weapon and tucks it into his waistband. "Give me your cell phone." I get my phone out of my back pocket and he says, "Slowly," as I hand it to him. He slinks into the passenger seat and tosses my phone to the ground before shutting the door. "Drive north," he says.

The light from a streetlamp fills the interior and I can see him clearly. The dark roots of his hair are growing out and sharply contrast with the odd yellow color that his hair has been bleached. His right wrist is unbandaged and looks like it could possibly be infected. His nose is also unbandaged, laying awkwardly to the side, and looks like something I drew with my left hand. He has two black eyes.

"You realize you were just caught on camera and people will look for you?" I ask.

"Nobody has a clue where we're going and I'll be long gone by the time they figure it out," he says. "Now shut up and drive like I told you to."

"Why are you doing this?"

"You're a loose end I need to tie up. The Sheriff is too busy with his war on drugs to come looking for me when I'm gone. But you? You're a different story. From what I hear, you're like a dog with a bone. I ain't planning on spending my time looking over my shoulder for your pretty little face," he says.

"I won't, I promise. You can walk away right now and I won't even say that I've seen you."

"Ha! You and me both know that's a lie. I'm real disappointed, Elle. I thought we had a real connection the first time I met you. Imagine my surprise when I found out all about you."

"Really? I thought we had a connection, too!" I lie.

"Do I look stupid?" he asks.

I suppose I hesitated a split second too long before replying, "No! Of course not," because he becomes furious.

"You think you're so smart! We'll see how smart you feel soon!" he yells. Then adds in a normal tone, "Besides, everyone knows you're knocking boots with the Sheriff."

"I am not and have never knocked boots with the Sheriff! I'm not even allowed to be investigating you anymore. So, see? You can let me go and I'll be quiet."

He laughs his wicked laugh and says, "It's a shame I already have plans for Lexie, or I might just take you along with me." He reaches over with his gun and traces it down my breast. I shiver and feel bile rising up my throat.

The bargaining phase is not working and now I feel terrified thinking of worse things he can do to me other than shooting me. I know I am likely not getting out of this alive. I also know that if I allow him to take me to a second location, I could possibly endure things that will make me wish I am dead. My thoughts race, trying to come up with a plan.

I take my foot off of the gas pedal, and he asks, "What are you doing?"

"Slowing down for the red light. You don't want me to get pulled over, do you?" It is after one o'clock AM and there is practically no traffic on the road.

"Hmm," he says suspiciously.

When the light turns green, I push the gas pedal to the floor, then slam on the brakes, causing his head to snap back and forth. He is not wearing a seat belt. I hoped his face would hit the dash, but he stopped short of that happening. "Sorry. My foot slipped."

"You bitch! Do that again and see what happens!" Once again, I stomp on the gas pedal and the brake, this time much harder. His face still stops short of the dash. He slams my head against the steering wheel, breaking open the stitches on my forehead. "You want me to shoot you right now? Cause I will!"

"No, you won't," I say. I cannot believe those words just spilled out of my mouth or that they shot forth with a calm that I certainly do not feel. I think I may be having an out-of-body experience.

"What do you mean, 'No, I won't?' Are you crazy?"

I put the SUV in park and say, "I mean, *no, you won't!* If you were going to shoot me now, you would have already. You don't want to shoot me here. You want to take me somewhere else and torture me! I would rather die right here than be subjected to whatever you have planned. So go ahead! If you're planning on shooting me, get it over with!" I close my eyes and wait for the bullet to come. When it doesn't, I squint one eye open and look at him. He is sitting there with a menacing look on his face.

"How about this? After I shoot you right here, I'll go kill your ma-ma, your grand-ma-ma, the old lady *and* her mangy mutt. I may even throw the sheriff in since I don't like him, anyway. How's that sound? That sound better than you just driving like I told you to?"

I swallow hard, a knot forming in my throat. I put the vehicle in drive and slowly pull out. I try to keep him talking. "Why did you kill Kurt?" I ask.

"No more talking!" he yells.

"Are you seriously going to kill me without telling me?" It is a moment before he replies.

"I didn't like having to kill Kurt. I really liked him. He was becoming a problem, though, and had to be dealt with. And that's all I'm going to say about that. Now, shut up. No more talking."

I fall silent. I know he has no qualms about killing. He sounded sincere about liking Kurt. If he is willing to kill someone that he is fond of, then he will certainly be willing to make good on his threats toward the people that I love.

I spend the rest of the drive thinking about those people and the things that I will miss. No more spending Saturday mornings with Mama, weekends with Colt, seeing Art daily, or Sundays at Gran's. No more visits with Gertie and Buddy. I will even miss my bantering with Jack. Actually, I will just miss Jack, period. I hope I can come up with a way to escape this situation before becoming an obituary at the age of thirty-two. Even if Art figures out that Clay has taken me, it's like Clay said—nobody knows where to look for me. I can't believe that I was careless enough to find myself ensnared in this situation. My only chance is to fight like hell when we get out of this vehicle.

CHAPTER THIRTY-FIVE

C lay tells me to turn off onto a road that leads to the new rehab center that construction started on recently. I drive slowly up the rutted graveled lane, realizing that I am probably driving myself to my death. Ironic that I will meet my demise at a place that will be used to help people get their lives back. "Park here," he says, directing me to the area in front of the trailer that serves as a construction office. Different pieces of heavy machinery are parked about and I wonder if the cement truck will be used to pump cement over my body after he kills me. *Don't keep thinking like that, Elle. You have to figure a way out of this!*

"Cut the engine," he says. I turn off the engine and try to slip the key into my pocket. "Nice try. I see you learned your lesson about leaving the key in the car," he laughs. "Give it to me." I grudgingly hand him the key. He produces a zip tie and says, "bind your wrists." He watches like a hawk as I put the zip tie around my wrists and use my teeth to tighten it. He reaches over and pulls on it to make sure I have it tight enough. "You sit there until I come around," he says.

I watch him skirt the front of the vehicle, approaching my side. I have felt nothing this close to hatred for an individual in my life. The headlights are still glowing and the rain has started again. I can recall Gertie's account of the night at the creek, with the rain falling and the headlights shining, and I wonder if this same scene played out before Kurt's eyes.

There is a wooded area beyond the small trailer. If I can make it to the other side of those trees, I know there are houses located there. If I perish tonight, I will much rather meet that fate trying to escape than just cowering and letting Clay go about it easily. I spot the lighter that Lester from the convenience store had given me. I shove it into my pocket, thinking it could come in useful.

Clay tugs my door open and says, "Get out and start walking toward the office." I cannot let him take me inside. If I do, then I know that my chances of making it out of there are zero to none. "And no funny business. Don't think I've forgiven or forgotten about my nose!"

I start walking slowly across the gravel lot. I imagine this is what people feel like when faced with walking the plank. "Pick up the pace. You like getting rained on?" he says, as he kicks me lightly on the rear. I despise him more with each passing second. I wish I could go back in time and shoot him behind the shed during our last encounter. I have never liked the thought of taking another person's life. I have always felt that people should leave this earth on God's terms, not mine. However, if I had felt that day, how I feel now toward Clay, I would not have hesitated to kill him.

I stop walking and ask, "What? Are you afraid you will melt in the rain?"

"Bitch, I said walk!" he says and kicks me in the rear again. This time, when his foot lands on my backside, I fall to the ground on purpose. "I didn't even kick you that hard. Get up," he says, grabbing my hair as he pulls me to a standing position. As soon as he releases me, I take a couple of quick steps, turn, and sling gravels at his face as hard as I can throw them with bound hands.

He is caught off guard and reaches up to shield his face from the assault, but doesn't release the gun. I do a leg sweep and knock him off his feet. He still holds to the gun. Damn it. He lands on the ground, on his side, with his back toward me, making it impossible to kick him in the groin or face, as I had hoped to do. I stomp down on his calf with my full body weight. He screams, curling into a fetal position. I kick him in the kidney area and then connect my shoe with the back of the head for good measure.

I flee toward the cover of the heavy machinery while he lies on the ground groaning. He recovers enough to fire off a shot, missing me. The bullet ricochets off an excavator, making a loud pinging sound. I race behind it before he can shoot again. I weave my way through the construction machinery, intent on making it to the wooded area. Breathless, I round the back of a bulldozer and almost collide with Lexie.

"Lexie. Thank God, you're okay! We have to get out of here now!" She has a fresh bruise on her face, her cheekbone has a knot on it, and her lip is split. I take two steps, intent on the wooded area, but she doesn't follow. "What are you doing? We have to go NOW!" I grab her arm, trying to pull her along.

She digs her heels in, hesitating. I do not understand why until she raises the shotgun she has been holding to her side. "I don't think so, Elle. You need to start walking to the office over there."

"I don't understand, Lexie. Why are you doing this?" I doubt she will actually shoot me, but I am not brave enough to take that chance.

"I don't have a choice. I don't want to shoot you, but I will. I'm real sorry, Elle, but Clay said he'd hurt my kids if I didn't help him and I know he means it."

"Lexie, you're holding a shotgun! Why not just shoot Clay and we'll get out of here! Or give it to me and I'll shoot him!"

She looks like she is weighing her options. "You don't understand. He said he has people that will make good on his threats if something happens to him." Clay seems to take a twisted enjoyment out of playing on people's emotions over their families. This must be his last resort to force people to go along with him.

Clay limps up behind Lexie. The temporary light I see at the end of the tunnel disappears with his pained gait. "Good work Lex." He takes the shotgun from her hands. He yanks me by the hair of the head yet again, shoving me violently toward the trailer. "Walk!" He pokes the shotgun barrel into my back sharply. Tears fall from my eyes as I reconcile myself to my imminent fate.

He pushes me up the metal steps leading to the door, causing me to stumble. I hit one of the steps with my shins, and they feel like they are being split in two. I go down, hitting my chin on the metal hard enough to rattle my teeth. I raise my bound hands to brush at the wet trickle flowing from my chin, the sticky crimson sight confirming that it is blood running down my neck, not rainwater.

Wrenching me up by my arm, he thrusts me roughly into the trailer. He picks up a roll of duct tape, directing Lexie to tape me to a chair. He props the shotgun behind the door after he carefully inspects her handiwork. Next, he tosses a zip tie to her, telling her to bind her own wrists.

"What? You said you'd let me go if I did what you wanted!" she says.

"No. I said I wouldn't hurt your brats if you did what I wanted. And I won't. But you ain't leaving until I do. I told you; you're going with me."

"You're insane! I don't want to go with you!"

"Don't make me change my mind about your kids," he says, and she falls silent. He pushes her into another chair and duct tapes her to it. She doesn't try to fight back. The worry and panic for her children are written clearly on her face.

I can feel the blood from my forehead cascading down my face, and the flow from my chin is dripping, dotting my gray t-shirt. "Damn girl. You ain't looking so pretty now," he says, jerking my face up to look at it. He takes his finger and dips it into my blood and traces a heart on my cheek. I shiver. "Did you get my note earlier? You were a hard one to get my hands on." He leans in close and I can feel his hot breath mingling with the metallic scent of my blood. "I've been watching you all week. Someone always hanging around. I would've had the perfect opportunity several times if that Yeti hadn't shown up and started keeping a check on you. I took his motorcycle just to piss him off." He laughs evilly, standing up, and limps his way over to the window.

"What's your end game, Clay?" I ask. "You have me bound up. Nobody knows you're here, so you're free to leave. I promise I won't look for you. Honestly, I'll be glad to be rid of you. I hope to never see your face again. Surely, you don't want to make Lexie walk out on her kids the way your mom walked off and left you, do you? Do you want her kids to always wonder why their mother left them the same way that you probably always wondered why yours left?"

"Did Cammie tell you that?" He laughs bitterly and says, "My mother didn't walk off and leave me! My father, piece of shit that he was, killed my mother in a drunken rage, buried her in the backyard, and made me and Cammie tell everyone that she ran off and abandoned us. Don't worry, he got what was coming to him. Died a horrible death. I made sure of that!"

"I'm so sorry to hear that. I cannot imagine how terrible that was. Tell me about your mother," I say. *Keep him talking. Make him think you sympathize with him.*

"Oh no. You ain't using your reverse psychology bullshit on me. Besides, I turned out just fine." I am wise enough to remain silent. I try to calculate what move I can make next. He seems to be waiting for something. He keeps looking out the blinds hanging on the small window. If I knew what he is waiting for, perhaps I could use it to my advantage.

"What are we waiting for?" I ask.

"You'll see soon enough."

I look over at Lexie. She is softly sobbing, almost hyperventilating, and shaking uncontrollably. She will be no help to me getting us out of this situation. I survey the small space. The chairs that we are bound to do not have wheels, so any movement made would have to be done by scooting. There doesn't seem to be anything nearby that I could use as a weapon, unless I could give him death by one thousand paper cuts. The shotgun is propped behind the door, with him being between me and it. If I could manage to get myself unbound, and Lexie could call him over, distracting him, I could make a move for the shotgun. I try to work my fingers into my front pocket for the lighter, thinking if Lexie can distract him, maybe I can burn the zip tie in two.

Headlights beam through the blinds. Clay says, "It's showtime." Cammie comes through the door, the headlights from her Jaguar haloing her as if she is the new light at the end of my tunnel. Perhaps she can talk some sense into her psychopath brother.

She slams the door and asks, "What's going on, Clayton? Why are they here?"

Before he can answer, I say, "Please talk to him, Cammie! We won't say anything about this if he lets us go. We promise." Lexie is nodding her head in agreement. Cammie grabs the roll of duct tape and stomps over to my chair.

She slaps the tape across my mouth forcefully and says, "I know what you're thinking. Why is Cammie doing this? Money, of course. You wouldn't know anything about that though, would you? You had yourself a rich husband and were too stupid to even take half his money. So many plans that you and the crazy old lady have ruined for us. Imagine, for instance, this rehab. If A.J. were out of the picture, I could turn this place into a real money maker. It would open up a world of opportunities, serving as a cover for anything I choose to pursue. Drugs? Maybe. I would have the right clientele here. I could probably even get reimbursed from insurance for their rehab treatment. Wouldn't that be irony at its best? Girls? Maybe. Money laundering? Maybe again. But, you just had to believe the old lady and get the sheriff involved." Gone is the sophisticated air of a rich, socialite wife. In its place is the icy demeanor of a manipulative bitch.

I murmur responses unfit for a lady. I just wish she could hear and understand them. If she had not used the tape, she would be getting an ear full of insults. That glimmer of hope that I had died as quickly as it appeared.

"Now, I repeat, why are they here, Clayton?"

"Lex is here because I'm taking her with me. You told me to take care of Elle. The last time you told me to take care of someone, you got mad when I done it, so I figured I'd better get you to give me real clear instructions this time."

"You idiot! That's because you left a witness and the body to be found!"

"How was I to know the old lady would be there snooping? And I didn't want to throw Kurt's body in my truck. That would have left all kinds of blood and DNA!"

"And the old lady and A.J.? They're both still alive and well," Cammie says.

"The old lady's dog about ate me up! How was I to know she has the devil's spawn protecting her? And how was I to know A.J. can hold his breath like it's an Olympic sport?"

"Obviously, you've never heard him talk," Cammie says, sarcastically. "He gets plenty of practice never taking a breath."

"You know what, Cammie? You try shooting someone and see how easy you think it is. Always ordering me to do the dirty work! Why don't you try getting your hands dirty for once!"

"I guess if I want something done right, I will have to do it myself. I told you to take care of her days ago and make it look like an accident, so she wouldn't be around to snoop when A.J. met his end. It would've been a nice little package. Art would be too busy mourning over her to stalk me like A.J. hired him to do."

She pulls a small twenty-five caliber pistol from her purse. *Great. She's going to shoot me and she'll probably have to shoot me multiple times using that gun. I don't want to die but I'd prefer to do one and done if it's going to be death by gunshot.* I close my eyes, waiting for the bullet to come. I hear her shoot, but don't feel any pain. I at least expected to feel something. I hear Clay give a shrill cry and I open my eyes.

He lands on the floor, yelling, "You bitch! You shot me!" He has his hands wrapped around his knee, blood flowing through his fingers and soaking his pant leg.

"Yeah, it's not nearly as terrible to do it as you were letting on," she says. "That's for taking out the life insurance policy on me!"

She's crazier than he is! Dropping the small pistol back in her purse, she reaches down and gets Clay's gun, as he lays writhing in pain on the floor. She turns toward me. I brace myself. I take in a deep ragged breath, close my eyes, and the next thing I know, the door bursts open.

CHAPTER THIRTY-SIX

It only takes one step before Jack has his gun pointed at the back of Cammie's head, telling her to drop her weapon. The gun clatters to the floor and he places her in handcuffs. Art, Ford, and Teeny also enter, guns drawn.

"Oww! Could you not be so rough? You almost broke one of my nails!" Cammie says to Jack. He jerks her unceremoniously, handing her off to Ford to be loaded into the squad car.

Teeny and Art are handling Clay. Jack walks over, freeing Lexie before me. She jumps up too quickly and almost falls to the floor. "Easy now," Jack says as he hands her off to Art. He then comes over to my chair, squats down and says, "Under any other circumstances, I would probably really enjoy doing this," as he rips the tape off my mouth.

"Ouch! Son of a mother trucker, that hurt!" I exclaim. "What took y'all so long to get here?"

He stands up and says, "Always the hard way, eh? I'm glad we got here in time." He then cuts all the tape and the zip tie loose, unbinding me. Art tosses him a handkerchief and he wipes some of the blood from my face, worry creasing his brow.

"I'm not mad at you anymore," I say.

"Good." The corners of his mouth lift. "I would hate to have to duct tape your mouth shut again."

Clay is loaded into an ambulance with two armed officers. Cammie is being taken to the Sheriff's Office, cuffed in the back of Ford's squad car, with Officer Keith riding shotgun. Lexie is loaded into Jack's car after being checked out by the paramedics. After a brief assessment by the EMTs and a few stitches, I assure them I am fine, and I get into Art's older model Lincoln Town Car to be taken to the station so I can give my statement.

Art details the events that led up to my rescue. "I was staking out Cammie. A.J. said she had been getting text messages and he thought she was going to try to sneak out for a rendezvous tonight. I had Teeny doing surveillance at your apartment. He reported everything seemed to be quiet, so I had him come to swap out with me. I was planning on crashing on the couch at the office for an hour or so. I got your message on my way to the office and tried to call you to talk you out of leaving. My call went to voicemail. I called Jack. When I got to the office, I found your phone laying in the parking lot. I knew something was wrong. I went back and watched the security footage and seen Clay taking you."

"Jack went to Lexie's. Her jeep was there, but she wasn't and neither were you. The deputy that was parked up the road said he hadn't seen you or anyone else enter. It's assumed Lexie walked through the woods to the adjoining road and got picked up there. Jack had the entire force out looking for you."

"Teeny called me, saying Cammie was on the move. I called Jack to let him know, then I fell in behind Teeny, tailing her here. Your Bronco was here. Jack and

Ford arrived right behind me and Teeny. And 'the rest is history'."

He reaches over, patting my hand with a relieved sigh. "I don't know whether to hug you or throttle you," he says. "If anything happened to you Elizabeth…." He let his words trail off. He didn't have to finish the sentence. I could see his feelings on his face and in the moisture gathered in his eyes. I swallow back a lump that has formed in my throat, and for the second time this week I become a sobbing mess in front of Art.

CHAPTER THIRTY-SEVEN

Ford had taken my statement. I went over every detail, no matter how small, because I do not want for any issues to arise when the case goes to court.

I am now standing over the sink in the restroom drying water off my face with paper napkins. The door opens. I see Jack through the reflection in the mirror. He walks in and takes a seat on the closed lid of the tall metal garbage can. I turn to look at him and he studies my face. Normally, I would have some snarky remark about him barging into the ladies' restroom. I just don't have it in me right now.

"You all done giving your statement?" he asks.

"Yeah."

"Good. Daphne has a hot cup of coffee with half a jug of creamer waiting on you. Just the way you like it."

He continues, "Cammie lawyered up quicker than you can say boo. Clay is in surgery. I suspect he'll ask for an attorney from his hospital bed. Given enough time, the two of them will no doubt turn on each other. Lexie sang like a songbird. You want to watch the recording?"

I nod and he says, "I'm sorry you didn't get to play bad cop. If it makes you feel any better, I went super bad cop, and I wasn't acting."

I give a forced smile and say, "I no longer have the desire to play bad cop. I just never want to play victim again."

"I never want you to play victim again either," he says as he takes a paper towel, wets it, and gently dabs at a dried spot of blood that I missed.

I follow him out the door, where Daphne is waiting with the steaming cup of coffee. She extends the cup to my outreached hand. Neither one of us says a word, the love between two old friends' hearts communicating silently.

Jack leads me to another room. He pulls out a chair for me, then sits down across the table and presses play on the recording. I watch as Lexie's image fills the screen, putting a few of the puzzle pieces of Kurt's murder in place.

Lexie and Kurt had been high school sweethearts. She gave Kurt a job remodeling the trailer for her parents and doing odd jobs. That's where Kurt had gotten money, but he did not want to tell Fiona that he was working for Lexie because she has always been jealous of Lexie. Lexie did not disclose that Kurt had been working for her family because she knew people would start asking questions after his death.

One day, as Clay was leaving a rendezvous with Lexie, Kurt saw him. Kurt warned Lexie away from Clay. While in prison, he had bragged to Kurt about killing Cammie's first husband, and revealed how they had plans to murder her new rich husband when he got out of prison so that Cammie would inherit all of his money.

You could imagine Kurt's incredulity when Clay showed up here, and he found out that Cammie is Clay's sister. Kurt intended to turn the pair in. Lexie let it slip that she knew Kurt planned on turning in Clay and Cammie before they could fulfil their plans. This is what led to Kurt's murder.

Lexie became terrified of Clay after he killed Kurt and tried to break off their relationship. Clay was not so willing to give up Lexie. He had decided to claim her as his property, and he also knew that she could turn him in for Kurt's murder. He threatened her kids, and she knew he was crazy enough to make good on the threat.

She was caught off guard the day that she showed up at the office for the interview. She made up the story that she gave as she went. She knew better than to make Clay sound innocent, but she also knew if he were caught, it would become clear that she knew he had murdered Kurt. Her conscience was bothering her though. That's why she showed up at my apartment. She intended to tell me all that she knew, but when Jack pulled in, her fear of being arrested outweighed her good intentions.

Gertie, witnessing Clay's crime, set in motion a series of events that fouled Clay and Cammie's plans. Had she not been at the creek that night, nobody would've ever known anything about who murdered Kurt. Except Lexie. Chances are, Clay would have eventually killed her, too. Clay's failed attempts of murdering Gertie and A.J. further fouled any plans the pair had.

Clay was to leave town, but he refused to leave without Lexie. Cammie wanted Clay to kill me because she was afraid that I would uncover the truth and she would never be safe, regardless how innocent she had made herself look.

Clay was more than happy to kidnap me. It fit squarely into his M.O. I cringe as I think of the zip ties he purchased earlier in the week, the eerie feeling I've had and Cammie's words days ago telling him to take care of me.

"Wow," I say, after watching the video. "I don't know if it should flatter me that people think that I'm such a good investigator."

"I guess I'm not the only one who thinks you're too tenacious to leave things alone," Jack says.

"What will happen to Lexie?" I ask.

"I couldn't say. I suppose that's up to the County Attorney to decide what kind of charges to bring against her. I hope impeding an investigation, and aiding and abetting a murderer," he says.

"*If* her story is true, then I can understand that she feels she didn't have a choice. She was protecting her children," I say.

"People always have a choice to do the right thing. She had an affair that ended up putting her children in harm's way. She isn't responsible for Clay's actions, but it was her telling Kurt's plans that caused Clay to kill him. Was it truly an accidental slip when she told Clay of Kurt's plans to turn the Butchers in? Did she maybe think that she would profit from the Butchers, too? Is she a con artist, too? She had plenty of opportunities to tell about Kurt's murder. She chose not to. She could have spoken up yesterday at your place. We would've had her family in protective custody in an instant. Maybe she enjoys playing victim. I still don't trust her," he says.

"You always see things in black and white, seeing no gray area, don't you?" I ask, thinking of the gray area in which I had wished that I shot Clay when I had the chance.

"I believe in right and wrong, and good and evil. It's us people that make it more complicated than that."

He makes it sound so simple. What one views as wrong could seem right in another's eyes. Would he think I was wrong or evil for wishing I could've killed Clay? I could justify self-defense, but the truth is that I felt a burning hatred for him that made me wish he were dead. Does that make me a terrible person? Or just human?

The world is full of terrible people created by the actions of others. Humans can be monsters. If Cammie and Clay weren't subjected to their father's cruelty, they may have turned out much differently.

One thing that I have learned from this case is that I am much too trustful of people. I fell for Cammie's sob story act of innocence and did not realize how deep into the mix Lexie was. I, like Jack, will always wonder about Lexie's motives. I never want to encounter people like the Butchers again, and I am determined to never be so naïve going forward. I know that the world is full of people that are far worse than Clay and Cammie. I hope that those far worse people never decide to call Justice their home.

CHAPTER THIRTY-EIGHT

MEMORIAL DAY

Today is Memorial Day. It has been a month and a half since my kidnapping. I have spent much of the time in a melancholy state that I cannot seem to pull myself out of. My inability to shake it off makes me angry with myself. I have never been one to wallow in miseries. Most days since that night at the construction site have consisted of routine and no drama, other than Colton and I ending our romantic relationship.

He showed up at my apartment about three weeks ago. I knew that something was wrong as soon as I answered the door and saw the look on his face. He said that he knew I would never want a serious relationship with him. He was ready to settle down. After the phone call in which I reminded him that we could see other people, he started dating someone that he met while working in Alabama. He thought it had the potential to turn into something serious.

I should have suspected. He had stopped coming home on weekends and our phone calls became less frequent and somewhat awkward. I could not be angry with him. It was what we had agreed upon when we first started seeing each other. I had thoughtlessly reminded him of that agreement, without knowing that he had not been dating anyone else because he wanted to become serious with me. I thanked him for telling me and wished him well. We remain friends.

Even though I felt the sting of losing him, I know it was for the best. I adore Colt, but I cannot picture myself spending the rest of my life with him. The longer the relationship went on, the harder it would have been when it ended. He deserves to be with someone who can picture forever with him. And I deserve to allow myself the opportunity to find my someone that I cannot imagine waking up without each morning.

My relationship status is not the only thing that changed in the last month. Gertie went to live at the Senior Living Complex to be closer to Oscar, her new boyfriend. She has her own apartment there, a community center, she is allowed to drive the golf cart, and she even purchased a bikini to wear on pool days. I consider myself lucky that I do not have the job of a lifeguard at the facility. I fear it is only a matter of time before she drives the golf cart into the pool. It is an accident waiting to happen.

She seems to be very happy there. I did not agree with Joe Jr. wanting to force her into the nursing home, but this new living arrangement suits Gertie. The only downside to her moving into the new residence is that she was very sad that she could not take Buddy along, but Jared promised to look after him.

Teeny Tulane has decided to make Justice his home. I suspect that his decision to ride solo has something to do with taking the fall for tax evasion and serving the time for it. Despite his cracking skulls persona, he really is a gentle giant. He now works for Art. I have yet to find a suitable secretary for the office, but having Teeny around has helped to lighten the load. Teeny is dating Sally now. The moment he stepped in the Troubadour, it was love at first sight. The pair have been glued together like a couple of sticky spaghetti noodles since then.

Today, I am getting ready to spend the day at Mama's with the entire family for a cook-out and swimming in her pool. I slip into a new maxi dress I bought last weekend at Anthropologie. It is white with a print of little blue flowers. The dress is very feminine, classy, and comfortable. It also accentuates the summer tan that I have acquired. I purchased the dress on a shopping trip that Mama and I took last weekend. We drove three and a half hours outside of Justice to Chattanooga, Tennessee. We went shopping at Warehouse Row, walked along the riverfront, ate dinner at a Brazilian steakhouse, and spent the night at a Jazz Age hotel. We had a lot of fun, particularly after I talked her into drinking margaritas.

I slip on a new pair of sandals and take extra time with my hair and makeup. My gold necklace and simple earrings complete my outfit.

I double-check to make sure that my hair iron is unplugged and the coffee pot is turned off. Then, I scan the security monitor. A habit that I have gotten into since the night Clay abducted me. I grab my new purse and head for the door. I see the Dollar General shoes on top of a bag of donation items sitting next to the door. I grab them to bring along. My Uncle Mike wears Crocs most of the time and is sure to get a kick out of the shoes.

* * *

I swing into the coffee shop to grab an iced coffee on my way to Mama's and I see A.J. The usually upbeat, exuberant A.J. is gone. A less verbal version of himself that hides his sadness behind a fake smile has replaced his normally outgoing personality. Cammie and Clay may not have succeeded in murdering him, but they did kill his spark.

"Hi, A.J. How are you?" I ask, sincerely.

"Oh, you know, Elle, just takin' it day to day. I'm fine though. How are you?"

"I'm okay," I say, and it comes out sounding more like a question than an answer. After some small talk, I say, "If you ever need anything, A.J., just call. I'm free to talk anytime."

"Thanks, Elle. But that's what I pay a therapist big bucks for. You have enough to deal with of your own because of Cammie, without having to listen about the number she done on me."

"The offer still stands. You take care A.J.," I say before walking out.

"You too, Elle."

I roll the windows down and turn Eric Church's "Springsteen" up, careful to watch my speed on my way to my mother's house.

* * *

I step out onto Mama's back patio. The scents of pool chlorine, barbequed food, and coconut suntan lotion fill the air. It is the smell of summer. It may not officially be summer on the calendar, but it's warm enough to swim, so that makes it summer here. The conversations taking place all around me are relaxed and the children squeal with delight as they splash water aimlessly.

I clear my throat to get Uncle Mike's attention. He turns his head in my direction when he hears the "Ahem" and starts cackling at me modeling my Clogs. "I'm glad to know you got your sense of humor back!" he says. Apparently, I haven't been hiding my melancholy mood nearly as well as I had thought.

His remark leads to my Gran saying, "Elle got used to too much excitement and doesn't know what to do with herself now. And I'm glad the excitement is over!"

Mama inserts that she thinks, "You're sad about Colt, even though you say you're not."

My cousin Renee advises that, "Colt is a man-slut and you're better off without him. And his new girlfriend isn't that pretty."

Uncle Mike simply says, "You sure know how to pick 'em."

And Teeny offers to crush Colt's skull.

I met Colt's new girlfriend, and I found her to be beautiful and delightful. At least I did, until Teeny figured out a couple of days ago that she was my nuisance caller and vehicle vandalizer. She had set her sights on Colt. He kept dismissing her advances. When she found out that I was the reason for him spurning her, she made a trip to Justice to do some stalking. When Colt agreed to start seeing her, the strange calls stopped. He broke up with her yesterday when he found out about her stalking and vandalism. I have not enlightened my mother with this new information. It will only lead to her trying to orchestrate a reconciliation between Colt and me.

My phone rings and I am glad to have a reason to step away from the conversation about me and my life.

"Hello," I say, plugging my other ear so that I can hear.

"Elle, honey, it's Dottie."

"Oh hi, Dot. How are you?"

"I'm fine, but I could use your help," she says.

"Of course. What do you need help with?"

"Well, nobody's answering the phone at Gertie's. Buddy has been on my back porch for three days now. He's a sweetheart, but he's becoming a nuisance. I know Gertie would always call you about him. I'm not sure what to do. I don't want to call animal control."

"Oh no, please don't do that. I'm on my way now," I say.

"Thanks Elle."

"No problem. I'll see you soon," I say.

I let Mama know what is going on, while wrapping up a hot dog and a hamburger in foil as I'm on my way out.

CHAPTER THIRTY-NINE

When I pull into Dot's driveway, Buddy gallops out, excited to see me. He is disheveled, dirty, and looks like he has lost some weight. Dot comes out of the house, thanking me for coming, and says that she suspects Buddy wasn't getting fed regularly anymore, and that's why he has taken to staying at her house. She had been feeding him, so he stayed.

I thank her for calling me, load Buddy into my Bronco, and give him the food. He makes quick work of the burger and hot dog. As he inhales the food, I give him lots of petting and puppy talk.

I then drive to Gertie's house, so angry that I can barely see straight. My knuckles are white from gripping the steering wheel so hard. I feel hot anger coursing through my veins. Jared is about to become the recipient of my ire. He is an adult, he can live his life how he chooses, but he agreed to care for Buddy, and he isn't doing what he said he would.

There is a "For Sale" sign in Gertie's yard. Joe Jr. wasted no time putting the home on the market when she went to live at the senior complex. A.J. is no longer interested in buying the property. He said he would not feel right about purchasing it after his wife tried to have Gertie murdered.

Pulling in, I leave an angry trail of gravel dust in my wake. I lower my window and leave Buddy in the vehicle. I yank the gate open, storm up the steps, and pound on the door. After several minutes, Jared finally swings the door open, shirtless, yawning, and rubbing sleep from his eyes. "What!" Then, he sees me standing on the porch and slowly takes me in, starting at my feet, and working his way up to my breasts, where his eyes settle. He props his naked arms on either side of the door frame and asks, "Sup, Elle?"

"Sup! Sup? I'll tell you what sup!" I say, grabbing one of his nipples and twisting.

He yelps. "Ouch! Why'd you do that for?" as he jumps back, swatting at my hand.

"Because you are a...... how old are you?"

"Twenty-nine," he mumbles cautiously.

"You are a nearly thirty-year-old man-child who cannot take care of a helpless dog!" I hike a thumb toward my Bronco and twist to see Buddy slinging my new purse around like a rag doll. I wince and turn back around. "You can't even make sure he's fed!" Hands on my hips, I shoot daggers at him with my eyes.

He looks around me and I follow his gaze to see a bowl of dog food sitting on the porch. The only thing making a meal of it is the trail of little black ants teeming around the nuggets. "Bet ya feel pretty dumb now," he says with a smug look on his face.

"I don't know. Do I, Jared?" I take my hands off my hips and cross them over my chest. He covers his nipples with his hands at my sudden movement. "Do you bother to leave the gate open so Buddy can come home to eat his food? Or come home, period, for that matter. Or here's a thought: keep the gate closed when he is home so he can't get out!"

His mouth forms a silent "oh" as realization sets in behind his bloodshot eyes.

"You promised your grandma that you would take care of Buddy! You should be ashamed of yourself. Did you even notice that he has been gone for the last three days? You know what? I'm taking Buddy with me. He's now my dog."

"Harsh. But okay, whatever. He's a pain, anyway. But just so you know, you'll have to take him to see Grandma once a week." He lifts his arms to the doorframe again and parks his eyes on my breasts once more. "You can ride with me if you want," he says with a wink.

I make a step toward him. He quickly lowers his arms, tucking his hands under his armpits, to protect *his* breasts, and says, "What? Stevie told me you were asking about me when you interviewed her." He cocks his head to the side.

"Ewww!" I grimace. I turn and stomp down the steps, stooping at the bottom to heft the mooning gnome statue. Jared ducks, expecting me to hurl the lawn ornament at his head. "And you know what else? I'm taking this too!" He raises up, relieved that I did not try to bash his head in, and shrugs.

When I get back in the vehicle, Buddy has thrown up the food and is eating it a second time. The meal looks intact, aside from the fact that it is swimming in stomach bile. He had swallowed everything whole. I gag at my first lesson as a dog owner—do not let him scarf food down so quickly.

* * *

I will need to pick up supplies for Buddy. I am not sure what the rules are for owning a pet, but I'm certain that I should not leave him in the vehicle on this hot day, while I go into the store. I take Buddy to Mama's and explain what happened. After giving me a lecture on how much responsibility he will be, she agrees to let him stay there while I go to the store and buy supplies. Buddy is in heaven, playing with the kids and trying to steal food from off of people's plates. As I am closing the gate, everyone is yelling, because Buddy has jumped into the swimming pool. At least I won't have to bathe him now.

While driving, I make a mental checklist of everything I will need to purchase. Food, toys, food and water bowls, leash, and a big dog bed. This leads me to thinking where I am going to put Buddy's bed, which trails into thinking that maybe I was too rash in my decision to claim Buddy. Maybe my mother was right. I had not even considered how small my apartment is.

I suppose I will have to look for a house with a yard big enough for Buddy to roam and play in. Perhaps the decision wasn't too rash after all. I wouldn't mind buying a house. After all, I am in my thirties and I do not plan to leave Justice. Maybe I should buy Gertie's house. Nah, maybe an old farmhouse to fix up!

I look up and see blue lights flashing in my rearview mirror. Although I was distracted, I do not think that I was speeding. I have been making an earnest effort to obey the limits lately.

I pull over to the side of the road. Jack gets out of his new truck and strides toward my SUV. *You know what? This is ridiculous,* I think, as I get out of my vehicle instead of waiting for him to reach my window.

"Are you kidding me, Jack? I almost get murdered, helping you catch not one, but two murderers, and you're pulling me over! I could not possibly have been going more than a few miles per hour over the speed limit!"

"Are you done?" he asks. "You weren't speeding, Elle."

"Oh. Okay. Well, why'd you pull me over?" I ask, confused. I take in his appearance. He is casually dressed in a white tee shirt stretched across his perfect pecs, blue jeans, sneakers, and a ball cap. *Yep, the Original Officer Sexy.*

"I heard you and Colt broke up?"

I arch a brow. "You pulled me over to ask me about my love life?"

"No. I pulled you over to ask you if you wanted to have dinner sometime," he says.

"Oh," I say, smiling. Honorable Jack has been waiting for me to be single to ask me out. "Why Sheriff, are you using your official vehicle for unofficial business?"

"I knew this was a mistake," he says, throwing his arms out.

"Jack! I'm teasing. I would love to have dinner with you."

"You would?" he asks, smiling, his dimple on full display. He tilts the bill of his ball cap back and his blue eyes are shining.

"Yes, I would. I just have one question, though." I place my finger on my chin, tapping it thoughtfully. "If we end up sleeping together, does that mean you can get me off the hook with those speeding tickets?"

"You're impossible," he laughs. "I'll text you the details," he says, jogging back toward his truck. He stops and turns around halfway, saying, "Oh, and you might not want to wear your DGs. I'm planning on taking you somewhere nice."

I look down at the shoes that I had forgotten I was wearing and smile.

EPILOGUE

I t is 10 A.M. and I am deep into working on an article when my phone rings. It is my mother calling.

"Hi, Mama."

"Hi, Elle. Did you hear the news?"

"I guess not. What news?"

"Someone shot and killed Clayton Butcher as they were taking him into the courthouse this morning!"

"No, I had not heard about it! I wondered what all the sirens that I was hearing were about. Do they know who did it?" I ask.

"Nope. Whoever done it had been hiding in the space above the old newspaper office, shot him from the window and was long gone by the time the police got there."

"Did anyone else get hurt?" I ask.

"No. Just Clay. Whoever done it must have been a skilled marksman."

"Sounds like Jack is going to have his hands full again. Who would have ever thought there would be two murders happen in Justice in such a short time?"

"I know, right? Well, hon, my appointment just arrived, so I'll hop off of here. I just thought you would want to know."

"Yes, I'm glad you told me. Thanks for calling, Mama."

The list of people that Clay has an extensive history of scamming and conning is long. The list of people that he has murdered is no doubt longer than the ones that are known about. Not to mention the list of female enemies he has made as a result of his stalking and abusing. This makes the list of people that would wish him .dead extremely long, too. I cannot say that I blame those people for wishing him dead.

However, I do still believe in letting the wheels of justice turn and allowing the

court system to work as it was designed to do. If the court system failed, then I might be more agreeable to an eye for an eye—in Clay's case, anyway. There was an instance when I wished to kill him myself. If he had taken the life of someone that I love, it may have been me lurking in the shadows, waiting for an opportunity to seek revenge.

I understand the gray area much clearer than our Sheriff does. Jack still sees everything in black and white. He arrested Clay and entrusted him to the justice system. He will hunt his murderer with the same scorched earth passion that he hunted Clay. The thin line between right and wrong remains uncomplicated for Jack, because without law, there would be chaos. I think the line between right and wrong may become a bit blurred at times, but the difference between good and evil is a bold, black line, with no room for a gray area. Jack falls on the good side of that bold line.

I wonder if the Good Sheriff will need my help to find the killer?

ACKNOWLEDGMENTS

First, thank you to my husband, James—my biggest supporter and encourager of following my dreams. To my sons, Tristan and Ethan, who have (patiently) listened to me endlessly about this book and given me their feedback/editing tips—You are two in a million!

My friends and family who have supported me and the ones who served as my beta-readers, I love you all. I have heard it said that "it takes a village to raise children." It also takes a village of supporters to encourage an author to publish their first novel. I am grateful for my village.

Thank you, Cathy for always being my sounding board and my personal photographer.

Thank you George. Daphne was always one of my biggest supporters. I can just imagine her laughter if she could hear of Elle and Gertie's antics. She had the greatest laugh. I miss her so.

www.ingramcontent.com/pod-product-compliance
Lightning Source LLC
Chambersburg PA
CBHW060307260626
47160CB00007B/2530